THE UNDYING ILLUSIONIST

TALES OF THE FEISTY DRUID™ BOOK 2

CANDY CRUM

MICHAEL ANDERLE

LMBPN

DISRUPTIVE IMAGINATION

LMBPN Publishing
PMB 196, 2540 South Maryland Pkwy
Las Vegas, NV 89109

First US edition, August 2017
Version 1.02, August 2017

DEDICATION

From Candy

To my boys, thank you for
being my reason for everything.
To my family who support me
no matter what.
To the fans and readers--thank you!

From Michael

To Family, Friends and
Those Who Love
To Read.
May We All Enjoy Grace
To Live The Life We Are
Called.

The Undying Illusionist Team

JIT / Beta Readers

Kimberly Boyer
Alex Wilson
Kello ODonnell
Joshua Ahles
Melissa OHanlon
Paul Westman
Micky Cocker

Thomas Ogden
John Findlay

If we missed anyone, please let us know!

Editor
Lynne Stiegler

THE UNDYING ILLUSIONIST

"**A**rchers, *hold!*" Arryn shouted.

Her voice was the only sound that could be heard, other than the gentle shifting of feet and the slight creak of the bows as they were pulled tight.

The early Spring temperatures were still frigid in the mornings. The air was cold enough Arryn could see her breath. But that didn't matter. There were other things—far more important things—to focus on.

A light fog had descended upon the area that morning, creating the illusion that everything was calm. Peaceful.

But it wasn't.

This particular morning was clouded over by more than the fog. Several guards stood ready on the ground and several more stood on the wall with Arryn, bows in hand, as she tried to remind herself to breathe.

The possibility of a remnant invasion on the city had become a reality.

Several weeks after Samuel's group had been rushed, another crew further south than that had been as well. Unfortunately for them, they didn't have Samuel and Andrew and had been completely overrun.

There were *no* survivors that time.

Still, half the city had felt confident the remnant had only been protecting their lands. That the men—both Ren's group as well as the second—had been working too close to the Madland's borders and incited an attack. But Samuel had far more experience with them than anyone, as did his friend, Ren.

Most had believed the Capitol Guard was ever vigilant and capable of handling an incursion, but more importantly, they never believed such a thing would happen.

Arcadia was just too far away from the Madlands and too heavily protected for the remnant to risk attacking and failing. While they were incredibly strong and lived only to destroy, they *were* still capable of higher reasoning. They would know not to advance on a city so well-armed, or so the most Arcadians had believed.

Arryn sighed as she thought back to the first conversations regarding the invasions. What some hadn't taken into consideration was that it didn't matter how well-armed the city was.

The Guard was untrained and underprepared.

Nearly the entire Arcadian Guard was brand-new. Almost all of them lacked sufficient training with weapons of any kind, let alone magitech weapons and hand-to-hand combat. It would require a hell of a lot for any single member of the Guard to take down a remnant, more so if there was an army of them.

The only way they would be able to survive such an onslaught would be to have skilled archers on the walls to thin out the horde before it reached the gates—and Arcadia didn't have a single one.

Given the growing fear of the remnant, after talking to Amelia and getting her blessing, Arryn, Cathillian, and Samuel had taken matters into their own hands, fixing that problem after they had rounded up a few men who were interested in learning extra skills. Brave men who took their job seriously and would stop at nothing to protect their city.

They weren't the best archers in the world—*yet*—but they knew how to shoot, and they occasionally hit something... Especially if that something was an approaching big-ass horde.

It was a hell of a lot better than what they'd had before.

As Arryn stood on top of the wall that separated Arcadia from the rest of the world, she stared outward into the fog as she tried to see anything that might be coming their way.

"Hey, bitches," Arryn said, holding tight to her bow and taking aim at what seemed like nothingness. "How lucky are ya feeling today?"

There was a laugh beside her from one of her archers. "Lucky enough not to fall off the wall and on my ass. Anything else, ask me later."

A smile crossed her face. "Fair enough. Let's just hope Cathillian doesn't get hit on by one of their chicks. They might be ugly, but Cathillian can't deny a girl that thinks he's prettier than she is."

Everyone laughed, and Arryn sighed, happy she could bust up the moment.

There were five bowmen to her left and five to her right, spread evenly apart to defend the eastern wall. Given the last remnant attack, Cathillian, Samuel, and Arryn all believed they'd be coming from that direction.

Unless they were smart enough to change directions to throw them off, of course.

Samuel seemed to think that might be possible, too, so he and Cathillian took the northern wall. The Arcadian gates had been closed, but only after some heavy convincing on Arryn's part.

After a man covered in blood from head to toe had raced his horse into the city, screaming about yet another remnant attack, one would think he'd have been believed. But because he came to warn them the remnant were planning to come for Arcadia, the guards and those that had discovered the news hadn't been so convinced.

The man lived on a small farm several miles south of Arcadia. The remnant had overrun his home, killing his entire family in the process. He'd been the only one to survive and had made haste toward the city after hearing one of the beasts mention Arcadia.

Though the Chancellor had been hesitant to cause fear and chaos, Arryn and the others believed him, and Amelia decided subtlety was their best chance.

Unfortunately for them, things had already escalated, and the attacks were controlled by outside sources. Now, the only thing they could do was hope for the best and do their best to protect their walls as the horde grew closer.

The fog seemed to thicken, and Arryn found herself wishing that the druid Chieftain's daughter, Elysia, was there. She would have been capable of lifting it. Arryn could only control the weather when she was pissed off.

But the fog wouldn't matter.

She knew she didn't need to see the enemy coming. No one did. According to Samuel and Ren, the enemy was more than happy to announce themselves.

And they did…

Loud gravel-voiced screams ripped through the air, chilling Arryn to the bone. She looked at the men beside her, only to see them glancing toward one another with fear on their faces. They turned to Arryn for direction, afraid of what was about to happen.

She knew how they felt. It was up to her to be their backbone.

"Archers, *aim*!" Arryn shouted. She heard the wings behind her before she saw the large Golden Eagle who was Cathillian's familiar fly overhead. "Echo, warn Cathillian. The remnant are here. Oh! And that the ladies *will* eat him alive, and *not* in the good way."

CHAPTER ONE

Two weeks earlier

T hings were changing very quickly, and Amelia had started to feel even more hope. It was almost like the old Arcadia again.

Well, minus an evil dictator.

It had been a couple of weeks since they'd tracked down and killed Doyle—a situation Amelia had regretted on behalf of Arryn because she'd wanted answers about her father, but it was a development the city rejoiced in. Knowing he was gone was a blessing.

The Governor had yet to be found, even after identifying the bodies at the farmhouse. It was no matter. Amelia would find him, too, and put an end to his plans for vengeance.

The men the city of Cella had sent were more than helpful. The factory building had been rebuilt, and now they were finishing everything on the inside. Within a few days, work would start again and the city—as well as its families—would be able to bring in money for the economy.

It had been quite an effort for Arcadia to feed and shelter so many extra people after the Battle for Arcadia, but luckily, plenty of vacant homes had been available and several local farms had been willing to donate food.

Given the impending reopening of the factory, extra men poured back into the city, no longer searching for work outside with the nobles that were building homes. Even the unemployed had lent a hand to the effort, knowing they would soon be receiving regular pay.

The factory was small, but not as small as they had anticipated. With the donated supplies and the added help from Cella, nobles, Boulevard men, and stray Arcadians returning home, they had been able to build larger and faster due to most of the wood being harvested locally.

Amelia's largest concern now, other than the factory, was getting the Arcadian Guard fully trained and ready to go. Because there were so many recruits and so few experienced fighters, the training was going very slowly.

Still, she was confident everything would turn out fine. They had to do well. It was Arcadia, after all—the grandest city in the valley, and its namesake. She needed her residents to feel safe and secure.

"Ah, Chancellor," Samuel said as Amelia approached the factory site. "It's good ta have ye. We're almost ready. I'm gonna say three days, but we might get done early. We have some magicians here installin' the magitech lightin' right now. We had more than plenty of glass from the old buildin' ta melt down into enough panes ta make sure this bitch is well lit. It won't remind anyone of the old place."

"I've never seen anything so incredible. Everyone really cooperated and put it together so quickly." She shook her head, trying to hold back her emotions. She was overjoyed and relieved, grateful to see everyone so happy. "I look forward to the reopening. I just came by to check on everyone. Do you or anyone else need anything?"

"Aye," Ren chimed in. "I could use a nice night at the Dragon's Lair. That ought ta set me right."

Amelia laughed. "I don't think that's on the menu, rearick. Not on my coin, anyway. But you're more than welcome to head there this evening. I'm sure you'll find nothing short of plentiful entertainment there."

"Aw, ye ain't jealous now, are ye?" Ren asked. "I know how shy Arcadian women can be sometimes. No need ta be shy around old Ren."

Amelia shook her head, still smiling. "Samuel, I think you need new friends. This one's old and broken."

"Hey, Chancellor!" Andrew said as he walked out the factory's front door. "Is Marie here with you?"

Amelia excused herself from the rearick and took a few steps forward. It made her happy to see an attractive, hard-working, and very kind man like Andrew asking about her sweet assistant, Marie.

She wasn't sure if it was simply platonic curiosity, but she couldn't help but hope for something else.

"Why, no, she isn't. I'm here alone. Should I give her a message? I'm sure I'll see her in just a few minutes."

Laughing nervously, Andrew looked down at the cobblestone walkway and ran his fingers through his short, dark hair. "No, that's okay. I don't want to bother her. I was just curious if she was here. She's been down here every day, but she hasn't stopped in yet today. Wanted to make sure she's okay."

He was so adorable, Amelia couldn't help but smile knowingly. "I assure you she's fine, but I'll be happy to let her know you asked for her."

There was a nervous pause as he looked anywhere except into Amelia's eyes. It was obvious he was embarrassed to ask about her.

That was rather cute on a man as attractive and masculine as he was. She'd heard the story about what he'd done with the remnant. Hopefully he'd use that brawn for something a bit more fun with sweet Marie.

Andrew was about to say something else, but he stopped, smiled, and pointed behind Amelia. "Well, there she is. I guess she surprised us."

Amelia turned, not having expected Marie to show up since she'd been working with someone on plans for the Boulevard. From the look on the woman's face, Amelia was expecting whatever information she carried even less than her presence.

"I'm sorry to break this up," Marie said. "I know you came down here because you're excited, but I have news."

Before she walked away, Amelia turned to Andrew to say her goodbyes. "Thank you again for all your hard work. I know you and Samuel have been at the head of this, and that you've been working at the factory *and* in the Boulevard. It couldn't have been easy, so thank you. If there's ever anything you need, please let me know."

Marie shot a quick smile toward Andrew as she led Amelia away. Given the connection they had seemed to share with one another, Amelia thought Marie was acting strangely. She was usually so very excited to see the tall, dark, and handsome man.

Once they were out of earshot, Amelia started the conversation, knowing that mood would be lost if she let her assistant talk first. "Before you unleash whatever darkness is in that brain of yours on me, I need to say I think that man is adorable. He obviously likes you. I think you'd be a crazy person if you didn't at least entertain the idea."

"Amelia…"

The Chancellor put her hands up in defeat. "I don't mean to intrude. I just know you're single and you worked for Adrien for years, so that means there was absolutely no time for you to date. It's not my business, but I had to say it, because if you *weren't* thinking it, I figured maybe you should, that's all. *Now* you can go on with whatever terrible news is causing that awful expression on your face."

"I don't mind you butting in. I'm not upset by that in any way. Actually, it feels nice to have someone looking out for me, and I especially like having a woman around to talk to. Unfortunately, you're right. There is bad news." Marie paused for a moment, wringing her hands and frowning. "There was another remnant attack about three miles south of the last one and five miles farther west. Farther into the valley."

"So, it was farther from their home territory, is what you're saying?" Amelia clarified.

Marie nodded. "Yes. And this one was far worse."

Closing her eyes, Amelia sighed as the weight of that news pressed on her. A remnant attack was terrible under any circumstances, but as Chancellor, it was her responsibility to make sure that everyone remained safe.

"Were there any survivors?" Amelia asked.

Marie shook her head, pausing for a moment before she continued, "I'm afraid not. Twenty-five dead. Some of those men were ripped apart. The Hunters and Border Patrol came in this morning with carts full of corpses. They were lucky that a nearby village allowed them to commandeer the carts, or they'd still be out there. From what they could tell, all but five of them were Arcadian. The rest were just outsiders looking for work."

"I can't believe this," Amelia cried, incredulity clear in her quiet voice. "Have the families been notified?"

Marie shook her head again. "I'm sorry, Amelia, but I think we're going to need you for that. Like I said, some of those men were ripped apart. Others had their skulls crushed. It's—" Marie stopped.

Amelia frowned, knowing just how hard all this must have been on someone as kind as Marie. The Chancellor had a good heart, but she was no stranger to carnage—unfortunately.

"It's impossible to identify some of them, is that what you were going to say?" Amelia asked.

"I don't know everyone here, certainly not the Boulevard people. Even with Adrien in the Academy tower, I was locked away in the Capitol building for years. I did my best, but I'm ashamed to say that I couldn't even hold my lunch, let alone stand there long enough to identify someone I've probably never met. I'm embarrassed, but that's how it was."

"Don't worry, Marie, I'll take a look. And don't be ashamed for not having the stomach to look at all that. It just means you have a pure heart. If I hadn't seen so much blood myself recently, I doubt I'd be able to either." Amelia stepped forward and pulled the girl into a reassuring hug, then moved back. "It'll be okay. Why don't you go home for the day? Either go home, or go talk to that sweet man back there who's more than likely been staring at you this whole time. I can take care of the rest."

Amelia was happy when Marie didn't argue. Knowing what she was about to have to do, the Chancellor had no desire to stand there and try to convince the woman to leave work.

Though she had to admit, she was very proud of Marie for trying to solve the problem herself before running to her. She'd certainly come a long way in a very short amount of time.

CHAPTER TWO

Things in the Girard house were becoming more familiar to Arryn and Cathillian once a routine had been set up and their training had resumed.

Today, however, things would be a little bit different for them.

With Arryn wanting to get more serious about training and improving all the time, Cathillian wanted to give Arryn what she'd asked for—to train like a traditional warrior.

On top of that, Cathillian wanted to work on his own skills. Teaching Arryn new things or helping her get stronger was always great, but he wanted to make sure to challenge himself as well.

After the big fight with Doyle, Cathillian had realized Arryn was more than ready for the harder training that warriors took part in.

That, and he wanted to do anything she asked for to make up for killing the man who had possessed information about her father before she could ask him even a single question.

That morning, the plan was to go just outside the city walls, where they would have a wide-open field to train in without hurting anyone.

Having the late Lord Girard's nice big house to live in while in the city was one thing, but the lack of a large enough yard to train in was something else, though his home had certainly had one of the biggest yards in the city.

According to Amelia, that was where Hannah's small group had trained, but with as active as the druids were, they needed more room—especially when long range weapons were brought into the mix.

For what they had planned, they needed a much larger area where they wouldn't accidentally kill the neighbor's chickens.

When they arrived out by the trees that Cathillian had been growing with his new students, they set their things down and prepared themselves for what was to come.

The sun was only beginning to rise, and the early spring air was crisp and cool, though they would warm up quickly enough once they began training.

"Just don't shoot me in the head or chest and we should be fine," Cathillian cautioned, smiling a bit as he pointedly locked eyes with her.

"Damn. With all these rules, you're just taking the fun out of *everything*, aren't you?" Arryn replied.

Cathillian smiled as he lifted a hand, signaling for her to stay put. "Oh, I know. Don't turn your back on an enemy. Don't shoot Cat in the face. There are just *so* many things to remember! How will you ever remember them all?" he quipped. "That being said, if you *do* shoot me, it just means my ass was too slow. Don't worry too much about it, just don't aim anywhere vital."

Arryn stretched her back and arms, reaching as high as she could and brushing the tips of her fingers against the underside of the leaves on one of the lowest branches of a tree.

She smiled. "I didn't plan on it. The worrying about it part, I mean." Picking up her staff, she began twisting it in circles, allowing the weight to relax her wrists. "I *totally* plan to shoot you. This is the best opportunity I've had in a long time!"

Laughing as she pulled her bow from her shoulder, she asked, "Is this gonna ruin my arrows? I spent a long-ass time making these. Your mom even helped a little. Speaking of which, have you sent a note back with Echo this week? We don't need her tearing down the Arcadian gate."

Cathillian looked at her incredulously. "Do you honestly think I'd forget something like that? Of course, I did, because even though she doesn't know physical magic, I'm still not sure she wouldn't rain hellfire down on everyone if she thought we were in danger." They both laughed, having fun joking about Elysia and the terrible temper she displayed when she was angry. "I sent Echo back this morning. And I think your precious arrows will be fine."

Arryn pulled an arrow from her quiver and nocked it, waiting for further instruction. She knew exactly what he wanted to do, but she had to wait for his go-ahead or risk hurting him worse than anticipated.

He planned to make himself a moving target while she attempted to shoot him. He would deflect her arrows by any means necessary—dodging, jumping, ducking, or by sword.

With anyone else, it would have been truly dangerous. It was for them as well, but since Arryn was great with a bow and they could heal, it made the exercise far less threatening.

Cathillian drew his sword before nodding. Arryn wasted no time and began shooting. One after another, Arryn loosed a barrage of arrows at him, each one missing: either flying past him as he dodged, or was cut in half by his sword.

"You lying bitch! So much for not destroying my arrows!" Arryn pouted, nocking another arrow and shooting it only a moment after it had been pulled back.

The druid moved so quickly as he spun out of the way of one of her arrows that she nearly missed him pulling a knife from his belt before throwing it directly at her.

She jumped to her right before dropping and somersaulting

once to come back up, bow drawn. She shot another arrow, this time hitting him in the thigh.

"*Fuck!*" Cathillian yelled before hissing in pain. "You actually got me! *Damn*, that was a good shot."

He snapped the end of the arrow off without hesitation, allowing him to pull it the rest of the way through as he once again hissed in pain. He threw the broken shaft to the ground and placed his hand over the wound.

Arryn looked behind her and found the knife he had hurled buried in one of the trees Cathillian had helped the loggers grow during their magic lessons. Their magic was still weak, so it was mostly him, but they were learning.

Still, it was a pretty impressive tree.

She turned and made her way over to Cathillian, who had been gathering up arrows. As they met in the middle, they traded weapons.

"How is the class, by the way?" she asked, nodding toward the tree. "Seems like it's going well."

Cathillian shrugged. "It could be better, but I can't complain. It's taken a couple weeks to teach them, but they're learning. It's slow, but as you can see, the trees are growing nicely. Unfortunately, only two of them have been doing most of the work, other than me, of course. The rest are a lot like you were when you first started."

She smacked him in the chest with her free hand. "Hey!" she scolded, her angry expression belied by the smile on her face. "I'm an excellent student, I'll have you know. And a fast learner."

"Yeah, *now*. Before, you completely sucked at it. You got better, though." He winked as he turned and began heading in the opposite direction. "Go again?"

Arryn laughed. "You're the one being shot at here, not me, so you call the shots." She paused for a moment, thinking over her last sentence, and laughed. "Damn, I'm witty without even trying. How can you stand it?"

He rolled his eyes. "I just do my best, I suppose. Sometimes it's *really* hard."

She smiled. "But seriously, you only have two good students out of all of those who've taken to nature magic? That's too bad."

"Well, there *would* be another, but he avoids learning magic at all costs. He wants nothing to do with it. And yes, we will be going again."

Arryn was confused. She couldn't imagine why anyone wouldn't want to learn, especially when the men Cathillian was working with were no strangers to hunger, death, and struggle.

"What do you mean he doesn't want to learn? Did you tell him that it could save his life? That it could save the lives of others he cares about?"

Cathillian smiled. "It's your friend, Samuel."

Arryn's eyes widened, immediately knowing the significance of his statement.

"He's a rearick. You know how much they hate magic. There's no way in hell he's gonna wanna learn, but he still shows up every day, and he still plants. He just makes somebody else do the magic part. Now, get ready. We're beginning again."

Arryn had knocked the dirt from her salvageable arrows and put them back in her quiver. She drew one and waited for his signal.

Cathillian ran at her, but Arryn saw him coming and was easily able to move before he slammed into her.

She twirled around him as she dodged his attack, then headed in the direction he'd just come from. Dropping to her knees, she slid across the grass before turning and releasing her shot.

She only barely missed Cathillian, but he was quick to return fire.

The grass around Arryn quickly grew, wrapping around her right arm before pulling it to the ground and pinning it there. She looked up to see Cathillian charging and quickly pulled the knife from the sheath strapped to her thigh, cutting the grass

CANDY CRUM & MICHAEL ANDERLE

before diving out of the way, leaving her bow on the ground in the process.

Looking back at the tree she'd been standing in front of when they'd first arrived, she saw her staff leaning against its sturdy trunk. As she ran for it, an unmistakable, searing pain ripped through the back of her leg.

Arryn knew Cathillian's knife was buried in her thigh.

She stopped and pulled the blade from her leg, spinning to throw it with surprising accuracy at her opponent.

Not waiting to see if it made contact, Arryn gazed back at the tree and extended her hand, her eyes going black as she used physical magic to levitate the staff.

The weapon launched toward her with impressive speed, and she was quick to catch it, whirling it around and bringing the end to the ground in front of her.

Cathillian charged after her so quickly she barely had enough time to conjure a barrier before he slammed into her.

The force of the impact threw her back a couple of steps, but she recovered quickly, dropping the barrier and planting a foot in his chest, kicking him back even farther.

Once there was enough distance between them, she swung her staff low, connecting with his knees and causing him to fall. She ran again, heading for her bow this time.

Arryn dropped to the ground before picking up the bow, nocking an arrow, and loosing it. The first one missed, Cathillian spinning out of the way at the last moment yet still somehow not losing footing in his run.

She quickly sent another, this one grazing his shoulder as he once again tried to dodge it.

Jumping up, she pretended to brace for the impact but instead lassoed his head with her bow and pulled as she spun out of the way, catching him hard around the neck with the wood and easily taking him down.

She wasted no time stepping down on the wood, knowing it

was unbreakable under her weight, and she quickly dropped next to him, pulling an arrow from her quiver to point it just above his left eye.

"I win!" she cheered, moving the arrow away and taking her weight off the bow.

"What the *shit* was that, and where the hell did you learn it?" Cathillian asked, a large smile on his face.

"Honestly, I thought that was fighting pretty dirty, but after you ran my leg through with that damn knife, I didn't really care much. I just wanted to take your ass down."

Arryn collapsed back onto her left hip, careful to avoid putting pressure on the right leg because of the knife wound.

"I planned to stop once I hit you with the knife, but you kept going, so I did, too. I didn't even mean to hit you, so I'm sorry. Don't hate me." He gave her a cheesy smile, and she laughed.

"It hurt like hell, but you guys are all rough-and-tumbly. I'd also just shot you with an arrow. You didn't even whine like a little girl at all like I'd expected, so I wasn't about to let you make a little bitch outta me. So, no hard feelings. Like you said, we deserve it if we're slow enough to get hit."

Cathillian laughed and shook his head. "I did say that. And yeah, I suppose we're a little extreme when we train, but it's all for a good cause. If anything bad ever happened to you, I'd never forgive myself. I'd rather you take a knife to the back of the leg because you turned your back on me and learn the lesson never to do that again. It might save you from taking an enemy's much larger knife to the back because you *didn't* learn. Now, turn over so I can heal you."

Arryn rolled onto her stomach, exposing the large wound in the back of her thigh. She jumped a little as she felt his large hands gently caress her leg on either side of it.

A blush rose to her cheeks since she hadn't expected to react in such a way, especially with the significant amount of pain she was feeling. But then the pain quickly faded, and all that was left were his hands.

They lingered for a moment before pulling away.

"There you go!" he chirped before slapping her on the ass. "All better!"

Arryn rounded on him, punching him in the arm as she did. "Hey! Uncalled for!"

He put his hands up in surrender. "Don't act so angry. You know you loved it."

Cathillian's brows rose in shock as he jumped back, knowing she was about to come for him. She only narrowly missed him, but that didn't stop her from getting to her feet and readying herself to go after him again.

"I'm sorry, I'm sorry, I'm sorry! Don't beat me up. Truce?"

Arryn rolled her eyes. "Fine. But next time you slap my ass, you get a foot to the balls."

He laughed. "Okay, deal. It's time for us to quit for today, anyway. About time for you to get to class. Speaking of which, how is *that* going?"

Arryn gathered her things, still feeling a bit awkward about her reaction to Cathillian. She shook her head to clear her mind as she hung her bow over her shoulder and began walking back toward the city gate, staff in hand.

"It's not too bad. I brought some flower seeds in—you know, something small. I'm trying to do essentially the same thing you are, but using things that are far easier to grow. My students are still having a hard time, so don't give your guys too much shit when they can't grow big-ass oaks. As for physical magic, it's been going well, too, though it's mostly remedial at the moment."

"That shouldn't be too bad, since you already have a handle on the basics. I think you'll do fine," he reassured her. "Just relax. You'll learn the big stuff soon enough."

Arryn thought that over for a few moments, debating just how good her physical magic was. Just how good *any* of her magic was. She wasn't exactly sure if she would ever really master the different forms, but she had decided when she came back that she was sure as hell going to give it her best shot.

"I'm nervous, but I know it'll get better over time."

The guards at the gate smiled and nodded as the twosome walked through. They had become very accustomed to seeing Arryn and Cathillian going just outside the gate to train every morning.

They'd watched and even complimented her on her form, and one mentioned his interest in archery. Arryn understood why he'd want to learn, especially after she found out the city didn't *have* any archers.

The city had always relied too heavily on physical magic and magitech weapons. Adrien saw no reason to have them because the Hunters were well trained and the Guard was nothing to be messed with.

The need for archers was never there. After the Battle for Arcadia, it was something that hadn't yet been thought of, but with the Guard being *highly* inexperienced and lacking even the most basic knowledge of physical magic—for most of them—the need for archers was there.

When the guards had shown interest, she told them their best bet was to go to Amelia and tell her. She thought talking about the interest in further training would do more good coming from them rather than an outsider who had only been in the city for a few weeks, even if she and Amelia had gotten much closer after the fight with Doyle.

Knowing Amelia and her desire to do right by everyone, Arryn was quite sure the Chancellor wouldn't turn down additional skills for her army.

When Arryn and Cathillian got back to the house, she ran upstairs to jump in the shower, needing to wash the blood off her and relax herself and her mind before going in to teach at the Academy.

Celine, Arryn's aunt, had breakfast waiting on them as she had every morning lately. She'd moved in after everything that had happened with Doyle. For the first week, she'd been staying over quite a bit anyway, so it was the logical choice for her after finally having someone in her family back in her life.

It had only made sense for them, and Arryn loved having her aunt with her.

As Arryn got out of the shower, she groaned. While she loved her job, she hated going there and seeing Talia. Every day, she still had to psych herself up to be able to face the *seemingly* perfect Dean of Students, without giving away her discomfort—a discomfort that hadn't been alleviated but rather had only worsened as time went on.

As she finished getting dressed, Arryn decided there was only one thing to do about that situation.

She needed to talk to Amelia.

CHAPTER THREE

S amuel considered himself an easy-going rearick, but he wasn't someone to mess with when he was on a mission.

The job at the factory was almost finished, and he and the others had decided to go to Sully's to have a few drinks to celebrate. He could certainly use the drinks after all the—free—hard work he'd been putting in for a city he wasn't the biggest fan of.

Unfortunately for him, he quickly found he wasn't in a celebratory mood once one of the other laborers had told the group what he'd overheard Marie relate to Amelia.

They were concerned about the men that had been killed down south, and Samuel couldn't say he blamed them. The remnant were nothing to scoff at.

It had been too late the night before to walk into the Capitol building or track down the Chancellor at home to say anything, but he had plans to do it now. Something had to be done.

The remnant needed to be dealt with, and if his fellow workers were correct, the city was under the assumption the Guard was more than capable of handling them—and they weren't.

Marie was sitting at her desk as he walked into the Capitol

building, smiling as soon as she saw him. She was a beautiful girl, one who was capable of making even an old dog rearick like Samuel blush, but he knew his friend Andrew liked her, so that was enough for him.

He wasn't in the habit of trying to steal a woman from another man, even if they weren't actually together and she was a sweet and beautiful girl like Marie. Still, he didn't mind admiring her a little.

"Samuel, it's good to see you again," Marie told him as he approached. "What can we do for you?"

The rearick cleared his throat as he smoothed his beard. "I believe I need ta talk ta that Chancellor of yers. I received some startlin' news, and I need ta know what she intends ta do about it."

Marie's brow furrowed as she looked at him. "What's happened, Samuel? Is everything okay?"

Samuel paused, trying to keep his worry under control. No matter what, it wasn't poor Marie's fault. "I know yer just doin' yer job, lass, but I think ye know what I'm talkin' about. Those people down south all losin' their lives ta those overgrown sacks of shit."

She exhaled, pausing for a moment before nodding. "It's terrible. All those men. All those families who lost their brothers, sons, fathers." She shook her head, her expression full of sadness. "I'm no expert on the subject, but I agree. Something needs to be done. I just don't know what."

"Hopefully the Chancellor knows. She available?" Samuel asked.

Marie nodded, walking to Amelia's office door and knocking softly. As she opened it, Samuel could hear a voice from inside, but not what was said.

Marie had obviously heard her, however, and she opened the door to poke her head inside. There was a pause before she turned back to Samuel and smiled.

"Amelia said to come on in. She's ready for you."

Giving a curt nod of thanks, Samuel stepped into the office and closed the door behind him. "Sorry ta bother ye, Chancellor, but I have some questions fer ye. I heard there was another remnant attack farther south. What exactly do ye plan ta do about it?"

Amelia's eyes were wide. "Well, hello to you, too!" She motioned to the chairs in front of her desk and paused as she waited for him to sit. "I know what you're talking about, and it's a tragedy. I would love for the Arcadian Guard to be able to ride into the Madlands on horses and use swords, magitech weapons, and fireballs until they're all dead and gone, but they can't."

Samuel stayed quiet as he listened intently, formulating his argument.

The Chancellor leaned forward, clasping her hands on her desk. "The truth is, we don't know how many remnant there are in the Madlands. We don't know much of anything about them except they're brutish, mindless scum that feed on death and destruction. We can't go picking a fight if we don't have enough information. We'd be sending them to their deaths."

Doing his best to keep his voice calm, Samuel said, "All due respect, Amelia, they ain't mindless. Not by a longshot. They're so obsessed with death and carnage they ain't thinkin' long-term, but they understand battle strategy. And make no mistake, lass, they have one."

"What are you talking about?" Amelia asked.

"They're always ready fer battle, no matter what. They focus on blunt force, and they're damn good at it. My people've been fightin' 'em fer years. Yer right that no one in this damned city should go pickin' a fight they can't win. Biggest reason is because I can promise ye those men ye have down there—" he shook his head "—they *won't* win."

Amelia nodded. "Unfortunately, if they went looking for a fight, you're absolutely right. It wouldn't end well for them. I'm confused. If we both agree we shouldn't send the Guard to the Madlands, then what are you suggesting that I do? We have our border walls, and we have the Guard. In fact, I just increased the Guard's numbers. I'll fight to the end for any person in this city, but I won't send men outside to their deaths."

Samuel ran his fingers through his beard as he leaned forward. "What I'm tellin' ye is, yer men ain't ready—even for a home invasion. And it's only a matter of time before the bastards from the Madlands come this way."

"What makes you think that?" Amelia asked.

"Experience, lass. Somethin' has 'em all riled up. Somethin' ain't right. How long have men been loggin' over there? Months. Ever since those spoiled nobles fled the city. Fer months they've been cuttin' down trees over there, and there ain't been a problem. But two attacks within just two weeks of each other now? The second was even further in the valley. I'm tellin' ye, somethin' ain't right. We need skilled soldiers, and we need a plan."

"You think something is agitating them and bringing them farther into the Valley?" Amelia asked.

Samuel nodded. "If it'd only been a single occurrence, I'd never think twice about it. But they spread their shit out. They're brutes, but they ain't exactly tryin' ta die. I don't have a clue what could be crawlin' up their arses, but somethin' is."

"I've had my own experiences with the remnant, and it's not something I'd want to see happen to anyone. The only thing we can do is continue to increase numbers, the Scouts and Hunters that patrol the Arcadian Borders especially, and educate everyone."

While Samuel was sure the Chancellor believed what she was saying, he'd seen the city Guard training.

They spent all day knocking each other on their asses, but that was about it. They had no idea how to properly hold a weapon, or even how throw a proper punch.

"I know ye think those are good choices, but there ain't

nobody good enough anymore to train those lads. They're all a bunch of babies. If the remnant come this way, yer men will fall. Ya ain't even got any archers. Never been a fan of 'em meself, but if an army approaches, especially an army of remnant, ye'll need ta stop 'em before they make it ta the gate."

Amelia sighed, forcing a smile as she nodded. He couldn't blame her for not enjoying the topic of her city potentially falling.

"I know you've saved the lives of several men, so I don't doubt your knowledge of battles or of the remnant. Put your mind at ease, rearick. If something happens, we'll stop it. I'll work on coming up with a better training strategy."

She was a brand-new Chancellor, taking over the chair after one hell of a bastard dictator. She was afraid to crack the whip too hard, and she was afraid to scare her people unnecessarily—but he knew she'd do what needed to be done.

Amelia was a strong woman, and he knew she was deadly serious when saying she'd fight to the end for anyone in her city. He nodded, putting his faith in her hands.

But that didn't mean he wouldn't also put faith into his own. Samuel had a plan to make sure training was done and done properly.

Samuel stood, gave her a nod, and walked out the door, hopefully leaving the Chancellor to think about a strategy that would make men out of those children in Guard's clothing.

ARRYN SAT at her desk waiting for everyone to fill the classroom. It was still strange to see the people she was responsible for, knowing she was to teach them all about her magic when she barely knew more than the basics of theirs.

Her class had been focusing on using magic to grow, much

like what Cathillian had been doing, except on a much smaller scale.

Cathillian was focusing on necessity and on a single topic: trees.

Arryn, on the other hand, had been focusing more on the bigger picture. Learning to grow smaller things and bond with the life inside of it. Teaching them how to harvest and connect to nature as a whole instead of simply willing something to grow.

Arryn had been teaching the students how to grow potted plants, something they were still working on.

Just as she had predicted, the Boulevard students were having an easier time learning the skills than the physical magic students.

One student had even gotten so frustrated that he accidentally set his flowers on fire. That had made the entire classroom laugh, even Arryn.

She decided to give them a little bit of a break today. She wanted to work on healing. It was harder to do, but she hoped it would reignite their interest in nature magic to learn something that valuable.

As everyone sat down, Arryn looked around the room and studied them for a moment. Something seemed very different. The entire class seemed distracted, worried, upset about something. "Good morning, class. I'd ask how everyone's doing, but it looks like you're all in a pissy mood."

One of the girls from the center of the class, Megan, raised her hand. "Did you not hear about what happened to Joel's dad?"

Arryn's forehead wrinkled as she looked around for Joel, but came up empty. She hadn't heard any news, good *or* bad. She shook her head. "No. What happened? Is that why he's not here?"

Megan nodded. "There was a remnant attack. Another one, this one farther south. Joel's dad was down there with a group of loggers, and the remnant killed everyone."

That certainly wasn't a good way to start the day.

Arryn felt terrible for Joel. He was one of the newest students —from the Boulevard, of course. He worked hard in class, and Arryn could see just how dedicated he was to learning any form of magic. He was particularly proud to be learning nature magic.

"I'm sorry to hear that." Arryn momentarily looked down at her desk before standing to address the class. "Joel's a great guy. I know what it's like to lose a parent, especially to violence. We should do something nice for him before he comes back."

A young man named Mark who sat to the right of the class spoke. "What exactly do you expect us to do for him? He just lost his father. Nothing's gonna make that better. Everyone's scared shitless the remnant's gonna come this way. What happens if they attack our city?"

"I don't think she meant doing something nice for him would fix his problems, Mark," Megan interjected. "She just meant it would be thoughtful. I think we're *all* sensitive to this and worried the remnant might come this way."

Arryn was about to speak when she felt a familiar tingle in her mind, reminding her of the day she'd met Amelia. She'd felt something that day—a buzzing feeling in her head—and Amelia had told her she'd felt the effects of the Chancellor looking into her thoughts. It was a mystical magic ability.

But that wasn't the problem.

Arryn had felt it again the day she met Talia, just before Amelia had pulled her out of class to hunt down Doyle. Once she'd returned to teaching after her week of being in a magically induced, coma-like sleep, that feeling had crept over her multiple times.

Amelia? Arryn thought, hoping that it was the Chancellor checking on her.

There was no answer.

The initial tingle went away, but she could still feel a light buzz in the back of her mind. It was very strange; something she couldn't quite describe.

Arryn shook her head, clearing her thoughts and bringing herself back to the conversation. "So, how far south are we talking?" Arryn asked. "If you mean farther than the last remnant attack, then I'd say we'll be fine."

It was Megan who spoke again. "It was, but it was also farther into the valley. It was the house farthest south before getting close to the mountain just north of Craigston. I don't know why they'd stop at the patch of forest, why they wouldn't climb up to Craigston. From what I hear, they can take anything they want."

"Yeah! I heard they're almost fifteen feet tall, built like bears, and just as strong, and they have magic. With that kind of combination... If they come here, we're screwed." That came from Jack, another student to the left side of the classroom.

Though Arryn had never seen the remnant herself, she knew about them from the Chieftain. She'd also heard Samuel's story, and she trusted both of those men, especially since both their descriptions matched the other.

"First of all, that's not right," Arryn corrected, standing and walking around the front of her desk. Suddenly, she felt like an Elder instead of a peer. "Second, why do you think we'd be screwed if they came to Arcadia?"

Jack snorted. "You're joking, right? Our military sucks. The Guard was a bunch of corrupt assholes before, but they were strong. We had over a thousand, but they were either killed or they left the city when they realized their shit wouldn't fly anymore. Now, to sum it up, we have hundreds of barely trained recruits who have no magic to back up what little martial skill they have."

She hadn't realized just how far off schedule the city was. With all the progress, it had seemed everything was on track. She'd been there for a few weeks, but she'd been so lost in the Academy and training with Cathillian that she hadn't even thought to check into the military aspect. She'd just assumed all of that was under control.

Clearly, the city was badly in need of help. Amelia could only do so much alone.

"Okay," Arryn began. "There's not much that I can do about the military, though I can talk to Amelia about it—"

"Yeah, do that," Mark said. "You're a druid. Aren't you guys supposed to be badasses or something? How do you guys train?"

Arryn thought back to her training session that very morning and smiled. "I trained with the druids for years, but I didn't start *actual* warrior training until recently when I decided to come back to Arcadia. The druids train all their people how to fight, not some, not just a select few. *Everyone.* Though, if someone decides to be a warrior, the training becomes *much* harder. Painful, really."

"Well, if the remnant are as awful as they say, we're gonna need a bunch of badasses, not toddlers in armor," Mark retorted.

"Yeah, I think the druids have it right. Everyone should know how to defend themselves. None of us knew anything until the worst happened with the Battle for Arcadia, and we barely made it out. If the remnant come, we're fucked, plain and simple. There's no way we can defend ourselves against them," Megan stated.

"Okay, I'm gonna put your minds at ease. You're right to fear the remnant, but your facts are wrong. The remnant aren't fifteen feet tall. They aren't built like bears. They sure as hell don't know magic. Their ancestors were regular, human men and women before the Age of Madness, so they're built like men and women, and are extremely strong. And I'm not going to lie to you, they do eat humans. They'll kill and eat anything."

"I'm not sure that makes me feel any better," Megan replied, a disgusted look on her face.

"Yeah, I'm pretty sure that's just as piss-your-pants scary," Mark agreed.

They were right. She realized she'd have been scared, too, if someone had told her what she'd just related to them when she was already worried about being attacked.

"I'll talk to Amelia. Like you, I believe everyone in the city should know how to defend themselves. Given that she was one of the people who helped train combatants for the revolution, I think she'll agree, so don't worry. Amelia seems smart when it comes to this stuff. She understands. You're right to prepare, but don't allow yourself to be sick over it. I'll take care of this."

"What about training with you?" Jack asked.

Arryn smiled. She couldn't deny that she really enjoyed the feeling of being respected, even if she was the same age or even younger than some of them. "If Amelia's good with it, I'd love to, even if I can only do it in private and not at the Academy."

Arryn made her way back around her desk to sit once again. "Let's get on with the day. How about I teach you a little about healing today? I had planned to anyway, but now I think it's the perfect topic."

She grew excited as everyone in the class perked up, happy to be taught something new and beneficial. She'd told them the truth, except for one thing.

She was just as worried as they were that the remnant might come their direction, though she couldn't deny that it would be exciting to test out her new training.

As she pondered her worries, the buzzing in her mind faded completely. If it wasn't Amelia, who was it? Arryn knew she needed to talk to Amelia, and soon.

CHAPTER FOUR

E lysia led a small group of warriors toward the border. She'd kept them busy maintaining the barrier ever since the first warning they'd received from the traitor, Aeris.

Aeris, with the help of his sister, Jenna, had come into the Dark Forest and left a warning—some dark arrows. While it didn't seem like much, the Elders knew that it was symbolic of war.

Jenna had allowed her brother in through the barrier before leaving the Forest herself to join them.

It was important for the warriors to continue ensuring no more breaches were made, but she didn't like forcing them to do it alone.

She and the Chieftain had decided to take turns, swapping out patrol leadership to keep everyone in good spirits and to make sure if anything *did* happen, one of them was there to see it firsthand.

So far, nothing had been found inside the barrier since the initial dark arrows, though they assumed that would change soon enough. They knew what the message had meant.

They would receive more than that initial visit, and the

threats would get progressively worse until an official war was declared.

The Chieftain had decided to allow Jenna and Aeris' parents, Flynn and Amara, to stay as a bargaining chip. The couple hadn't wanted to leave the tribe, but what they'd done had made them worthy to be called traitors.

Unlike their treacherous children, their only crime--thus far-- had been allowing the love they held for their offspring to cloud their better judgment.

They'd kept Aeris' presence—as well as their daughter Jenna's visits with him—hidden. They worried their son would be hurt or killed for his crimes, but it had gotten worse when Jenna had left to join him.

Now, Flynn and Amara were prisoners inside their own home, unable to be trusted, but having had committed a crime large enough to be banished.

Still, Elysia and the Chieftain knew Jenna and Aeris would be more likely to remain cautious out of worry for their parents. They would be less likely to declare an all-out war if their parents were still in "enemy" hands.

As they patrolled the southern border, Elysia's gut began to roil. Her connection with nature told her something had, in fact, breached the wall, so she held her hand up, signaling for everyone to stop their horses behind her.

Everyone halted and waited as she listened to the area around them. Off to the west, toward the Kalt River, in the direction they were traveling, she could hear the sound of small footsteps.

Her eyes turned darker green as she closed them, focusing on the plants and animals around her. Though her connection to the birds and other animals couldn't be as strong as the one she shared with Chaos, as powerful as she was, she could still coax them to allow her to see or, in this case, sense what they did.

Soon, she opened her eyes, looking back to her men and

women. "Move slowly. Something's inside the Dark Forest, but it isn't human."

Elysia used their bond to silently urge Chaos to pace forward, and he obliged, every step surprisingly light for a horse as large as he was.

As they got closer, Elysia could hear the faint sounds of growls and whines. Wolves. Chaos stopped and knelt, telling Elysia that he wanted her to get off.

She climbed down and waited for him to alert her, knowing his senses were even better than hers. Chaos suddenly ran forward at full speed, leaving Elysia behind. Through their connection, she could see him approaching several wolves.

They were disheveled, their fur matted and filthy. Their eyes were clouded over, and they looked sickly, their teeth longer and sharper than those of a normal wolf. These weren't just any wolves.

They were *familiars*.

Dark familiars. Elysia imagined Jenna had used her pure nature magic to open the border, something dark druids were unable to do—even Aeris after having been gone for so long— and allowed the wolves, the companions to their dark masters, to come through.

It was nothing shy of treason.

Elysia turned to her warriors. "Jenna has opened the wall, and the dark druids have sent in their companions. Chaos has gone after them. Let's move!" she ordered.

Faylinn, one of the other warriors, rode forward and reached down to pull Elysia onto his horse before heading in the direction Chaos had run. Within moments, they were upon the enemy wolves.

Elysia watched as Chaos bucked, kicking at the pack with his large hooves. There were seven in total, and Chaos was about to be overrun, though he was causing a lot of damage on his own.

They growled and snapped at his legs, leaving deep gashes

from their elongated teeth. Their saliva was full of bacteria and would no doubt cause great illness to anyone they bit into if it wasn't quickly healed—including Chaos.

Elysia jumped from the back of Faylinn's horse and ran forward. One of the wolves broke free of Chaos and charged at her, but she pulled her bow from her shoulder, nocked an arrow, and took the shot in one fluid movement.

The arrow flew straight through the wolf's open mouth and pierced the back of its throat and head as it jumped at her, ready to bite into her neck.

It fell to the ground and Elysia stepped over it, moving onto the next. She shot another one through the side of the head as it dove for Chaos. The other warriors were now running past her to fight them.

Elysia heard a growl to her right just before she saw the wolf in her peripheral vision. An eighth familiar had been hidden off to the side and had now jumped out of the thick brush, diving straight for her.

Without even breaking her stride, Elysia lifted her right hand, causing thick vines to burst from the ground and wrap around its neck. She swiped her hand downward, the vines slamming him to the earth before she closed her fist.

They snapped his neck as they tightened.

"Behind you, Chaos," Elysia warned. Her voice wasn't loud, but he was able to hear her through the bond.

A wolf bit at his hind leg, but because of her warning, he was able to kick it in the face, sending it flying back into the barrier surrounding the forest.

Elysia pulled a knife from her belt and charged toward a wolf that was heading for one of her warriors. She jumped on its back, wrapping her arm tight around its throat and pulling its head back so it couldn't snap at her as she rolled it to the ground. Wrapping her legs around it to pin it down, she sliced its throat before throwing it off her.

Faylinn reached a hand down to help her stand. As she rose, she saw one of her fellow druids taking down the final wolf with his sword.

They stood there and took a few moments to collect themselves. The death of any animal was not something to take lightly, especially when a druid had to be the one to do it.

But this... This was something else entirely.

They'd sacrificed their own familiars. Not in a great battle where lives were at stake, but as an *experiment*. It made Elysia sick and also saddened for the lives lost there today.

But there was nothing she could do. As dark familiars, they would never listen to her.

"What should we do, Elysia?" Arabella, a high-ranking warrior, asked.

Elysia paused, looking from the bodies to the barrier. "They sacrificed their own familiars to test our strength and vigilance. They wanted to know if we were patrolling, and they wanted to see how effective we would be. I'm betting if we opened the barrier, they'd be standing right on the other side."

"How could they do that? How could they sacrifice their own companions?" Arabella exclaimed.

Elysia had no answer. All she could do was shake her head, thinking of what it would be like to coldly sacrifice Chaos just to test the enemy. She felt like throwing up, but she couldn't allow her emotions to take hold. This wasn't over yet.

"I don't know how they did it, but it doesn't matter now. We can send their fallen companions back to them. Follow my lead," she ordered. "We're gonna give them a message of our own."

Elysia turned and faced the barrier, lifting her hands as she did so. Her eyes turned dark green as she focused on the thorny vines intertwined in the barrier, which began to pop as they broke away.

Soon, several were hanging free in the air. With graceful, fluid movements of her hands, she brought the thorn-covered vines down to wrap around a few of the wolves. Then, with a thrust of her hand as if she were throwing something, the vines whipped across the wall, launching the dark familiars back to the other side.

She heard voices shouting as the men and women on the other side were pelted with the bodies of their dead companions. As Elysia had ordered, her warriors did the same, throwing the rest of the wolves over the wall and back to the ones who had sent them to their deaths.

It hurt her heart and her gentle nature to do so, but she couldn't open the barrier as she was certain they expected her to do.

"*Elysia!*" a dark voice shouted. It was loud, brutally angry, and filled with hate.

Elysia knew that voice.

"Aeris! So lovely to hear your *traitorous* voice again!" Elysia called.

"You *will* pay for this!" he cried.

A dark smile spread across Elysia's beautiful face, making her look terrifying even to her fellow warriors. She was a good woman, but when anyone threatened her tribe, she became fearsome.

"Oh, but Aeris! It was *you* who sent them to their deaths. Go home, boy. Know that their blood is on *your* hands, and anyone you send through this barrier will meet the same fate!"

Elysia turned and walked toward Chaos as he knelt for her to climb on. She laid her hands against his neck, paying special attention to him right then as she allowed her magic to flow through him to heal whatever damage the wolves had done. The rest of the warriors followed suit, mounting their own horses.

When Aeris didn't reply and she felt the retreat of the dark energy, she sent one of the soldiers back to summon the next watch. It was decided. When she returned, she planned to double the number of warriors patrolling and spread them out to monitor larger areas.

Anyone who was left would begin battle training immediately. There was no longer a question in her mind.

A war was coming.

"HEY!" Samuel shouted at Ren who had just thrown his arms up in victory. "Yer a damn cheater if I ever saw one, mate."

Ren looked offended for a moment before smiling and wagging his eyebrows at a barmaid as she sat down two more glasses of ale. As soon as she'd walked off, he turned his offended expression back on Samuel.

"Yerrr a summa muh bitch," Ren slurred, pointing at Samuel as he tipped up his own mug and chugged half his ale.

"Did you just call me a son of a bitch? Because I couldn't understand ye over the sound of ye not bein' able ta hold yer ale," Samuel spat back.

Ren nodded. "That'sss whut I said, mate! Summa muh bitch. *Youuu*," he said, carefully enunciating the last word without his normally thick accent. "Yerra smmmbitch."

Samuel rolled his eyes. "*Scheisse*, man! Yer actually gettin' worse!"

"Pffft." Ren made the loud noise through closed lips while waving a hand in the air, spitting on the table in the process. "I ain't gettin' worse at nnnuthin', mate. Yer da one callin' people *cheaterrrs*. Yer just mad cuz I beat ya at arm wrestlin'. My ol' arm is ssstrong'r than yers."

Samuel shook his head before finishing off his glass and picking up the new one that had just been brought to their table. "I'm gonna need ta be as drunk as ye are just ta deal with yer belligerent arse. And yes! Yes, ye did cheat!"

"How?" Ren asked, leaning over the table, nearly-finished mug in hand.

"I damn near had ye pinned and ye kicked me under the table, ye old bastard!"

Ren laughed loudly. "Ah, yeah. I rrrmber now," he slurred before belching loudly and laughing again. "Ye hear that? That'sss how a man does it. *Youuu* sound like a prepubescent little girl."

Samuel stared at him incredulously. "Yer two seconds from gettin' drawn an' quartered in the street, mate. An' why do ye keep doin' that?"

Ren sat his mug down after another more modest drink, wiping his beard of some that had escaped. "What's that, Sally?"

Samuel ignored his reference back to the prepubescent comment he'd made before. "Minus talkin' like a damn drunk mule, ye keep sayin' yer words weird."

Ren nodded. "Ye ever done it? Try ta talk like the Arrrcadiansss? It sssounds stupid."

Samuel dropped his forehead to the table for a moment, tapping it a few times in annoyance before looking back up. "Then why do it?"

Ren laughed. "Because I get bored easy when I drink, lad. Ye know what that says about ye, don't ye?"

"I sure as piss know what it says about *youuu*," Samuel mocked. "I want a rematch when yer sober, ya prick."

"I think it'sss time fer anotherrr. I found da bottom of me glass," Ren said, picking it up and looking through the bottom at Samuel.

"Like hell ye do!" Samuel said, yanking the glass out of his friend's hand. "Yer a rude drunk."

"But I'm funny," Ren said with a smile.

Samuel laughed. "Funny lookin' maybe. I have shite ta do tomorrow, old man. Let's get yer arse home before ye pass out on the table and ye need ta be carried there."

"Ye'd do that fer me?" Ren asked. "Even after I kicked ye in the shin and cheated?"

"Pffft. I never said a fool thing like that, mate. I said we needed ta get ye there before ye *needed* ta be carried home. Me leg hurts. I ain't carryin' yer drunken arse anywhere."

Ren laughed, and Samuel walked around the table to help his friend out of the bar, making sure to leave some coins on the table as he did.

While it had been a long time coming, Samuel needed the night to let loose and have fun, though Ren did far more *letting loose* than he did. As they made their way down the street, both men drunk as hell, he reminded himself to let go more often.

CHAPTER FIVE

As soon as class had ended the day before, Arryn had gone to Amelia's office in hopes of talking to her, but Marie had said that she was too busy. With everything going on, she wasn't too surprised to be dismissed.

So, Arryn decided to go see Amelia the following day. Not only was the remnant weighing heavily on her mind, but she had other problems as well.

Someone in the school was snooping in her thoughts with mystical powers. It was very unsettling, to say the least.

Amelia was the only one who knew the story of her past. Her students knew she'd left the city, but she had never explained why. She wanted to keep it that way, for her own safety.

No one knew if she was a noble or from the Boulevard, and no one knew about her total disdain for Adrien. She'd been careful to keep all of it under wraps.

Amelia's door was wide open, but Arryn knocked anyway. Amelia looked up from her desk, then smiled and waved Arryn in.

As Arryn came over to sit down across from her newest friend, she was well aware that her own expression wasn't nearly as happy as Amelia's. When Amelia's smile fell, it was obvious that she had noticed.

"That doesn't look like excitement to see me," Amelia said. "What's wrong?"

Arryn hadn't meant to worry her, so she forced a smile. "I apologize. I didn't mean to look so pissed, but I had a rather interesting conversation with my students, and I thought you should know."

Amelia nodded, closing a folder on the desk and sliding it to the side. "Of course. I'm assuming it's regarding the remnant, because that's been the running theme for the last two days."

There was a pause as Arryn hesitated, debating what she should say. She didn't want to bombard her with more about problems she already knew about, but she did need to know the students felt worried.

She straightened herself, deciding to continue. "Seems like you've probably already heard everything I'm about to say, but if I didn't say it I'd make myself a liar. I told them I'd talk to you."

Amelia nodded. "No, don't worry about that. I understand. Tell me everything."

Arryn sighed, clasping her fingers as she debated how to start the conversation. "First of all, I think Amos' murder is playing a big part in their reaction to the latest news of the remnant attacks."

Realization struck Amelia's face. She'd taken the death of Amos, the Boulevard student that had gone missing for several days before being found with his throat slit open, particularly hard. She'd promised his mother she'd find him and bring him home, but instead, she'd been led to his corpse.

The Chancellor seemed to be lost in thought for a moment before finally speaking. "I'm sure you're right. That's a lot to take in within a short period of time. I hadn't planned to release any information on the remnant *because* of the murder and the initial attack on Ren's group. I wasn't expecting the students to know."

"I had a student miss school today because his father was one of the men who was killed. That's how the others found out. They had a lot of misinformation about the remnant, so I cleared that up—though, I don't think I actually helped. But I saw no benefit to lying to them."

Amelia smiled, but it was more a sympathetic smile than a genuine one. "I wouldn't have lied either. Sometimes, the mind creates something far worse than the real thing, but in this case, they're just as scary as we can imagine."

"Exactly. And they want to be prepared for the worst. I don't think that's wrong," Arryn replied.

"I know they're worried. Luckily, those other attacks were almost at the southern edge of the Valley. Granted, the rearick and his friends did an excellent job fighting them off and keeping everyone alive, but the others farther south had no protection whatsoever."

Arryn grew excited as she saw a perfect entrance into what she had come to discuss. "Exactly. The students know the Guard is understaffed and undertrained. We know you just hired a lot more, but those recruits are just that—*recruits*. They aren't even trained in magic, so their lack of martial expertise isn't backed up by anything. The students have real worries, and I think they're right."

Amelia sat back, tapping her fingers on her chair. "I know, and I understand. While I'm hoping for the best, I know the possibility is there. When we came back after the Battle for Arcadia, I didn't want the people of the city to feel like they would always be at war. I didn't want them to feel like they *had* to protect us anymore. That's what the *new* Guard is for. I figured they should feel safe inside the city they had protected during the Battle for Arcadia, but now, it seems the remnant have other plans. I've taken steps to increase training, but I'm open to ideas. What did you have in mind?"

Arryn told Amelia what she had told her class about the

druids and went into even more detail, explaining the intensity with which they trained. Everyone learned and everyone knew how to protect themselves, and not just when an emergency happened.

After taking a moment to let Amelia process what she'd said, she continued, "They want to learn how to fight. They want to know how to save themselves and their families. To ease their minds, I even taught them a bit of healing yesterday. It was abysmal, which was to be expected since I'm not the best healer either, but it certainly made a difference in morale."

Amelia stood, running her fingers through her hair as she paced slowly back and forth behind her desk. It was a lot to take in; Arryn was certain of that.

Not only did the woman have the weight of the city on her shoulders, but she also had a murder to solve, rebuilding to complete, jobs to fill, and now remnant to worry about.

"I think you're right," Amelia responded. "Once things get settled and we have the funds to hire more teachers, we should use one of the downstairs great rooms in the Academy as a training area. It would be a terrific addition, and anyone who wanted to attend, even moms and dads, would be more than welcome to take the class. Right now, we need to focus on training up the Guard. If we spread too thin, there will be a city full of mediocre fighters instead of an army full of great ones."

It was hard to say when things would be settled, and Arryn knew the fear of bad things happening sooner rather than later. Maybe she could do something to help with that. Arryn believed Amelia was right about focusing on the Guard. They were the most important to train.

"That's a great solution," Arryn agreed, smiling. "Let me know if I can help you figure anything out, especially the timeline. We might be able to help train guards, too."

Arryn decided to end the conversation there, knowing it was best not to talk to her about mental magic right then with everything else on her plate. She needed to do a bit more investigation anyway.

Amelia's voice stopped Arryn as she stood to leave. "One more thing. I know everything is still raw about Doyle. I know you missed your shot there, but I wanted you to know that it isn't over. There's someone else you can still talk to. Elon—Adrien's chief engineer. I mentioned him before, but don't forget. As soon as I'm done interrogating him about Doyle and what he may or may not have said, I'll take you down there so you can ask him anything you want. Promise."

Arryn smiled in response. "Thanks. I appreciate that. I've actually been *trying* to forget. Otherwise, I start to feel overly excited. I don't think you want that on your plate right now."

Amelia laughed. "Get some rest. I'm sure you could use it."

She needed to talk to Cathillian about the possibility of getting a group together. It wasn't going to hurt anything, and it would go a long way to helping Amelia.

With her bad feeling about Talia only growing stronger over time, Arryn wondered if it could be her that possessed the mental magic.

From what she'd been told about mystics, they could convince anyone to see anything they want. Maybe Talia wasn't capable of physical magic at all. Given that her head was being messed with, she had a feeling whoever Doyle had warned Amelia about was already inside the Academy.

Arryn didn't want to wait any longer to get training underway.

THE SUN BEAT down on the Dark Forest, peeking through the tiniest breaks in the thick leaves of the canopy above. Elysia crossed her arms as she watched the three tribes' warriors gather.

In the Dark Forest, there were three separate communities.

Each had its own warriors, though they were all trained the same way. Though the two southernmost tribes specialized in magic and expert combat, the tribe farthest to the north—the *Schatten*—specialized in subtlety.

All druids were exceptionally quiet, but the *Schatten* were the quietest.

Elysia stepped forward to address all the men and women before her. "Everyone here is one army! We're initializing battle training right now. As you all know, each community usually drills only with its own warriors. This time, we have an actual threat, which leads me to call for full-on battle challenges."

She paused as voices erupted. They talked amongst themselves about the threats from the dark druids among other things.

She raised a hand, and everyone quieted so she could continue. "All three tribes' warriors will split into two groups. As you can see behind me, I have thirty healers. If you're down, call for help and you'll be retrieved and healed. If you're not too weak and haven't lost too much blood, you'll be thrown back in."

The Chieftain stepped forward, looking over the tribes as they counted themselves off and broke into two teams. They did so without further instruction, another sign of just how incredible these warriors truly were.

Once they were split into groups comprising more than a hundred in each, the Chieftain gave further orders.

"The group to my left will stay put. The group to my right will head north. You'll start at the village farthest from us. You'll know the battle is to begin as well as ends when you hear the crack of my thunder overhead. Now *move!*"

Every warrior placed their fist over their heart before following the instructions. Team Two headed toward the north and Team One stayed put, turning to face north.

Elysia made her way to her father, looking at their prized fighters. "What do ya think? Should we play, too?"

The Chieftain laughed. "Really? *You* wanna go against *me*?"

Elysia could only grin. "You know it, old man. It's been a while since you and I fought against one another. I think it's about time, don't you?"

"I think I'm about to kick your ass all over the place. Maybe you should go ahead and designate your healer now. Wouldn't want you to waste any energy healing all the ass-kicking."

"How many times are you gonna say ass-kicking in one sentence?" she asked.

The Chieftain looked up for a moment as his lips moved, but no sound came out. Finally, he shook his head. "No. It was two different sentences, and they were separated. Smartass. So, you wanna take bets or not?"

Elysia nodded. "Absolutely."

The Chieftain's jade green eyes glowed an almost neon green. "Then you better run, daughter. Your men in Team Two have already left you. This is *my* domain. I'm Number *One*, remember?"

Elysia shook her head, sighing at her father and his ridiculous sense of humor.

At a loud whistle from Elysia, Chaos ran to her side and knelt. She climbed onto his back, and they raced for the northern village. Before she made it completely out of earshot, she heard her father call out, "*Zobig*!" before a loud roar echoed through the woods.

TALIA HAD ONLY BARELY MADE it in the front door of the Academy when Jackson came over to stand in front of her. The recent beating he'd gotten at the hands of his fellow students—Boulevard students—had changed him.

The physical evidence had almost disappeared. The bruises had turned a sickly yellow, and would be gone in a few days' time. The scratches and open wounds were still there, but in another week the scars would be their only reminder.

Emotionally, those scars were much deeper.

Jackson no longer had a single shred of respect or trust for the Boulevard students; what fragile bit he'd possessed had shattered with the first punch. All of that had worked in Talia's favor, and he had come around to her way of thinking much faster once she'd claimed loyalty to his cause.

But he wasn't great at being the bad guy. In fact, he was terrible at it. Jackson was a terrible liar and always obvious—at least to Talia. She hoped that he wasn't so transparent to others.

On top of being over an hour early for class, he acted very odd for a normal visit, looking around and over his shoulder several times as he approached.

It made her want to smack him for being so suspicious.

Except for the teachers, the building was supposed to be empty. Talia didn't even want to be there.

From the look on his face she could tell he needed to talk about something. "Good morning, Jackson. You seem upset."

He took a deep breath and smiled, hands clasped and fidgeting in front of him. "Actually, I'm not upset at all. I, well, *we* wanted to extend an invite to you. I'm sorry for the unannounced visit, but I wanted to get here early to catch you privately."

"We?" she asked. "You mean the group you've been telling me about?"

Jackson nodded. "We've talked about it for a couple of weeks, debating the pros and cons. Obviously, it's a significant risk for us to trust just anyone. We have to be careful, especially after what happened to me. But it's obvious we need the help, especially from someone like you. So, if you want to, you're more than welcome to attend tonight—but you don't have to. We realize the risk you'd be taking. Ten p.m. It's a couple hours after dark, so it'll be easy to sneak around."

Talia couldn't help but smile. It was exactly what she'd been waiting for. All that time she'd spent talking to Jackson about *feelings* hadn't been wasted at all. He just wanted to see the Boulevard students go down at this point, and apparently, his friends in the group did as well.

"I'd love to," Talia told him. "Just tell me where to be, and I'll be happy to meet you there."

"There are some abandoned houses in the center of the city. The Guard doesn't go down there, and it's secluded. We usually meet in the auditorium here since it's pretty useless now that Adrien doesn't give *grand* speeches, but we didn't want anyone to see you with us just in case. We wanted to protect you if you decided against helping us."

Well, that was shocking. He was lost further in her charm than she'd thought. And his friends must have been impacted in some way as well. Whatever the case, it was a good plan.

"How will I know which house?" she asked.

"It's the only one with red curtains in the window," he told her.

Talia nodded. "I'll be there. Now, run along before someone sees us talking. If anyone has—"

"It's about our counseling." He smiled.

Talia gave a quick nod in acknowledgment and made her way down the hall to the stairs before heading to her office. Things were going her way, and she couldn't be more excited. As long as she continued to tread lightly and gather the help that was necessary, she would have everything she'd planned for.

CHAPTER SIX

E lysia sat on the back of her over one-ton steed, Chaos, listening to him snort and scrape his large, front hoof against the forest floor in preparation.

Everything was deadly silent as the warriors in Team Two stood behind their fearless leader, waiting for the crack of thunder overhead to signal the beginning.

All around her, Elysia could hear the rustling of wolves, foxes, squirrels, raptor birds, and other familiars as they awaited the same call.

"*Schatten!*" Elysia called out to the shadow warriors that specialized in subtlety. "My father will undoubtedly send your counterparts to the trees. He will keep them low enough to engage, but high enough not to be seen. Make sure they don't find their targets."

"Then we'll go higher, Elysia," Rae, one of the *Schatten* said from behind her.

Elysia turned in time to see several druids raise their hands to the sky, vines unraveling from the trees and wrapping around them before pulling them upward.

Had she not seen it herself, she never would have heard them.

During training, those men and women spent most of their time learning the intricacy of the plants and how they grow. As much as a normal druid knew, these warriors knew far more.

They were able to control and shift anything within the plant, allowing those movements to be almost silent.

The Chieftain had once explained it to her in a way she hadn't understood then, but as she grew, it made perfect sense.

"When you ask a tree to move, you ask its permission to *allow you* to move it. You do all the heavy lifting, and it's noisy and clumsy, even when it looks poetic to someone else. Now, imagine connecting to that tree so deeply that it *helps* you. You become one with one another and the movements become seamless and silent. Like a familiar to her master druid. It takes incredibly hard work and years of study. Not even I am capable of such a task, but that's why we have them. Because you and I are just *way* too hyper. Mostly me… but you're not much better."

She'd been offended then, but he'd been very right. No one in the Chieftain's bloodline would ever be capable of such a feat.

Especially Cathillian.

His mind was far more scattered than anyone she knew.

A deep, grim *Boom!* sounded out overhead, bringing a smile to Elysia's face.

"Just a friendly warning! Anyone that let's my father win…" Elysia began.

There was a laugh beside her. "We love our Chieftain, but he's a goofy, old man. We can take him," Faylinn said.

Elysia smiled and shook her head as she wordlessly told Chaos to step forward. "He might be senile at times, but he's still strong. Don't underestimate him, or we lose. And then I have to go against all of *you* to reclaim my honor."

Those that were closest to Elysia laughed, knowing her sense of humor, while others wore their fiercest war-faces and nodded in understanding.

Chaos was slow at first, but then began to move faster,

leading the small army behind them into battle with his master druid.

There was quite a distance between the southernmost village and the northernmost, but both approaching from each direction made the distance much shorter.

First blood was spilled from above. There were no sounds in the canopies to mark the "kill", only the *Schatten* that fell, a vine snatching him up at the last moment to carefully lower him the rest of the way to the ground.

Within only a few moments, a healer pulled him free to heal him, but Elysia did not see if he was sent back out, only that he wasn't one of hers. Her team had successfully gotten their first target.

After tapping Chaos on the shoulder, Elysia jumped off, not waiting for him to kneel. She lowered herself into a crouch and ran forward, using trees and brush to hide her as best as she could.

With a wave of her hand, she motioned for everyone to fan out.

More men and women dropped from the trees, vines catching them in their falls as designated healers came to get them.

Soon, Elysia could hear the sounds of battle commencing.

She stood, looking around as her ears were bombarded with the clashing of metal, the gnashing of teeth with the larger animals growling and snapping at their enemy familiars, and the thunder gently rolling above.

Where are you, old man? Elysia asked herself.

She decided to fight her way through until she drew him out.

Running at full speed, she arched backward, narrowly missing the swipe of a sword through the air as she slid to a stop.

Turning, she saw a terrified druid from her father's team that was in his early twenties standing there, sword raised and suddenly shaking.

"Elysia! I'm sorry! I didn't see that it was you!" he shouted over the chaos, his light green eyes wide.

She smiled darkly before lifting her hand. A vine shot from the ground and wrapped around the sword, and with a flick of her fingers, it thrust the sword backwards, the handle punching him hard in the stomach. Then, she lifted her hand, the handle then rising to smash him in the face.

Releasing the vines, she ran forward and backhanded him, sending him stumbling back into a tree.

As the man collapsed, struggling to catch his breath, she came to stand over him. She smiled as she leaned over.

"This is battle training, young man. I'm not your superior. I'm your enemy, and you just let me take you down. Next time, don't treat me like I'm helpless. Punch me in the face, or I'll do far worse to you."

A healer ran up and dropped by their sides.

"See to it he gets his ass back out there," she said to the designated healer before turning back to him. "Next time, I expect you to forget my title. Battle training is life and death."

He nodded nervously as she gave him a smile and a wink before standing.

Taking a few steps back, she looked above to the tree with low branches. She jumped hard as her eyes turned an even darker green, the lowest limb popping and cracking as it moved down to meet her.

She grabbed hold and pulled herself up before running farther down the limb and jumping to the next tree, again moving the branches to meet her.

This time, she scurried higher, making sure to watch for any *Schatten*. Placing both of her hands against the thick trunk, she connected to the life within, pushing outward to feel for the life all around.

The birds in the trees scattered from branch to branch and

the squirrels hid in holes in the trunks, watching the war below them.

As she looked around, using her magic to feel for what she needed, two things were brought to her attention.

Elysia jumped back several feet as a *Schatten* dropped directly on top of her. This one was fearless and didn't care who Elysia was. The warrior only saw an enemy.

A smile spread across Elysia's face as the *Schatten* moved forward, her eyes glowing with power.

The woman charged, pulling a large knife from her belt as she did. The *Schatten* weren't quite as skilled in hand-to-hand combat in comparison to the other warriors, though they were still terrifying.

It was their magic that killed.

Elysia knew if the woman got hold of her, she'd lose, and she'd just found her father. She couldn't lose yet.

Without hesitation, Elysia jumped down, her hands catching the branch as she used her momentum to swing herself back up and over. As she came back up, she wrapped her legs around the *Schatten* and jerked, pulling her off the branch entirely before dropping her to the ground.

Vines shot from the tree like lightning, wrapping around the shadow warrior and pulling her up and deep into the tree where Elysia could no longer see her.

Breathing a sigh of relief, Elysia dropped back down to the ground and began running, deciding she didn't want to risk another run-in with a *Schatten*.

The sound of hooves echoed through her ears as Chaos charged forward, knocking several enemies out of Elysia's path before she jumped, only barely making it high enough to lie on his back so she could pull herself the rest of the way up.

"To my father," she breathed out before Chaos rose on his hind legs, causing everyone in their immediate area to step back for fear of being trampled.

The horse galloped through the woods, easily clearing others out of the way and jumping over anything that didn't move.

The thunder grew louder as they neared the Chieftain, and Elysia knew he was aware of her approach.

Lightning shot from the sky, bolt after bolt raining down around them in a large circle, stopping them hard in their tracks.

Chaos rose to his hind legs again before slamming his front hooves down hard on the ground, his head nodding up and down fervently as he huffed and snorted his annoyance.

The Chieftain's lightning was strong enough that Elysia knew she'd never be able to stop or reroute it with her own magic, so she decided to take another road to disturb it.

Sliding off her horse, Elysia pulled her sword from its sheathe and threw it, the metal passing through a bolt of lightning and disrupting its path.

Using the disruption, she used her magic to finish redirecting it toward her father.

It blew past, hitting a tree and creating a large scar in its bark. It missed her target, but it did what she'd hoped: stopped the barrage of electricity from raining down from above.

As Elysia ran forward, she heard someone call her name out from the side. It was Arabella, one of her friends.

The woman threw a staff to her that was made from the *Heilig* tree, a tree that grew stronger and sturdier with every natural death of a druid in the Forest as they channeled what was left of their power into the massive trunk until their final breath was taken.

Elysia caught it just in time to swing it around and block the attack from her father as he brought his own staff crashing down.

The wood from the *Heilig* tree was unbreakable to anyone other than an Elder druid—power both father and daughter possessed.

The wind whipped around them as Elysia struggled to push

back against him. He may have been old, but he sure as hell wasn't weak.

Realizing she was getting nowhere fast while pushing against him, she quickly dropped and tumbled out of the way, narrowly missing the end of the staff as it came down hard on the ground next to her.

Rolling back onto her heels, Elysia's eyes turned darker green and she grunted loudly as she swung her staff upward, a root just under the ground breaking free of the earth and bringing with it several large chunks of earth flying toward the Chieftain.

Twirling his staff like a fan, a heavy gust of wind blew forward, shooting the pieces of earth back at Elysia, hitting her hard and sending her back onto the ground with a loud *Oof!*

The Chieftain stalked toward her, but she was able to throw her hand up, a root lifting from the ground and bringing him down.

Taking the only opportunity she knew she'd have, she jumped up and kicked his staff away before wrapping the root around his waist, squeezing him.

A smile spread across her face as she was about to declare her victory, but she hadn't noticed his eyes glowing.

His free hands dove into the dirt around him, the ground under Elysia shaking as large roots moved and shifted, opening the earth below her feet and swallowing her up to her shoulders.

A deep, hearty laugh echoed out as he moved the roots back into place, pinning her there. She watched her father effortlessly unwrap himself and move to sit on his knees.

"Oh, child. That was pretty good! But I keep *trying* to tell ya! *I'm* number one!" he laughed.

Something patted her hard on the top of her head as she squirmed around in the dirt, trying to move. He'd only given her enough space to breathe.

She struggled to look up and saw Zobig pull his enormous front paw away, having been the one to pat her. The black bear made several noises as he made his way to stand by the Chieftain, and Elysia wondered if the bear was laughing at her.

He was quite the smartass, so she didn't doubt it for a moment.

"Zobig says he's taken out several of your men," the Chieftain said with a smile. "Ready to accept defeat?"

Elysia laughed. She'd managed to wiggle her hands up into the open space her father had left for her ribs to expand.

"Chaos has taken out just as many of yours. Maybe more!" Elysia shouted.

She twisted her fingers, willing the roots to loosen the area around her as a vine shot down from the tree to lift her out before her father could seal her back in.

Within seconds, Chaos was by her side, his head low as he stared down Zobig. The black bear stepped forward and roared in response.

"Elysia, Chieftain," Moira, the captain of the designated healers said as she stepped forward.

Father and daughter never allowed their eyes to leave one another.

"Yes," the Chieftain answered.

"We have exhausted our healers. Everyone is safe, and there have been no casualties, but I sent word to those further out that the battle would have to end. As instructed, I ended the drill once our magic began to wane," she said.

The Chieftain smiled. "Well, daughter, I guess we'll have to call this a draw. Until next time?"

Elysia rolled her eyes. "Yeah. Sure. But I know you. Until we get an honest rematch, you're going to keep saying you beat me."

He shrugged. "Well, I trapped you *way* better than you trapped me. Oh! And my familiar could *eat* yours. So, while I'm going to say it's a draw, like you were so kind to point out, *yes*. I'm the winner." He gave a big, cheesy smile. "After all—I *am*..."

"Yeah, yeah. Number one," Elysia interrupted as she waved a

hand in the air. "Now, why don't you sound the thunder to signal the end before anyone gets injured, and they can't be healed."

The sound of loud thunder cracked overhead, echoing through the skies as it did. "Don't be sad, Elysia. You shouldn't be intimidated by my awesomeness. You did pretty good out there."

Elysia looked at him incredulously. "Awesomeness? You've been drinking too much wine with the young people."

In a move that reminded her of her son, Cathillian, the Chieftain dropped his jaw in feigned shock as his hand lazily came to rest over his heart. "What? Never! They think I'm cool! I can't let 'em down."

Elysia laughed, unable to hold it in any longer. Her elderly father was just as much of a child as any kid in the village—but she knew better than anyone that day that he was still quite a force to be reckoned with.

CHAPTER SEVEN

The sun had just begun to set when Samuel headed toward Lord Girard's manor. With one hell of a hangover, he was already regretting the decision to move at all.

It had been a while since he'd had one, but Ren was far worse.

He'd thought it over repeatedly, and he wanted to make the city stronger. If someone—including the remnant—could just walk in and take anything they wanted because the guards were babies, well, that wouldn't benefit him at all.

It would take even *longer* for the city to get back on its feet, and his people would be even further burdened. They needed steady work.

Oddly enough, the only person in the city he felt comfortable discussing these things with was a druid. Well, a druid and his young friend. Their people trained hard, and Samuel knew it. They'd understand what he did about strategy and prevention.

While the rearick didn't go to such lengths in their training— in fact, they had no formal training at all.

They sparred and grappled and fought from the time they were very young. They were tough, and life in the mines hadn't done anything except make them stronger, more powerful.

They'd seen their fair share of fights with the remnant through the years, but the Arcadians hadn't. The druid people hadn't either, but they were serious fighters. Cathillian and Arryn were his last hope to protect the city—to protect a city he hated so his people could survive.

He walked up the steps and knocked on the front door. Arryn opened it and smiled. "Samuel! How are you? Come in."

Arryn stepped aside and Samuel walked past her into the elaborate living room. Cathillian came into the room then, a large smile spreading across his face.

"Samuel! What are you doing here?" the druid asked as he crossed the room to meet his friend. "Did that little sassy ass of yours finally decide to take me up on learning nature magic?"

The rearick didn't miss the sarcasm in the other man's voice.

Samuel shook his head. "Yer a real funny one, ain't ye? No, I came fer somethin' else. Yer the only ones I figured would take me seriously."

That got their attention. They looked at one another for a moment before turning back to Samuel, curiosity on both their faces.

Arryn motioned toward the couch, signaling for him to take a seat.

"I talked ta the Chancellor about this already, but I figured she's got enough ta deal with. Especially when we can do a pretty good job of it ourselves."

Arryn shook her head, confusion in her expression. "What are you talking about?"

"The remnant! I've fought those bastards more than a few times. They're smarter than people give 'em credit for, and I've gotta bad feelin'. That remnant attack ain't gonna be the last."

Cathillian sat down on the opposite end of the couch from Samuel. "Arryn came home yesterday telling me about that. I don't know a lot, but what I *do* know is they typically look for places they can rip apart easily. They like fighting and a challenge, but they don't wanna walk into a guaranteed loss. I highly doubt they know what's happened here in Arcadia. They probably still think Adrien is in charge, which works in our favor because they'll also think the army is strong and well-trained."

Cathillian paused as he thought over his next words. "That being said, while I doubt they'll come in this direction, I also think it's completely and totally irresponsible to leave the city unprotected."

Arryn nodded. "Same here. Don't just prepare for absolutes, prepare for possibilities. If the entire city is prepared all the time, then nothing can stand in their way. Cathillian may be completely right. Hell, we may never hear of another attack. But it would be stupid not to prepare for the possibility. Amelia agrees, and she's trying to help, but I think we can do a bit more."

Samuel smiled. "There's what I was lookin' fer. Well, this was even easier than I hoped, and I figured it'd be pretty simple. So, now that we're settled, what do we do about it?"

Arryn sighed as she came over to sit in a chair off to the side.

"Emotions are off the charts right now," Cathillian offered. "I think everyone needs to take a breath and slow down. As we've all agreed, or at least Arryn and I have agreed, the odds of another remnant attack are slim."

Arryn shook her head, leaning forward in her chair. "Yeah, we did, but we also agreed it's stupid to leave everyone underprepared. There've been two attacks. A murder. A change in government. And one of the students was attacked by several Boulevard students. Have you heard there have been some robberies as well? The poor have only gotten poorer and the nobles are being pulled down to middle-class. It makes sense that they would be so afraid.

"Everything in the city is completely unstable right now; Adrien left one hell of a mess. I don't care if it seems crazy or irrational, I think we need to do something to ease their minds.

Even if it's not *because* of an imminent threat. They just need to feel *some* control. Let's give them that if we can."

"Couldn't agree more, lass, so I propose we gather ourselves a group and see what we can do," Samuel stated.

"I already spend my entire day with you ass hats," Cathillian quipped. "What else do you wanna do?"

Arryn laughed sarcastically. "Is that a serious question? Well, for starters, the city needs archers. I would gladly teach the men how to shoot. I might not be the best at magic, even though I got roped into being a teacher, but *archery* I can do. The two of you can handle hand-to-hand combat. If we find them to be brave and fast enough, we could train them the druid way. No holding back."

Cathillian's eyes widened. "Are you insane? We heal, that's why we can train like that."

Arryn's left eyebrow rose as she looked at him incredulously. "We heal *each other*, dork. We can heal *them* if they get shot in the leg with an arrow. It'll be fine. And like I said, we only warrior-train those who want to learn hard and fast. Although, everyone we recruit should be of that caliber. We shouldn't be wasting our time on anyone who is only capable of mediocre skills anyway. That's the problem with the Arcadian Guard right now—they're too damn slow and dopey."

"I think we got ourselves a plan," Samuel told them. "If we can't get this taken care of the good old-fashioned way, we'll take care of it ourselves. I ain't never been one ta let a little thing like *rules* stand in me way, anyway. Don't particularly care fer 'em."

Cathillian threw his hands up for a moment before they fell back down to rest on his legs. "Well, I guess that's it then. That's the plan. Not that I had much say about it."

"Oh, hush, lad. Ya know damn good and well that ye'd have said yes anyway. Yer ass just stings because the lass agreed before ye did."

Arryn laughed. It always amused her to give him a tough time, and when someone else did it, it was even more special.

The trio launched into forming a plan to get some of the Arcadian Guard to follow them, to really learn how to fight for their city. Arryn just hoped it wouldn't get her arrested for treason in the process.

More and more every day, she found herself hoping she was making her parents proud.

THE EVENING WAS off to a beautiful start. As Talia walked through the quiet streets of the city, a city that would one day be hers, she thought over the plan she and the mystic had put in place.

After having discussed the meeting with Scarlett, they both decided it was time. Talia really needed to take control now. If things were going to go her way, and her plan was to continue working the way she needed it to, then she needed to get them on her side.

What better way to do it than by offering more power?

They'd decided to use an old legend to their advantage. This story said if one drank the blood of another, he or she would absorb their power. It was impossible, of course; Talia knew that, but their group of sheep didn't, and they didn't need to. All Talia required was for them to believe it.

Talia didn't mind doing the dirty work, but she hated wasting time on the hunt. She had far too much to do with running a school, keeping the Chancellor happy, and planning their next move to worry about much else, so she delegated the task of picking the next victim to Scarlett.

To Talia's surprise, Scarlett's answer had come rather quickly. The next victim would be one of the Boulevard students who had attacked Jackson.

Shaking her head and putting a hand in the air, Talia

disagreed. "No. Jackson had an argument with Amos before I took him, and it made him look guilty as hell. That's why he was attacked. If we pick another student he's been in an altercation with, he will *not* be overlooked this time. Not by the students and not by Amelia. It took a *lot* of convincing on my part to keep Amelia off his ass the *last* time," Talia had told Scarlett. "We won't be doing that again. We need him. Otherwise, I wouldn't give a damn."

But Scarlett had several points of her own.

"That's exactly right, we need him. It's *our* job to protect him. He's helping us, helping *you*. We should do this for him and show him *and* that group we won't tolerate violence against our own. Show them we are deadly serious about our plan and taking back the city. They'll trust you implicitly."

Talia had already heard enough, but she decided to hear Scarlett the rest of the way out and had encouraged her to continue.

Scarlett had smiled. "Jackson was far too weak to take the four of them on alone—obviously. Take a good look... Do you *ever* see those boys walking alone? No. They're always together. Therefore, Jackson wouldn't be able to take them on by himself now which gives us a great opportunity if you'll let us take it. If you ask me, I think we should stop doing things so subtly and let me take a more active role. I'm here. *Use me*," Scarlett had replied with a playful wink.

She was right. If Talia wanted to move further and make a difference with Jackson and the others, Scarlett was her best chance.

With a heavy sigh, Talia had decided to listen to her partner and take her advice. It was hard for Talia to do, but she believed Scarlett was onto something.

The mystic had already taken the initiative to arrange for two of the four boys to take a walk that evening just after sunset.

Talia would do the dirty work on one of them—their leader, Dallas—while Scarlett convinced the other he'd seen someone else. It would be dark outside, so they'd decided that only subtle hints would be required.

It was still early in their game, and they wanted to leave their options open. They weren't ready to pin things on any one person yet, though Talia certainly had a person in mind whom she'd love to see go down.

Arryn.

It would be easy to set her up, but the time needed to be right. As close as Amelia and Arryn had become in such a short time, it wouldn't be easy to take her down. She needed to study her enemy before she made any moves against her.

As Talia walked closer to what used to be a large park area, she saw the boys walking, just as Scarlett had instructed them. When she saw movement from the opposite direction, she froze, but her body relaxed a bit when she realized it was her compatriot.

Engage them, Scarlett said telepathically. *I have a connection to them, so pick whichever one you want. I have an image already in place. Dark and shadowy, female, and obviously* not *Jackson.*

Good, Talia replied. *Have the bottles ready. It's going be a busy night, and I plan to make the drinks extra special for our guests later this evening.*

Talia smiled as she stepped forward, her eyes locking on Dallas as she pulled a knife from her jacket.

CELINE STOOD in Lord Girard's back yard, Arryn's bow in hand and knives on a patio table next to her. She'd been staying with Arryn since they'd found one another.

The first few days had been slow, taking the time to get used to one another again, but soon after, they were inseparable.

Celine's world had changed the moment she saw Arryn standing in that old house. All the years of hatred and anger melted away the moment her eyes came to rest on the young woman's features—features so like her older sister, Elayne.

Now, the only thing that mattered to Celine was keeping her family safe, and that included Cathillian.

The only problem with that was she was the weakest link.

Celine had no weapons or formal fighting skills—only what she'd picked up getting into fights in the street over her *traitorous whore* of a sister, as they'd called her. The nobles had not been kind to Celine once Elayne's body had been recovered along with the Hunters she'd killed.

But none of that mattered anymore.

Celine knew how to throw a good punch, and hell, she knew how to take one, too. Her fighting style was raw, explosive, not unlike that of a rearick, but she needed skills with weapons.

Every night, after the house was quiet, and everyone else was asleep—including the rearick, Samuel, who was now taking up residence as well—Celine came outside, taking Arryn's bow and Cathillian's throwing knives to practice.

It was slow at first, learning on her own, but that's how she'd done everything since Elayne had died. Learned and grew on her own.

She thought about asking for help, but decided it was best not to. They already trained so hard, and now they planned to take on even more. Celine didn't want to hinder them, not when she could learn alone with lots of practice.

But, sometimes, things don't always work out as planned.

"What're ye doin' out here, lass?"

Celine jumped, missing her shot entirely when the rearick spoke.

"What'd the air ever do to ye? I ask because that seems ta be the only thing ye can hit." Samuel approached with a smile on his heavily bearded face, but his eyes appeared exhausted. He'd been asleep at some point.

Celine looked down to the pilfered bow then back to Samuel. "I practice at night. I didn't mean to wake you," she replied.

He waved a hand in the air. "Don't worry about it. But with the noise yer makin', I thought fer sure I'd find a mess of dead targets."

She shook her head. "I'm not that great. Not yet, anyway. But I'll get there; you'll see."

Samuel laughed. "In a few years maybe. I don't know shit about archery. That's yer niece's thing. Maybe the bigger lad, too. But I can sure as hell teach ye ta throw a knife. Maybe we should start thar before ye accidentally kill a squirrel, and its forest friends come ta tell the druids on ye."

Celine laughed before nodding. "That's a plan, rearick."

Samuel made his way over to the table and picked up the knives. Pulling one free, he pinched the bladed end of it between the side of his index finger and thumb.

"Don't squeeze too tight," he said, moving his wrist back and forth to show the blade swaying just a bit to demonstrate the tightness of his grip. "Don't death-grip it, or it won't spin. Just squeeze tight enough that it won't fly outta yer hand when ye pull back ta throw. Watch me."

Samuel stepped up, and with a firm, yet relaxed grip on the knife, he pulled his arm back, the handle of the blade falling back parallel with his wrist. He moved fast, his arm almost a blur as he threw the knife, the blade making a full turn before stabbing hard into the target she had set up.

"Wow!" she exclaimed. "Let me try."

Stepping forward, Celine took a knife and tried to hold it just as Samuel had. Laughing a bit, Samuel stepped forward.

"Yer not throwin' a ball, lassie. Yer arm is too far out ta the side." He gently took hold of her arm at the elbow and wrist, repositioning it. "When ye throw, yer hand will stay almost directly over yer shoulder, tucked in tight, but not uncomfortably so. Here—try this."

Celine threw the blade, but not hard enough. It spun too many times, and the handle hit the target first before falling to the ground.

"Hey!" Samuel shouted.

Celine grumbled. "What do you seem so happy about? I missed!"

He smiled and patted her hard on the back. "But ye didn't! Ye hit yer target, girlie. The only flaw here is ye didn't have the confidence to throw harder. Keep practicin'. I'll check on ye tomorrow, and ye better be hittin' somethin'. Got it?"

She smiled as she switched from looking at the target back to Samuel, nodding. "I will. Thank you for the help. That's the first time I've hit anything."

"Aye, no problem. Focus on the knives and leave the archery ta the nature users fer now. Seems the blades are what yer sweet on. Perfect those, and ye can't go wrong. Get 'em right and *then* try on somethin' else."

"Thank you," she said again, smiling as he made his way inside.

She picked up another knife and held the tip between her fingers, feeling the weight. Tossing the blade into the air, letting it tumble over, and then catching it by the blade again, she thought, *I've got this.*

CHAPTER EIGHT

Talia made her way through the streets to the meeting, keeping her eyes open for any Guard that might be lurking. So far, Jackson had been very accurate. This part of town was not only devoid of people, but the Guard was nowhere to be found either. She was able to walk around freely and do as she pleased.

She found the road Jackson had told her about, and turned down it. She walked quietly, making sure every footstep was completely silent. She inspected every window for the red curtains, until she finally found a beautiful house with deep red drapes.

She studied it for moment before taking several steps forward and testing the doorknob. It opened right away, and she looked inside to see that magitech lights were on. Pushing the door open farther, she saw a lot of people sitting in a living room with sheets over the furniture.

The interior was exquisite. There was a beautiful fireplace across from the couch. She could tell that a large picture once hung above it since the wall was a slightly lighter color in that spot. The entire house was full of dust. As she closed the door, she saw three swords sitting in the corner behind it. They were beautiful, ornately crafted.

"Dean Talia!" Jackson exclaimed. "So happy that you could join us."

Talia smiled and gave him a quick wave. Talia noticed there were more people than Jackson had told her about. He'd originally said there would be seven or eight, but it now appeared there were far more.

Jackson stood before the group and motioned to Talia. "Hey, everyone. As you can see, she decided to come. She hasn't promised to do anything yet, but Dean Talia, I'm going to let you introduce yourself properly and ask any questions you might have."

Before Talia could even respond, Scarlett made her way in the door. She sauntered across the room with a large smile on her face and a bag on her shoulder. "Greetings everyone."

One of the other teachers began to stand, but Talia and Jackson both put a hand up to still her.

"She's the one who pulled me away," Jackson said. "She's the one who saved me from those shithead Boulevard students. She's new to the Academy, so I'm not sure who does and doesn't know her yet, but this is Scarlett. Anyway, she's safe."

The teacher only nodded before relaxing and sitting back down.

"What are you doing here?" Talia asked Scarlett in a hushed whisper. "You were only supposed to drop the bag off outside for me to grab when I needed it."

Scarlett shrugged. "You didn't think I'd miss out on all the fun, did you? Besides, he invited me, and you need me here."

Talia stifled the urge to roll her eyes. She didn't *need* anyone. However, Scarlett could certainly be useful in such a situation. "Good. I expect you to work then. Get into their heads. I need to know if I can trust them, and quickly."

Talia turned to the group, studying each of their faces to see just how many of them she knew. Only two of them had been hired since she'd come to the Academy, which meant that all the others had been upset about their situation since the beginning. There were six other teachers, and nine students. With Talia and Scarlett, that made a good-sized group.

With all the people in the room, Talia decided to take note of everyone here.

First, the teachers: Victoria, Rebecca, Bernice, David, Daniel, and William. Then, the students: the twins, Caydon and Camdon, Lisa, Connor, Hugh, Leon, Brandi, Margaret, and Jackson.

"Good evening," Talia began. "I know it's probably strange to have me here. I've been very open about helping the city and also about staying a neutral party between the Boulevard students and the nobles. That being said, one thing I know for sure is that when I saw how badly Jackson was hurt, I folded. No matter how I felt before, at that moment I knew something had to be done."

Talia made sure to speak slowly and eloquently, doing her best to give Scarlett enough time to peek into the minds of everyone there. She turned to her companion, her eyes imploring the mystic to give her an update.

Scarlett smiled. "I've checked them all. They're all very clean. They're terrified of what the Boulevard students are capable of, but they refused to do anything for fear of Amelia. They'll only move if they have someone they can trust to win this for them."

Jackson's brows furrowed as he stood. "Talia, what's she talking about?"

Talia once again looked at Scarlett, who nodded. "It's safe. Spill it," Scarlett told her.

Turning back to her audience, Talia smiled, crossing her arms over her chest. "It looks like I'm telling you a few things sooner rather than later. Scarlett is a mystic. I'm sure all of you are familiar with the mystical arts, even if you don't know how to use them, yes?"

Everyone looked at each other for a moment before turning back to her and nodding.

"Good. I don't trust anyone. I'm sure all of you can understand that, given what we've been through. Scarlett here helps make sure I know exactly what's going on. I think it's time that I did as Jackson suggested, so let me introduce myself properly. My name is Talia, and I am the daughter of your past Chancellor, Adrien."

For a moment, looks of confusion swept across those in attendance. Everyone once again glanced at one another for answers, but slowly, as they gazed at her, studied her, those looks of confusion melted away, and their eyes reflected recognition.

Talia looked so much like her mother that it was hard to see unless you knew what you were looking for. Only then could you spot Adrien's obvious features on her beautiful face.

"Adrien had a daughter?" Victoria asked, her bright blue eyes glowing with excitement as she studied Talia's face.

Talia looked at her. "He kept it a secret because he was rather paranoid. He knew someone might use me against him."

Or—more accurately—meet an untimely end by some Boulevard bitch, she thought to herself.

"If he did, he wanted to make sure he had one person he could trust no matter what. Unfortunately, I didn't get my letter from Doyle until after my father died, but I vowed I wouldn't let his death be ignored. But make no mistake... I am *not* my father. I have no interest in power, or in building an airship, or any other exorbitant plan for dominance he may have once entertained. All I want is to continue ruling in honor of the man who gave me everything, who made me strong. All of you want that as well. Even if you hated my father, you know he was right. The people of Arcadia have their place, as does magic."

Talia was careful to choose her words, avoiding anything that sounded like revenge or that could induce terror. She wanted them to believe she wanted to reinstate her father's rules without being as violent as he'd been. She wanted them to believe she'd be the ruler they'd always wanted Adrien to be—though sacrifices *would* need to be made.

Jackson's eyes were wide as he stared at her. Talia gave him a reassuring smile, hoping that he would buy that she was sincere. "Jackson, I hope you don't feel betrayed or misled by me. That was never my intention. I never wanted to cause damage, only heal and do things the way they should have been done. Now that I've gotten close to you, and I've seen the devastation these people can cause. *My* mission no longer matters. Now it's *our* mission."

Jackson gave a small nod before looking at the floor. He seemed to be mulling things over. Finally, he looked at Talia and smiled. "I understand. I don't feel that you betrayed me. I guess I would've done the same thing in your shoes. It's not like you could just come in here and announce you were Adrien's daughter and have anyone trust you."

He sighed as he looked around the room to the other faces. "*We* would have, but everyone else would've hated you. You never would've even gotten the job in the first place, and we would be stuck. Your reasons for coming back to the city aren't important. Not anymore. What's important is that you found it in your heart to help us."

Rebecca, another teacher, stood then. Her brown eyes seemed dark, furious, though her expression was amused. "Those Boulevard kids are capable of terrible things. We can't let them destroy our Academy, and we can't let them hurt us. We all know as soon as they learn magic, they *will* use it against us. They will take all those years of imaginary abuse out on us, when it was never our fault."

"I couldn't agree more," Talia assured her. "So, the question is, will you trust me? Will you let me help you? I promise—if you do—the city will find its final transformation. It'll be everything it should've been from the beginning."

One by one, everyone stood, and one by one they pledged their allegiance to Talia.

Scarlett took a step forward, sitting the bag on a table and opening it up. She pulled a bottle of wine free and held it up. "To celebrate, I brought a *very* special wine for all of us to share while I tell you a legend. And if you know anything about mystics, you know we are *wonderful* storytellers. Some would even call us master illusionists..."

ARRYN AWOKE with a start as she did every morning, heart racing and sweat beading on her forehead. She took a few deep breaths to calm herself before sitting up and swinging her legs over the side of the bed.

She sighed heavily and took a drink of water from the bedside table before standing and making her way out of the room. As she headed downstairs, she smelled something burning.

Rushing into the kitchen, she saw Cathillian turn with a start and look at her with wide eyes, guilt all over his face. Arryn closed her eyes for a moment as she crossed her arms.

"What exactly are you up to in here?" she asked. "Are you *trying* to burn the house down?"

"Sorry! You get mad at me when I wake you from those dreams, so I thought I'd make breakfast instead. I would have asked Celine, but she's still passed out. She's always up early, so I figured she could use the rest. Quit giving me that look. It kept me busy and out of your hair, didn't it?"

Arryn crossed the room and sat at the table, laying her head on the cool wood. "Well, whatever it was, I'm *pretty* sure it's done." She smiled, but it was hidden from his view. "And I *do* hate it when you wake me from those dreams. I just wish I'd quit having them. I figured they would've stopped by now; they've never lasted this long."

"Do you want some blackened coal for breakfast? Because if you do, I'm a *damn* good chef."

Arryn laughed, looking up from the table. "Coal *is* black, dork."

"Yeah, but I blackened it more. It's like—twice blackened. See? *Talent.*"

Arryn rolled her eyes, her expression still very amused. "Even if it didn't smell like that, I still wouldn't eat it. I don't trust it. You'd trick me into eating a fried piece of dog shit if you could."

His brows furrowed as he looked down into the scorched pan before looking back to her. "So, you mean I snuck into the neighbor's yard this morning and waited for the dog to go back in for nothing? I nearly got punched to make you this fine breakfast."

Arryn was already beginning to feel better. Her heart had slowed to a regular rhythm, and the laughing was taking her mind off everything. "What did you *actually* try to cook?"

He smiled, but it was full of mischief. Arryn's face fell as she stared at him.

"Cathillian…" her voice a bit sterner. "What did you try to make?"

"Well, let's just say that I wasn't lying about nearly getting punched this morning." Cathillian only grinned again as Arryn looked at him incredulously. "Or about waiting in the neighbor's yard… I *might* have stolen some eggs."

"Holy shit, Cathillian! What's the matter with you? You didn't have to do that. I have money now, you know. By proxy—*you* have money now, too. We can *buy* eggs. Or chickens."

Arryn made a mental note to hunt down some chickens. Of course, she would have to pay the neighbor for the eggs her ridiculous friend stole, but then she could teach him how to properly cook them. It was obvious he'd never cooked a thing in his entire life.

"So, enough about my exciting morning and fine cooking skills. What are you up to today on your day off?"

"I think I'm gonna go see Amelia. She's convinced that either Doyle was lying, or she was delirious from blood loss. Either way, she doesn't believe anything she remembers, but I do. I think Doyle was very serious about someone coming to the city, and it's way too much of a coincidence to find out about it after having met Talia."

"So, you think the big bad is Talia?" Cathillian asked.

"I don't know. It's odd. The day we met Amelia I got a buzzy feeling in my head because she was looking inside my mind. That's a feeling I'll never forget, mostly because I feel it quite often at school."

Arryn crossed the room, filling a pot with hot water before setting it to boil. Though Arcadia didn't have kaffe like they did in the Forest, it did have tea, and that would have to suffice.

"It doesn't matter at this stage if I'm right or wrong. I just need to either prove it's not her so I can move on with my life and maybe even try to like her, or prove that it *is* her, so I can make sure she doesn't do any damage to the city. I've been there for a while now and that feeling hasn't gone away, but it's not like she's tried anything weird either. I just need to talk to Amelia. Maybe Adrien left some things that I can go through."

"Do you even know what you're looking for? Didn't you say Amelia told you Doyle didn't give her a name?"

Arryn shrugged as she turned and went back over to the table, waiting for the water to boil. "No, he didn't give her a name, but my dream isn't just a dream, it's my actual memory. It's everything that really happened that night, and it's exactly how I remember it. My father told my mother there was a big secret, something he'd found out about Adrien. He said something, but I didn't hear him that night because I was freaking out."

Cathillian looked at her incredulously. "Don't you think that's stretching? Maybe you're seeing what you want to see."

"Exactly!" Arryn exclaimed, her hands going out to her sides. "Don't you think I know that? That's why I need to get into

Adrien's stuff. I need to find out what that secret was. Maybe he was sending money or gifts or other stuff that could tell me something. There has to be something somewhere. I just need to talk to Amelia."

Cathillian nodded, his expression telling her he thought she was nothing shy of insane at the moment. "If it'll make your ass a little less nuts, then go see Amelia. I've been up for about an hour and already you're driving me *fucking* crazy. Also, I may have burned the eggs, but I'm pretty sure you're burning *water*."

Arryn rolled her eyes as she crossed the room, taking her pot off the fire and pouring the hot water into a mug. She'd let it get too hot, but it wouldn't take long to cool off. Then, after tea, she planned to go see Amelia.

AMELIA HAD BEEN FIGHTING the need to work all day. Everyone was gone from the Academy and there was no one in the Capitol Building, so she didn't want to be there either, but she couldn't get her mind off recent events.

It was hard for her to stay at home when everything was so close to coming together. Plus, she was still having a hard time with the Doyle episode. Nearly dying had affected her more than she'd like to admit—she'd never come that close before.

There was a knock at her door, interrupting her thoughts. When she opened it, she was surprised to see Arryn standing there. They had spent quite a bit of time together after everything that had happened, going over all that Doyle had said.

Finding out if Doyle had been telling the truth had become priority number one for Amelia, but Arryn had been suspiciously obsessed with it as well.

"Hey!" Amelia greeted her with a smile. "What are you doing here? Shouldn't you be enjoying your day at home?"

Arryn stepped inside. "I had another one of those dreams last night. They've been less frequent since the whole raid thing, but they're still happening, so I couldn't rest. I decided to come see you instead."

Amelia nodded as she made her way over to the couch. She sat down and patted the cushion next to her. Amelia decided it was time to find out exactly what was going on. She needed to know why Arryn was so interested in all this.

"Even though I know you can sense me doing it, I'm not going to look inside your head." Amelia looked at Arryn, who nodded. "That being said, I want you to tell me the truth. I know something's going on."

"Okay, ask away. I'll be honest."

"I know you have the sense of duty instilled in you by your parents. But Adrien is gone. Even with him gone, however, you're still obsessed with finding the person Doyle was talking about. I know I probably sound paranoid, but why are you so obsessed with it? You haven't even been here for ten years. This isn't your problem to solve."

"I can see why you would think that," Arryn replied, "but it's not true. I always thought my vow was to avenge my parents, but once I got here, I realized it wasn't. Now that the city is safe, or at least safer, I feel the need to make sure it stays that way. I still have to find my dad, but if there's a possibility some psycho is going to come and try to tear the city apart, then I need to make sure that doesn't happen first."

"Dreams are often our mind's way of telling us there's something we need to do. It's our own stress weighing on us. Protecting the city is literally invading your sleep. That's obsession if I've ever heard it."

Arryn rolled her eyes. "Damn, now you sound just like Cathillian. I told you I'd be honest, and I'm gonna be. The reason I'm here is because I need you to help me find Adrien's things. I need to go through them. I need to find out who this person might be. I know you don't wanna hear it, and I don't even wanna tell you, but the moment I met Talia my gut rolled over—and it wasn't the shitty Arcadian food. I don't like her. I sense something about her that just isn't right."

Amelia laughed. "Well, the funny thing is the day I told her about you, she suggested you might be the one who had kidnapped Amos. She had a point. You were brand-new to the city, and that was about the time he disappeared."

Arryn's jaw dropped, her expression revealing her shock. "Of course, *she* would say that! Why the hell else would she immediately start blaming me? Probably because she's *guilty*!"

"Relax, Arryn." Amelia reached over and gave Arryn's hand a quick squeeze. "I told you that only because it shows that we aren't the only suspicious ones around here. Talia is worried, too. If I choose not to trust her, I have to choose not to trust you either."

Amelia understood Arryn's hesitation. Her paranoia. Amelia felt same way. Still, she couldn't go around pointing fingers at anyone who was new in the city, because there were quite a few. It would take time, and she needed proof. She didn't want to alarm the city any more than she wanted to frighten off the new teachers at the Academy by accusing them.

"I don't believe her worries about you being a murderer any more than I worry about her. It's my job to make sure I investigate everything; even Doyle's claims, which I'm almost positive were ripe bullshit. I'm not even sure he said those things, let alone that I heard them correctly. Or possibly they just aren't true. Talia helped save the city, so maybe she's not as bad as you think."

Arryn sighed. "No, *you* saved the city. She's just doing some supplying because she wanted to look good."

"And you saved my life," Amelia argued. "Were you just trying to look good, too?"

Arryn sighed again, leaning back against the couch. She seemed exasperated, but she nodded. "I get it. And that's why I need to prove it. Right or wrong, I just want to get past this. Nature magic lets a person sense the overall intentions of the individual. It's not flawless by any means, but most times you can get a good sense of a person from it. Talia was just *wrong*. So, if you have anything of Adrien's, I'd love the chance to go through it, just to ease my mind."

Amelia understood that. It wasn't that she didn't believe Arryn; it was just that Talia had been such an asset and Amelia had spent so much time with her that if *she* was bad, then *anyone* in the city could be.

She didn't want to think about that possibility.

But if there was something to find, there was a chance Arryn would find it.

Amelia stood, went to her bedroom, grabbed a large box, and brought it back to Arryn. "This was Adrien's. I gathered these things myself out of his office in the Academy tower. I'm sure there's more in his old house, but this should get you started. I've looked and looked through here, but I can't find anything. Maybe you'll have better luck."

Arryn stood, taking the box like it was a delicate piece of glass. "Thanks. I'll start going through it tonight. I'm sorry to be so pushy. I just need to know if I should get along with her or kick her ass."

Amelia smiled. "Don't worry, I understand. I guess I'm no different because I've been tearing up everything in hopes of finding evidence that will explain things. I just don't have a suspect. That's the difference between us—you do.

CHAPTER NINE

Things had been going great. The students had all fallen in love with Talia. The Chancellor had fallen in love with Talia. The city had been told of the things that Talia had done to speed up the rebuilding, so they loved Talia, too.

Everything was exactly the way it should be. Everything had been perfect.

Until that bitch Arryn showed up.

Ever since the day Arryn arrived at the school and Scarlett had informed her that she was someone to worry about, Talia hadn't been able to think straight. Arryn was everything Talia was afraid of.

She was from out of town, supposedly very skilled, smart, and —most importantly—on a mission.

But that was okay… She could now focus on Arryn even more now that Amelia was preoccupied with the murder of yet another student.

The body of Dallas—the boy who led the group that had attacked Jackson and who had soon met an untimely end at Talia's hand—had recently been found and there was no lead to what happened.

The only clue available came from a frightened best friend that had hid in his house for two days because of the mysterious woman in a cloak that had come for Dallas and threatened him as well.

Scarlett's magic had worked perfectly. The boy had seen a feminine figure clad in a cloak but with no other discernible features. The Academy was in an uproar over it all, terrified of what another murder meant.

But things within the group were going perfectly.

Toward the end of the first meeting Talia had with Jackson's group, she found a rather interesting piece of the puzzle.

After perusing through the home while the others listened to Scarlett's grand tale about the ancestors and their bloodlust and consequent increase in power, Talia found another painting, one of a small girl. A small girl that looked incredibly familiar.

Looking more closely, Talia found a familiar name on the gold-plated tag at the bottom.

Arryn.

Jackson and his group had inadvertently held their very first meeting in none other than the house Arryn had spent the first half of her life in. At that moment, Talia made it her goal to figure it out exactly who Arryn was and why she was back in the city.

So far, Scarlett had found that none of the students had any idea. All Arryn had told anyone was that she was once an Arcadian who'd left the city and ended up being raised in the Dark Forest.

But who the hell would choose to be raised in the Dark Forest?

There was much more to the story, and Talia intended find out.

Talia sent a letter with one of the teachers in the group to give to Jackson. Talia wanted to meet with him and talk about the newest teacher on the block.

It would take a hell of a lot more than just her wishing for it to get what she needed.

Jackson was a very handsome guy, and she figured Arryn probably wasn't used to having guys falling over her. Perhaps Talia could teach Jackson to use his looks for her benefit.

Having become impatient, Talia made her way out of her office and down the stairs, heading toward the classrooms. Unsurprisingly, she found Scarlett waiting for her.

"*Shocker*. Am I going to have to tie a bell around your neck?" Talia asked.

Scarlett smiled. "Kinky," she declared with a wink. "You can tie whatever you'd like around my neck. But that's not why I'm here."

Talia rolled her eyes. "Well, it sure as hell isn't teaching. Do you even really *have* a job? Didn't I hire you for something?"

"You know, if I didn't know any better, I'd say you didn't appreciate my help. I work *so* hard to avoid my classroom, and this is the thanks I get?" When Talia didn't respond, Scarlett just continued, "Ugh. I have them trying to turn wood into glass. I figured if they could learn how to do that you could put them to use on the rebuild and look even more like a hero."

That earned a smile from Talia. "Now you've impressed me. Not just annoyed the piss out of me. Now, I assume you strained so hard to avoid your classroom to come see me for more than flirting, correct?"

"Maybe. But since flirting isn't getting me anywhere, I was wondering if you'd found anything out about Arryn and her noble quest."

Talia shook her head. "So far, all I have to go on is what you've told me, and I will never know if that's true or not. Not exactly sure if I can trust you. I still think that fight with Jackson was a little *too* convenient..."

"I told you I had nothing to do with it. I came across the fight, and I stopped it. Granted, I might've let him take an extra punch, but they were already trading blows."

Talia trusted *Arryn* more than she trusted Scarlett, mostly because Scarlett had the ability to make people think whatever she wanted them to. Talia wasn't exactly sure how sensitive to mystical magic she was, though.

Her father had taught her how to put up a barrier, but Scarlett had already been in her head once, though she'd been drunk at the time.

"It doesn't matter. At this point, I don't know if I have a choice. I need eyes and ears, or, in this case, your powers. Jackson should be coming to meet me at any moment and I'm going to tell him that I'm transferring him into Arryn's class with another student, Maddie. She elected into the class. Only half the school so far is required to take the nature magic class. I'm moving him into it to get close to Arryn."

Scarlett suddenly got excited, quietly clapping her hands. "Now, this is more my territory. Good plan. Would you like to know what I found out?"

Talia sighed, closing her eyes as her head dropped a little. "Why didn't you start by telling me you had information? Must you always play with my head?" Scarlett opened her mouth to say something, but Talia put her hand over it. "And if you say that you'll play with whatever I ask you to, I'm probably going to punch you."

Talia slowly pulled her hand away, revealing a devious smile on Scarlett's face.

"*Now* who's the mind reader? You can punch me if you like, I don't mind. But my discovery! I found out that Arryn came here with another druid. Not a fake one, though, a real one. In fact, one of the girls in one of her classes that I spied on has a dad who is training with Cathillian. He was among the first group involved in the remnant attack. They've been learning how to grow trees or some shit. Anyway, apparently, he's pretty hot, at least if the girl's thoughts were correct."

"And? She has a hot druid friend? This is your big information?" Talia asked.

"You mentioned using Jackson against Arryn. I assumed you meant having him flirt with her, act interested in her. What if you got close to the druid? He isn't gonna know how to deal with a woman quite like you. Use your charms on him, make him like you. I've been in Arryn's head. She *doesn't* like you. She definitely doesn't trust you. I'm telling you, you need to make a choice. Personally, I say just get rid of her."

Talia sighed again. "I told you I can't do that. I made a huge mistake when Amelia first told me she hired Arryn. I freaked out when she said Arryn helped her figure out that Amos hadn't been killed in the Boulevard and she might even be able to find the killer. I might have suggested in a very rushed manner that the new teacher might have been the one to do it, because the murder happened right about the time she got to town."

Scarlett grimaced. "Yeah, that's no good. It doesn't help she's been telling her druid friend just how much she doesn't trust you. If she disappeared, I suppose it would stand to reason that you had something to do with it. Dammit. Well, I guess we'll have to get rid of the nature bitch the hard way."

Talia jumped, her eyes wide as she saw none other than Arryn rounding the corner to head down the opposite hallway. Arryn's eyes briefly met hers as she made her way toward her classroom.

Talia turned cold, hateful eyes on Scarlett. When she spoke, her voice was low, barely audible, though the darkness in it could be felt. "Explain to me how in the hell that just happened. Explain to me how someone like you, a mystical magic user, could miss someone approaching, let alone the *one* person we are trying to get rid of."

Scarlett looked just as shocked as Talia did. "I have no idea. I guess I just got distracted. It's really early, you know. I've been using my powers a lot lately, and not getting much time to meditate properly. It takes a toll. You try conjuring fireballs all day every day and not sleeping, and tell me just how well *your* abilities work! Simple mistake. Do *not* snap at me."

Talia groaned as she considered the mystic's words. Put in that context, she could understand how it could happen. Grudgingly, she decided she could let it go.

Glaring at Scarlett, Talia said, "Don't let it happen again." Scarlett only nodded in response. Talia relaxed a little, crossing her arms.

Scarlett cleared her throat. "I've been thinking. The remnant have been quite a distraction around here, wouldn't you say?"

Talia snorted. "The kids are scared shitless of them. Don't get me wrong, they're scared of having a murderer on the loose, too, but the remnant seemed to be driving everyone absolutely *mad*, no pun intended."

Scarlett's expression turned thoughtful. Finally, she said, "Good. That's what I thought, too. Perhaps we should pay a little visit to the Madlands this weekend. What do you say?"

Talia's eyes widened. "The Madlands? What exactly did you have in mind?"

Scarlett smiled. "The remnant may be violent and seem stupid, but they aren't. They can even speak. I think it's time to pay them a visit, see if we might be able to strike a deal. If we can time their attacks and coax them a little closer to Arcadia, we might be able to control the city entirely. With everyone distracted, we can do pretty much anything we need to."

Talia looked impressed. "That's probably the best idea I've heard so far. It would divide the city between those who want to strike against them and those who want to stay inside the city walls and barricade themselves indoors. They're already arguing about it, and the remnant are as far south in the valley as they can go without running into the rearick. It's obvious they're only protecting their lands. But if we staged it that way, everyone would lose their minds."

Scarlett nodded. "Then it's settled. This weekend we'll go to the Madlands and pay the remnant a little visit. You're gonna need to be rested up, and so will I. I'll practice my meditation and rest my mind. You can use Jackson for information from now on unless you state otherwise."

Talia nodded, stepping to the side to reveal the boy in question approaching from down the hallway.

"Ah, Jackson." Talia beamed. "You have perfect timing. Come with me to my office, we have things to discuss."

CHAPTER TEN

E cho had just returned from the Dark Forest on an errand
to deliver a letter from Elysia when there was a knock at
the front door. Cathillian set the letter down on the table next to
the couch and went to answer it.

As he opened the door, his eyes nearly fell out of his head.
There was a beautiful woman standing there, holding a rather
large fruit basket and smiling.

"Hi! Is Arryn around? I brought her a welcome present."

Confused, Cathillian answered, "No, she's still at the Academy. She's a teacher there."

The woman laughed, the sound rich and beautiful. "Actually, I
knew that. I'm Talia, the Dean. I just thought she'd be home by
now. Anyway, I guess I can leave this here with you."

Cathillian smiled, unable to resist her charm. Just from
looking at the woman, he couldn't understand why Arryn hated
her so much. She was not only beautiful, but she gave off no
warning signs of any kind. That feeling that Arryn kept going on
about was completely absent for him.

He stepped back out of the way and motioned for her to come
inside. "Please, come in."

Talia shook her head, still smiling. "No, I couldn't impose. I thought to give these to her at school, then I realized that would be rather rude because she would have to carry them home. I didn't quite pay attention to the time, but I guess I left school early today. I was hoping to catch her, but this is okay. I'd rather you surprise her with them."

Cathillian heard the flap of large wings behind him, and he turned to see Echo land on the back of the couch and stare at their new guest. Her chest was puffed out, as she would in the presence of someone she didn't like.

Is it just a female thing? he asked himself.

"Are you aware that you have a large eagle in your living room? Or is that normal for druids?" Talia asked, amused.

Cathillian laughed and reached for the fruit basket. "I'll take this; it looks pretty heavy. I'm gonna go put it in the kitchen. As for the eagle, this is my familiar, Echo. She's a golden eagle."

Echo screeched, unfurling her massive wings and stretching to show off just how large she was.

"Well, she's beautiful. I'm pretty sure that's the largest bird I've ever seen in my life," Talia told him.

Cathillian walked back into the room, smiling at Echo before giving her chest a scratch. "Yeah, she's pretty incredible. We come to rely on our familiars quite a bit. She's saved my ass a time or two."

Talia crossed the room, cautiously reaching out. "A man with a very large... bird. Mind if I touch it?"

Cathillian laughed. "Sure. She's completely tame." There was a loud screech as Echo pointedly looked at Cathillian. "And a smart-ass."

Talia laughed. "Do you guys communicate with one another?"

Cathillian nodded. "We do. I've never quite understood how the bond works, but because of our magic, we just naturally understand each other when we bond. I guess it's like meeting someone and spending a lot of time with them when they don't speak your language. You may figure out exactly what they're talking about, but never learn how to speak it yourself. It's the same with us. When I talk, the bond somehow translates it into something she can understand, and vice versa. I can even look through her eyes and see what she sees when I need to."

Talia's expression turned to surprise as she looked from Cathillian to Echo and back again. "That's incredible! I can't imagine what it would be like to be so close to an animal of any kind. Does Arryn have a familiar? Is it a golden eagle, too?"

Laughing, Cathillian said, "No, Arryn doesn't have one, though, don't mention that to her, because she absolutely hates it. We don't search for familiars; it just happens. We have a natural ability to communicate with animals, though it's mostly through feelings. Basically, we can communicate that we're not hostile, and can even coax them to us once they realize we're safe."

Echo unfurled her wings, flying across the room to perch on the table. Cathillian could tell Talia made her uncomfortable, though he still couldn't understand why. She seemed nice to him. He wondered if it was out of sympathy for Arryn.

After all, they were close, too.

Ignoring the strange raptor, Cathillian continued. "Only the bond allows us to really understand each other, though. And sometimes while playing with an animal or interacting with it in some other way, a bond forms. Unfortunately, Arryn has never been able to seal a bond, though she has a much stronger natural gift with animals than most. She can talk to several at once. She doesn't have to work quite as hard as the rest of us, which is strange. It's like she has all the benefits of the bond except the actual closeness."

"And druids can bond with any kind of animal?" Talia asked.

Cathillian nodded. "Yep. My mother has a large Shire horse, and my grandfather, the Chieftain, he has a gigantic bear named Zobig."

"Zobig? That's funny. And your grandfather is the Chieftain?

So, he was involved in building the city in the beginning? That's so interesting. What brings you to the city? Everything I've ever heard is that the druids are completely elusive. I thought you guys loved the Dark Forest so much you don't leave."

Cathillian laughed. "Well, that's true for the most part. We do love the Dark Forest. But now that I've discovered hot showers, I'm having a hard time imagining myself back there. Those waterfalls are nice, but they don't hold a candle to hot water."

Talia smiled, looking to the floor before gazing back at him. "I can't help but find you interesting, but maybe I just have a soft spot for a guy with a big bird. Of course, I'm sure you expected that. Around here, you're rather exotic. I'm sure most of the girls have been giving you a... *hard* time."

Cathillian couldn't believe his pointed ears, his jade green eyes widening a bit. This beautiful woman found him attractive? He joked about finding himself sexy and always gave Arryn a hard time, but he only did it to get under her skin. He wasn't actually that narcissistic.

Arryn was wrong about Talia in many ways. And now that he'd met her and things were clearly going so well, he wondered if he'd be able to convince Arryn that she wasn't so bad.

At the moment, he couldn't help but find himself distracted by her. He couldn't seem to focus on anything other than her. He'd never met anyone like her.

"I've mostly been spending my time with men." He laughed again. "Nothing like that, though. Not that I wouldn't be flattered, but I'm just helping them learn how to grow trees so they don't have to go so close to the Madlands for lumber. And so they don't take from the Forest and not give back. As for girls, Arryn is a full-time job. She's my best friend, basically family. And even though she's capable of doing it herself, I've made it my duty to ensure she's protected while we're here, so I haven't really had a chance to go out for anything other than training purposes."

"Oh, that's too bad. I'm sorry to hear it. She's incredible. Very talented. Her class has been going well, and the students seem to really like her. She's a great asset to the Academy. And all of your teaching must be going for a good purpose. Still, it's a shame you don't get any time to yourself."

Cathillian waved his hands. "No, it's not an inconvenience at all. When you're as close as we are, it's normal. I just want to make sure I help her do what she came to do. She's waited her whole life to come back to Arcadia to find out what happened to her dad, so I wanna make sure I do what I can."

Talia covered her heart with her hand, her expression turning concerned. "What do you mean? What happened to her dad? We don't really know much about her except she grew up in the Forest."

Cathillian sighed as he looked at the floor for a moment, shifting his weight from one foot to the other. "I'm surprised you don't know. It's not really my story to tell, so I won't go into too many details, but her father was taken by Adrien ten years ago. She and her mom fled on horseback to the Dark Forest. Her mom was killed before she even made it, but she was able to save Arryn. My mother took her in."

Realization hit Talia in the face. "Oh, that makes sense. Now I see why she would spend ten years in the Dark Forest. Your mother must be a wonderful woman to have taken in a child she'd never met, and an Arcadian, no less."

Cathillian waved his hand again. "There's a lot more to the story, which I'll save for her to tell if ever she feels the need, but that's what happened. And here we are now."

Talia nodded before looking at the windows. "Oh my, I didn't realize how late it was getting. I'd better get out of here. I'm sorry to run, but with everything going on, I'm always trying to find new ways to help. The Chancellor can't do everything on her own, and even though I know she has a lot of help, two more hands aren't gonna hurt."

Cathillian smiled. "It's pretty great that you take so much on yourself like that. Running an entire Academy would be enough to drive me crazy. Trying to help the Chancellor on top of that would be even worse. Are you sure you have to go? Arryn should be here soon."

"Unfortunately, yes. I've taken enough of your evening. I should get out of here and tend to my duties. It was great meeting you... Wow, I didn't even ask your name."

"Cathillian. And it was nice to meet you, too, Talia. Thanks for stopping by, and for the warm welcome."

Talia smiled as she turned to head towards the door. She opened it, stopping for just a moment before turning back to Cathillian. "You know, Arryn is very lucky to have someone like you in her life. Someone so dedicated. Concerned. And... incredibly attractive, of course. After everything she's been through and everything she's lost, I'm sure you mean more to her than anything. I know I'd have a hard time not being close to you."

Cathillian wasn't exactly sure how to respond to that.

Before Cathillian could thank her, she gave one last smile, stepped out the door, and closed it behind her. He wasn't exactly sure what the hell had just happened, but whatever it was, he was happy it had.

As TALIA WALKED down the street, she watched for her friend to pop out of the shadows. It seemed to be what she was best at. She'd been traveling for several minutes when Scarlett finally caught up with her.

"Well?" Scarlett asked. "How did it go?"

Talia looked at her incredulously. "Shouldn't *I* be asking *you* that question? You're the one who was in his head."

"Luckily, you're charming enough that I didn't have to do a lot. All I had to do was suppress the inherent defense that all nature magic users have. He's pretty strong, though I doubt he knows how to fully tap into his energy. He sure as hell had no idea I was in his head. Anyway, I made sure he felt nothing but butterflies and excitement. You took care of the rest by laying it on so thick. He absolutely loved you."

Talia smiled, her satisfaction in a well-executed plan rising. "Good, now let's see what happens. When she finds out that he not only accepted a gift from me but he likes me, things are gonna go very badly for her."

"We just have to alienate her. Once we put her out of the minds of everyone around her, it'll be easier to take her down. All we have to do is pin something on her, and whatever residual trust everyone has in her will crumble. It'll take longer than just killing her like I'd like to do, but it'll be effective."

"I think this will end up being much more fun than just killing her. She's been planning to destroy me from the moment she met me. I'm going to enjoy watching her suffer."

WHEN ARRYN WALKED in the door that night after school, Cathillian was sitting on the couch reading a letter, Echo perched on the chair across the room. She must've brought back word from Elysia.

Arryn was happy that he was busy, because she was a woman on a mission. Once again, she'd felt that familiar buzz in her head nearly the whole day, and had then run right into none other than Scarlett and Talia.

The buzz in her mind had kept her distracted enough that she wasn't able to completely hear their conversation, but when she was close enough, she was almost positive she'd heard one of them say something about getting rid of someone. She thought she'd heard *nature bitch*, but that couldn't have been it, right?

"Hey!" Cathillian exclaimed. "You just gonna walk right by me? Not even say hi?"

"Sorry," Arryn told him. "Not really in the mood. I have a lot of shit to go through in that box. I'm trying to take your advice and even Amelia's and be patient while going through it, but not after the day I've had. My head is pounding, and I feel exhausted, but now I'm almost positive Talia is up to something."

"This again?" Cathillian asked, concern crossing his face. "Arryn, I'm starting to worry about you. You're obsessed."

"Obsessed?" Arryn asked, her expression turning angry. "I went downstairs between classes to check out the room Amelia had mentioned using as a training room for fighting class. I wanted to see if it was big enough, and how many students I could have. The entire time I felt like I was drunk on the Chieftain's wine. I felt so lightheaded, and I've felt that way the entire time I've been there. Not consistently, but at least once every day. Usually more."

Cathillian shrugged. "Maybe you're allergic to something in there. Have you thought about that? Maybe you're allergic to the city. We should just go back to the Dark Forest, I guess, right?"

Arryn put her hands on her hips. "Yeah? Are you ready to give up your hot showers?"

A disgusted expression went across Cathillian's face as he turned slightly in his seat. "Oh, *hell no*. I didn't really think that statement through. Carry on with going bat-shit crazy."

"I'm not crazy!" Arryn shouted, "though you certainly make me feel that way."

Cathillian strode across the room to stand before her. "What if I told you that I'd met her?"

Arryn's eyes narrowed as she studied his face. "What? What are you talking about?"

"What if I told you I'd met her? Not only that, but that she was actually pretty nice."

Arryn's jaw fell open, unable to speak as she contemplated his words. "You can't be serious. Are you? Or are you just fucking with me?"

Cathillian sighed, grabbing Arryn's hand. "Come with me. I have something to show you."

Cathillian led Arryn into the kitchen, where a large fruit basket was sitting on the table. For food grown without nature magic, the fruit looked surprisingly good.

"What the fuck is this?" Arryn asked.

Cathillian pointed at the elaborate basket on the table. "That was a gift from your *evil* boss. She came by here to drop it off for you for when you got home. She didn't want you to have to carry it all the way here. She said she wanted to give you a welcome not only to the Academy, but to the city."

Arryn couldn't help but stare at it, shocked that it was there. The fact that Talia knew where she lived bothered her, the gift even more so. At that moment, she noticed that the sheer fabric that had been used to wrap it had been tampered with.

"Did you open it?" Arryn asked.

Cathillian exhaled, clearly exasperated. "Yes, I did. I opened it a little while ago, and I even ate an apple out of it. Do I look dead? Because I'm assuming that's where you're going with this. That she could've poisoned it. There were at least ten other people on the street when she left here, meaning that there are probably just as many that saw her when she carried that basket here. If you or I died, it would have been obvious that she was the one who caused it, so stop that right now."

Arryn shook her head, tears threatening to fill her eyes. She couldn't explain it. She'd never been so sure of anything in her life. There was something inexplicably wrong with that woman, and hearing her talk so harshly about getting rid of someone, and with another teacher at that—especially a new one—just got under her skin.

Now, even Cathillian was convinced of Talia's innocence.

"I don't know what to say," Arryn muttered.

Cathillian gave a sad smile. "I know you got a bad feeling about her when you first met her, but I think it was just nerves.

Those dreams of yours are getting to you, and you are focusing too hard on your past. Maybe being back here is making you feel responsible for your parents in some way. Maybe you feel the need to save the city so much that you're creating a problem that isn't even there."

Arryn's jaw dropped, her eyes widening as she stared at him.

"You *do* realize that what you just said is almost the *exact* definition of insane, don't you? Dammit, Cathillian, I heard it. I heard her say something about getting rid of someone. She's up to something, and I'm gonna prove it. Whether I prove to you she's crazy, or prove to myself that she's the best person in the world, I don't care at this point. Someone is wrong here, and I'm not going to ignore my gut because you're an idiot and got all squirrelly when a pretty girl flirted with you and then you accepted some maybe-tainted fruit."

"No offense, Arryn, but I'm a native druid. I've been practicing nature magic my *entire* life. That little *gut feeling* that you keep going on about? Mine is way stronger than yours could ever consider being, and she is *not* a bad person. I would've known, I promise. I wouldn't lead you wrong."

Arryn shook her head and laughed, which was the only thing she could do, as angry as she was at that moment. "Thanks for trusting me. I'm going to my room. Don't come in there. Enjoy your not-poisoned-evil-hot-chick fruit. Try not to choke and die on it because I expect your ass to be up and ready for training at six. Food poisoning is *not* an excuse."

And with that, Arryn stormed up to her room to finish going through the box Amelia had given her.

CHAPTER ELEVEN

The following morning Cathillian was up early. After Arryn had threatened him, he didn't want to make the mistake of pissing her off again.

While he understood that she felt uneasy about Talia, he couldn't understand the blatant hatred with no proof, especially when the Dean had seemed perfectly harmless.

While he worried that she might be acting irrationally, he decided not to talk to her about it again until she'd found whatever it was that she needed. He also figured she needed to take out some frustration, so he'd gone extra hard in training that morning.

Arryn had been up even earlier than he'd managed to be and was running on little sleep. Having stayed up all night the night before, Cathillian had assumed she'd sleep in, but that hadn't been the case. She was up, ready and determined.

And she'd kicked his ass all over the place.

Yet another thing he shouldn't have been surprised about, given how pissed she'd been with him. Everyone had seen what she was capable of when angry. He was just glad she hadn't fried his ass.

Pissed or not, he was proud of how much she'd improved in such a short time. When she'd requested to train traditionally —with no holding back—he'd wondered how she would handle it.

That had been a mistake.

Hard, relentless training had been exactly what she'd needed. In only a few short weeks she'd nearly doubled her speed, agility, and skills. Since going even harder in the last week, she'd improved even more.

Now, Arryn was able to run and shoot her bow instead of standing stationary. Her accuracy while moving still needed work, but with more training, he knew she'd be just as good moving as she was while standing still.

The other added benefit had been strength. She was stronger than ever. Not having to hold back her kicks and punches had given her an increase in power, power Cathillian wasn't even sure if she was aware of yet.

He sure as hell was. She'd left marks of her improvement all over his body.

Even after healing, he still felt sore from their match that morning. But he hadn't wanted to use any more power than needed because he would be helping out his friends later.

Today, they were heading to the Boulevard.

Talia had sent word to the Governor of Cella, who had graciously extended the duration of time for which the one hundred men who had helped rebuild the factory were on loan. Now that the factory was nearly finished and only a few laborers were needed for what was left, the larger group was helping in other areas.

Within the last several days, the street had been torn the rest of the way apart, finishing the job that Andrew and his small group of men had started and leaving nothing more than the foundations.

It would be Cathillian's job to designate an area for a park of sorts; someplace nice and quiet for mothers to take their children to play.

The idea had been the druid's and Amelia had been quick to approve it when word had been brought to her by Andrew, a Boulevard man who was more than happy to have wonderful new ideas to make his home a better place.

"This is a lot bigger than I imagined," Marie commented, looking at the area Cathillian had sectioned off for the park.

A grin broke across the druid's face. "That's not the first time I've heard a woman say that."

Cathillian expected a snide comment in return, but was instead punched in the arm from the other side.

"Ouch!" he complained, rubbing at his shoulder as he saw Andrew shaking his head at him.

"You really can't help yourself, can you?" Andrew asked, his expression a cross between disbelief and amusement.

Shaking his head, Cathillian told him, "Not really, no."

Andrew nodded. "So, ya just open your mouth and out it pukes?"

Cathillian looked up for a moment before nodding. "Yeah, that's basically it. And look… Don't be mad because she complimented the size. I don't plan to stand in your way. I just accept the compliments and move on."

Marie punched Cathillian in his other arm.

"Ouch! Damn, guys. You have *no* sense of humor," Cathillian complained, now rubbing both his shoulders.

"You know, they say the more you brag, the more you're compensating," Marie told him, pointing at his pants.

"Yeah," Andrew added. "Ever wonder why I don't ever mention mine?"

"Ugh! I'm gonna go play over here. You guys are huge dicks today," Cathillian scolded, tossing his hair as he spun with an exaggerated movement.

"How would you know anything about huge dicks?" Andrew

shouted after him.

There was laughter behind him, which brought a smile to his own face. It was all in good fun, and he knew it. He was impressed that Marie had hit him, though. She was usually very timid, but over the past couple of weeks she'd grown used to him and his jokes.

It seemed like she wasn't so timid anymore.

A loud screech cut through the sky, alerting Cathillian. His smile faded as he looked up to see Echo overhead. He knew her calls, and that was a warning.

Cathillian drew on the magical bond between them, allowing him to wordlessly communicate with her. In moments, he turned to the others.

"I need a horse. Now," he ordered, his tone suddenly serious.

The others' smiles fell as Marie and Andrew glanced at each other before looking back at him. "There are stables three blocks down on the right," Andrew answered.

Cathillian didn't bother responding. He turned and ran at full speed toward the stables. He had no idea why, but he knew Echo wasn't wrong. He could feel the familiar presence of nature magic being used.

Jenna was outside the Arcadian walls.

It didn't take Cathillian long to reach the stables, and he was fast at coaxing a horse out. Jumping on its back, he used nature magic to will it to do as he asked and was happy when the horse obliged.

As Cathillian came up to the gates, he was met with a terrible sight. The four guards at the gate had all been killed.

What the fuck? Cathillian thought.

"Echo!" Cathillian shouted. The eagle called out in response. "Get Amelia!"

The golden eagle had accompanied Cathillian to the Capitol building before, and he hoped she'd be able to get in.

Cathillian stopped his horse at the gate, inspecting the men on the ground only to see he'd unfortunately been right.

They were all dead.

Confusion took hold of him as he studied them. Normally, the recently dead still had lingering energy surrounding them, but these men didn't. It was as though they'd been dead for days, but that was impossible.

Looking up, Cathillian saw Jenna standing roughly a hundred feet outside the gates, a dark smile on her face. A mix between disbelief and bewilderment gripped him as he began piecing things together.

Jenna was clad in black leather instead of the normal brown, green, or other earth tones the druids of the Dark Forest generally wore. The magical energy swirling around her was also dark and terrible.

Cathillian looked at the bodies lying on the ground around him, now realizing why it had seemed that they'd been dead for much longer than they had.

Jenna had used dark nature magic to suck the life from them.

At that moment, Cathillian realized that Jenna had joined the dark druids along with her brother Aeris. She'd always been rather slow and weak with warrior training as well as with nature magic, but it had now become very clear that her talents had laid elsewhere.

When it came to dark nature magic, she had been a very quick learner.

Cathillian took a few steps outside the gates toward Jenna. He stared her down, but realized that he was at a loss for words. He had no idea how to handle the situation, because it was obvious that she had come there for a fight.

"What have you done?" Cathillian asked. "How could you do this?"

Jenna's dark smile grew. "I never thought you'd actually leave the Dark Forest. Especially for an outsider. For an *Arcadian*."

Cathillian tightened his fist, doing his best to keep calm,

although instinct told him to tear her a new asshole. If she'd crossed the line from nature magic to using magic to drain the life out of innocent men, then in his eyes, she no longer deserved to live. But until he knew what had happened, he needed to keep his wits about him.

"Arryn spent more time in the Dark Forest with us than she ever did in Arcadia. She's a druid. You and your family were the only ones who didn't share that opinion. Don't you see that it's you who is the outsider? Can't you see that *you* are the traitor?"

When Jenna laughed, it chilled Cathillian to the bone. This girl was nothing like the one he'd known in the Forest. Even though she'd always been stubborn, rude, and very unforgiving about things she didn't understand, she'd still been one of them.

Now, she was something else entirely.

Something darker, far more confident, and far more power-ful. He'd never gone against a dark druid before, but he had heard stories. His grandfather told him about dark magic, and what they were capable of. It now seemed that he was going to find out first-hand.

Still smiling, Jenna called, "Cathillian, you are one of the strongest they have. You always have been. You could've been a lot more, but you wasted your time on the Arcadian. You know as well as I do that I was nothing in the Dark Forest. It wasn't until I left that I realized my true potential."

Cathillian narrowed his eyes as he took a few steps forward, further studying his opponent's appearance. Her green eyes had started to turn grey, and her beautiful, healthy skin had become lighter in color.

He and Arryn hadn't been gone very long, so her transforma-tion must have been a very fast one. As the years passed, her skin would turn more and more ashen, and her eyes would become cloudy or smoky in color, only a hint of their original green evident around the edges when she cast.

"You know, that sounds like a recruitment speech. You've

always been rather stubborn and unbelievable, but you must be absolutely brainless if you think the grandson of the Chieftain— the only *real* Chieftain—would join you."

Jenna's hands rose at her sides for a moment before falling back down. "Well, you can't blame a girl for trying. I always thought that you and I would be good together, but that Arcadian bitch was always in the way. One day, you'll come to see just how pathetic she is. That is, of course, if you're still alive by then."

"Why are you here, Jenna? Why did you kill these men?" Cathillian asked. His urge to punish her for what she'd done was rising, but he had to know more first. There was a reason she had come to Arcadia, and he feared she wouldn't be the last dark druid to do so. He had to know if the city was in danger.

"I had to see for myself. I had to see how far the almighty grandson of the Chieftain had fallen. The future Elder of our tribe."

Cathillian shook his head. "Not *our* tribe. Not yours anymore, traitor."

Jenna glanced at the ground before looking back at him. "I suppose that's true. Fair enough. But it's not like you'll have a tribe to go home to soon. And don't think that Arryn's precious Arcadia is safe either. Well, I guess I should say *your* precious Arcadia, *Arcadian.*"

That was all Cathillian could handle. Not only had she threatened the Dark Forest and by proxy his family, but she'd also threatened Arcadia and Arryn. Given the damage she had already caused, the lives she had already taken, he didn't plan to stand for any more.

"I'm sorry to hear you say that, Jenna, but I can honestly say I'm not surprised. You always were a piece of shit. You *and* your family."

Cathillian's hand was a blur as he pulled the knife from his belt and threw it at her. Jenna only narrowly missed getting hit in the throat when she dodged at the last moment. Apparently, whatever she'd been learning had made her even faster on top of being more skilled in magic.

Jenna ran toward Cathillian and he toward her, quickly closing the distance between them. As he ran, Cathillian jerked a hand through the air, causing a large chunk of dirt to break free of the ground and hit her directly in the chest. The newly-turned dark druid was thrown backward onto the ground, but she was quick to roll over and get back to her feet.

Just as Cathillian was about to make contact, she spun out of the way, yanking the sword out of the sheath on his hip as she moved. She hit him in the back of the knees with its broad side, taking him to the ground before kicking him hard in the throat and collarbone as he tried to rise.

Cathillian fell back, coughing hard as his hand involuntarily reached for his throat. Before he could reach it, Jenna had straddled him, knocking his hand out of the way and wrapping her hand around his throat instead.

It had been hard to take him down, especially for Jenna. There were a handful of warriors in the tribe that were stronger than he who could take him down with little effort on their part. They were the warriors he loved to train with most because they made him better.

Jenna had never been one of them.

In fact, she had always been the weakest. But there he laid, flat on the ground, barely able to breathe, Jenna straddling him with her hand wrapped around his throat. He didn't want to be bested by the likes of her, but he very quickly found himself unable to move.

As he did his best to throw her off, he felt his body growing weaker and weaker. Just as a druid of the Dark Forest connected to nature and used their power to push that pure energy toward their target to heal them, Jenna was using her power to pull energy from him.

Soon, Cathillian was unable to move, forced to lie there

staring into her cold grayish-green eyes as she looked down at him and smiled.

"I always wondered what it would be like to get you in this position. Well, with a little less clothing and a lot less dark magic." Jenna shook her head, her eyes never leaving his. "Unfortunately, we don't always get what we want, do we?"

Cathillian swallowed, the pain of that action terrible from both the kick to the throat and the dark magic flowing through him. Still, he found the energy to speak, unwilling to let her take him without some sort of fight.

"I always knew you were capable of treachery, just like your brother. In case you hadn't noticed, I was raised by the strongest woman in the entire tribe. There's no way in hell I would've chosen the weakest in the tribe to bring home to her. It would've been an insult to her and myself."

Jenna turned angry then, her expression revealing her rage as she leaned forward, her face only a breath away from Cathillian's. "You have no idea how sorry you are about to be. I would kill you, but you're my messenger. I need you to live."

Though it pained him, Cathillian forced a smile. "That's too bad. I guess that means I'll have to suffer through seeing you again. On the other hand, it also means I'll get the privilege of seeing Arryn again." He threw that last bit in just to piss her off even more, though he knew it was a bad idea, given that she literally had his life in the palm of her hand.

Her eyes widened as she sat back a few inches. Once the disbelief faded, her eyes narrowed again. "Let your mother know that we're coming. You have a choice, Cathillian. Stay with your precious Arryn in Arcadia, or save your family and the Dark Forest. Goodbye for now."

With that, she leaned back, her power increasing as it flowed through her hand and entered Cathillian, draining him. Within seconds his eyes fluttered closed and unconsciousness overtook him.

CHAPTER TWELVE

Arryn decided to take the box of Adrien's things back to Amelia, but only the things that had no meaning. Arryn had been rifling through them for a couple of days, but she'd not found much.

There were a couple of ledgers and some other things that she kept, but most of it was useless. There were also designs for a beautiful box with a magitech lock on it. Something far too pretty for Adrien to ever have possessed.

She'd hoped something would jump out at her, but she knew better. Adrien wasn't that stupid.

Other than seeing Amelia, Arryn wanted to finally talk to Elon. She'd waited long enough, having given Amelia enough time to question him about his whereabouts as well as the mysterious person that Doyle had mentioned.

Amelia still wasn't certain she'd heard it all, but that wasn't going to stop her from looking into it, which Arryn found to be a relief.

Cathillian had left early that morning to work in the Boulevard, taking a break from his normal classes just outside the walls. Since he was up early, she had decided that she should be as well. It was the perfect time to get everything delivered to Amelia without having to bother her at home.

When Arryn got to the Capitol building, she found that Marie was out and decided to just let herself in. Amelia smiled as Arryn walked through the door, box in hand.

"What's the verdict?" Amelia asked. "Did you find anything good in there?"

Arryn made her way over to the desk and set the box down with a grunt. "I guess I found just about as much as you did. Shit. I kept all of the ledgers, some plans for a lockbox, and a few envelopes because I thought I might find something in one of those, but other than that, no. I found a whole lot of nothing."

Amelia sighed and nodded, her smile fading a bit as she looked at the box. "I was afraid of that. Not unlike you, I can't seem to get this whole thing out of my head, and it only seems to be getting worse."

Arryn snorted. "At least you don't have someone telling you that you're crazy. I'm here, and I think you're right."

With a laugh, Amelia remarked, "You want it to be true because you want to blame everything on Talia."

Arryn grimaced for a moment. "That may be the case, but it doesn't make me any less interested in helping you find the truth. Speaking of which, I came for another reason."

Amelia took the box and set it just off to the side of her desk before sitting down. "What can I do for you?"

Taking a deep breath, Arryn took a step closer to the desk. "You mentioned a while back the possibility of talking to Elon. After everything that happened with Doyle, I wanted to give you the time you asked for. It's been a couple weeks, so I wanted to see if it was possible to speak to him now."

Sitting back in her chair, Amelia exhaled heavily as she stared at the wall, obviously deep in thought. Finally, she turned back to Arryn and nodded. "I don't see a problem with that. You've been very patient, and I appreciate it." Amelia checked the time. "Do you want to go now? You still have plenty of time before school starts."

Arryn's eyes lit up, not having expected to be able to speak to him so soon. "Yes! That would be great. Thanks."

Amelia waved a hand in the air before she stood. "Don't mention it. You've done more than plenty to help the city. I made you a promise to help if I could when you first came here; I've been the one slacking on my end of the deal. You've more than held up your end."

Arryn followed Amelia out of the room and down the hall to the stairwell. As they walked downstairs, Arryn decided that since luck was on her side, she should bring up another topic she'd been wanting to discuss.

After throwing her long hair back over her shoulder, Arryn said, "I've been getting my head looked into on a daily basis at the Academy. Before you argue, I honestly have no idea if I even think it's Talia. Of course, it *had* occurred to me. Regardless, someone in the school is using mystical powers, and I can feel it. Do you think you can teach me how to guard my mind?"

The magitech sconces on the wall lit up as they made their way downstairs, one after another clicking on as they got close enough for the sensors to pick up their movement.

"I know this is motivated by the whole Talia thing, but—" Amelia began, but Arryn quickly cut her off.

"Oh, no. Not you, too. Don't start talking like I'm crazy. Talia came over to the house and left a fruit basket for me. She spent enough time there to convince Cathillian that she was an angel."

Amelia laughed." Oh no! That *bitch*! How dare she bring you a gift?"

Arryn sighed. "Please, just stop and think for a minute. How many other teachers has she given a gift to? And personally delivered it to their home when she knew they were still in school.

Yes, I find it very strange. But all that aside, someone is in my head multiple times every day. They're after something."

Amelia threw up her hands in surrender. "Okay, okay, I get it. I'm not going to call you crazy like Cathillian apparently did, but I *am* going to tell you to talk to her personally. I'll make you a deal. If you go to her office, speak to her one-on-one, and *still* get bad vibes from her, I'll teach you how to guard your mind. See if you get that feeling while you're in there. If you do, it's her. Then again, if you don't get it, that doesn't necessarily rule her out either."

Arryn nodded. "That's exactly what I was thinking. Whoever is getting into my head has to know I'm aware they're in there. So, if it is her, she's not going to risk it in close quarters. At least, I'd imagine she wouldn't."

"I guess it just depends on how badly she wants information. If she wants to know why you're there, she'll risk it, especially if you go in there acting like you want to make peace. In fact, make that your experiment. If she's as bad as you think she is, then she knows you don't like her. Even if it's not her in your head, it'll more than likely be someone she's close to. Go in there and pretend that you want to be her best friend. Use that gift as a gateway. If she's a good person, she's going to buy it without question. But if she's everything you think she is, then you're either going to feel someone getting in your head, or you will very soon after."

"So, you believe me?" Arryn asked.

Amelia shook her head. Arryn couldn't see her expression because she was still following her, but she could read her relaxed body language.

"It's not that I do or don't believe you," Amelia told her, "but that I would be *very* irresponsible if I just let this go. If the content of my interaction with Doyle proves to be true, anyone around us could be the person who's seeking to destroy the city. I would be a fool to dismiss anyone—even you."

"I'll take it. It's not perfect, but it's good enough for me," Arryn agreed. "So, if she does get in my head, what should I do?"

Amelia laughed. "Well, that's the fun part. You have enough hatred for her that this should be easy for you. If she gets in your head and it's been her from the beginning, then she's up to no good. That means I don't give a shit what happens to her. It also means that you're justified in hating her. So, what you're going to do is put on your best performance. On the outside, you're going to be her brand-new best friend. On the inside, I want you to imagine all the terrible things you plan to do to her if she is, in fact, a traitor. Because if she *is* a traitor, we want her to know her fate."

Arryn smiled, the very thought of it amusing to her. It made her happy that Amelia was helping her, even if she wasn't a hundred percent sure. It was more than Cathillian had done for her.

The plan was simple enough. Be nice to Talia because she could be innocent. That made sense. However, if she was as bad as Arryn thought, and she was capable of mystical powers, then by Arryn thinking terrible things about her, Talia would know and more than likely give an indication that she did.

Easy enough, though Arryn wasn't a big fan of this kind of behavior. She was the up front and honest type. Sneaking around and lying made her sick, even if she was trying to be diplomatic for her friend and superior.

They had almost reached the cells under the Capitol building when someone came down the stairs and down the hall, screaming.

"Amelia! Amelia!"

Arryn and Amelia both turned and ran back toward the stairs, meeting one of Cathillian's students at their base.

"What is it?" Amelia asked.

The guy shook his head, struggling to catch his breath. "It's Cathillian," was all he was able to get out.

Arryn stepped forward, a jolt of fear rushing through her. "What about him? What's happened?"

He was out of breath, but he was trying hard. "He ran off... and stole a horse... from stables. He didn't... say what was going on... but we knew something was up." He took several more breaths before continuing. "Echo came for us and wouldn't stop screeching at us until we followed her. Four guards are dead by the gate, and Cathillian was unconscious just outside it."

"What?" Arryn asked, grabbing his arm. "Where is he now?"

"The other guys are bringing him to the medical building. I ran ahead to get Amelia. Her office window has been busted out, so I think Echo tried to get in that way."

Arryn looked at Amelia. "Cathillian must have sent Echo for you when he found the dead guards."

Amelia sighed, her eyes closing. "But we weren't in the office, and Marie was down in the Boulevard."

Arryn shook her head. "It doesn't matter now. Let's go."

Arryn ran past them, heading upstairs and through the halls to get out the front entrance. It no longer mattered that she was mad at him. Her best friend had nearly been killed, and there wasn't anyone else around who was skilled enough to help him. Not something she planned to let happen again.

IT HAD BEEN two days since Cathillian was attacked, and he was only now beginning to stir. Arryn had sat by his bedside for most of that time, with Samuel taking the watch during Academy hours, and Celine watching overnight to let Arryn sleep. During the twelve hours after class was over and before she had to go to sleep, Arryn sat by his bedside and wouldn't leave for anything.

Even with Arryn healing him, it was obvious that he wouldn't wake up anytime soon. She wasn't sure what had happened to him, and she knew she wasn't the best healer, but she tried anyway, every morning and every night.

On the third morning, Arryn woke up and made her way into his room. Celine was sitting on his bedside, placing a cool wash-cloth on his forehead. As his eyes started to flutter open, Arryn rushed over and knelt on the bed.

"Cathillian?" she asked.

A hand wrapped around hers, giving it a gentle squeeze. Arryn looked into Celine's eyes as the woman shook her head and gave a sad smile.

"He's been doing that all night. I don't think he's waking up just yet, but he's getting there. Maybe he'll be okay after another healing. This is definitely the most awake I've seen him."

Arryn nodded before rising to her feet. Celine stood and moved out of Arryn's way to give full access. After removing the washcloth, Arryn leaned forward and placed one hand on his forehead and the other on his chest.

Unsure of how much more of watching him lie there helpless without having any clue as to what happened she could take, Arryn began to feel desperate. She needed him to get better, even if it was just for him to argue with her about Talia. It didn't matter.

She felt her magic swirling around her as she tried to control it with her emotions high. Taking a deep breath, she decided to focus on the anger that someone had hurt him when she'd been nowhere around to help him, the sadness from having to watch him be so weak, and the desperation of needing him to get better.

Her magic felt stronger and far more powerful than any she'd called before while healing. Taking another deep breath, Arryn focused the energy and began channeling it through her hands into Cathillian.

She could feel the magic moving through him and pushing life into him. At that moment, she realized he hadn't been injured by any traditional means. Magic had done this. Magic had literally sucked the life out of him. But who would do such a thing? Who *could* do such a thing?

She heard a deep breath, which forced Arryn's eyes open. Looking down, she saw Cathillian staring wide-eyed directly at her. As she pulled her magic back, his hand came to rest on hers.

"Cathillian?" Arryn whispered, her voice unsteady.

"What happened?" he asked as he looked around and realized where he was.

Arryn sat next to him, wondering what to say because she wanted to know the same thing. "One of your men chased you down after Echo came to get help. They found you unconscious just outside the gates. Four guards had been killed."

Cathillian's brows furrowed, his eyes wandering around the room. He looked confused, like he was trying to remember.

"You've been unconscious for the better part of three days. I've tried healing you every morning and every night, but I'm not nearly as good at it as you. Something was different this time. It was like I could feel what had happened to you."

Cathillian's eyes met hers as he turned his head. His expression still looked confused, but now he seemed more curious. "And? What happened?"

"It felt like someone had sucked the life out of you. There weren't really any bruises on you. It didn't look like any real damage had been done on the outside to cause you to be unconscious for that long. But when I healed you, I could feel something dark in there. I don't know how to explain it."

Cathillian's eyes closed then as he sighed heavily. His hands lifted to his face, and he groaned before brushing his long hair back and pulling it out from under him.

"I remember. I remember what happened."

Cathillian tried to sit up, and Arryn moved to help him, but he smiled and waved her off. It seemed that he was able to move around relatively easily now.

Once he was situated, he continued, "Jenna has left the Dark

Forest. She joined her brother, Aeris, and went with the dark druids. That darkness that you're talking about... it's dark nature magic. It's essentially the total opposite of healing. My grandfather told me about it once, but it was a long time ago, and I'd forgotten about it entirely until you said you felt darkness."

"What was the darkness that I felt? Shouldn't it have dissipated as soon as your magic left?" Arryn asked.

Cathillian nodded. "If a magician throws a fireball, it will naturally burn hotter than normal fire, so you can tell the difference between the scorch marks the fireball leaves and scorch marks from an actual fire. The same thing can be said of nature magic. The actual dark magic she used was gone, but you could feel what had caused the damage. It leaves the equivalent of a scorch mark on anything that it touches, even down to the arrows they make. Touching a wound made by them, you can feel how the energy has been drained. It feels like death. That's what you felt when your magic touched me. Excellent job, by the way."

Arryn smiled. Always the teacher, even when he was the victim. "So, Jenna did this? What was she even doing here?"

"I need to send word to my mother. Jenna came here to give me a warning that I needed to choose between staying here and protecting you or going home and protecting the Dark Forest. It seems that both are in danger. She came here hoping that I would leave with her, I think."

Arryn rolled her eyes and shook her head. "That bitch always was crazy. So, what do we do?"

There was a pause as Cathillian mulled things over. "We carry on as normal. I'm not giving in to her. We send word to my mother. If there is any kind of problem or emergency, she'll let us know that we need to come back. Otherwise, the two of us are not gonna make a difference in the Dark Forest. But if something happens here, where the army is weak, we could make a huge difference."

It surprised Arryn that Cathillian wasn't ready to abandon the city and rush back to the Dark Forest. That was his home, and it was where his family lived. She couldn't imagine just letting it go, but then again, he was right.

The druid warriors were fierce fighters. There was no way they would go down easily, and a single druid and an Arcadian-turned-druid weren't going to make a difference. Well, as far she could tell, anyway.

"It's the shower, isn't it?" Arryn smiled. "That's the real reason you're staying in Arcadia."

Cathillian sleepily returned the smile. "Ya got me. That's totally why. I just really don't think I can give 'em up. It's how I relax after a hard day of dealing with you."

Arryn laughed. "Dealing with me? Sir, dealing with *you* is a full-time job."

He shook his head. "You don't know you like I do. Hell, I've been debating on going down to the factory and applying for a job. I'll go hang out with sweaty men all day."

Quirking an eyebrow, Arryn asked, "Oh! I get it... You're considering our business plan! Damn, I'd nearly forgotten. Rest that pretty face of yours, and we'll put it right to work. You'll make a fortune now that the Arcadian men have a solid income."

Cathillian sighed, his expression still amused. "Not even death excuses me from your prostitution jokes, I see."

Arryn shrugged. "Well, *death* would have." She patted him on the shoulder. "But you aren't dying. Not today, anyway. I saw to that. We all did."

She winked, but was quite surprised when he pulled her down into a tight hug. His body had been quite chilled the past few days, but he finally felt warm—very warm.

"Thank you," he whispered before letting her go after several long moments.

"I have to get out of here," Arryn told him. "I want you to get something to eat and drink, but then I want you to rest. Samuel will be here soon, and Celine is here, of course. I've been leaving the Academy early in the afternoon, so I will today, too."

"Well, look at you. Taking care of me even though you hate me." He laughed.

Arryn sighed. "Yeah, yeah. Don't remind me."

CHAPTER THIRTEEN

Amelia sat in her office, staring at the box that Arryn had brought back to her. Her eyes were locked on it as though it might grow legs and run away. The past few days had been quite eventful, and it didn't look as though there would be an end anytime soon.

Cathillian had been attacked, and she had no idea who or what did it. Four guards had been lost as well, and Amelia couldn't deny the signs any longer. The Guard needed to be more heavily trained, and someone definitely had it in for the city.

It occurred to her that since the attack had happened at the entry to the city, just outside its walls, it had been an outsider who had attacked, but that didn't matter as much as a few other things.

Were they gone?

Had they come into the city and stayed?

Were they from outside the city?

Was it a resident?

There were far too many variables, and she would have no answers until Cathillian was ready to talk. The Matriarch knew that the dead sure as hell weren't talking.

But that hadn't been the only thing...

That whole mess had started when Amelia had tried to take Arryn to see Elon. She wanted Arryn to be able to talk to him and try to get answers. After everything that had happened with Doyle, Amelia had needed time to try to get anything out of him that she could, but it was obvious he had no plans to help her unless she helped him first.

But her attempt to get him to talk to Arryn had been thwarted by the attack on the gate. She and Arryn rushed to the medical building to see Cathillian and find out what happened. There weren't many answers to be had, but Amelia had helped Arryn get the druid home safely.

When it was obvious that Arryn wouldn't be back to speak to Elon right away, Amelia had taken it upon herself to do it for her. As she sat there in her office, staring at the box that she had looked through a hundred times, she thought back over everything he'd told her.

Elon had paced back and forth in his cell that day, ignoring Amelia's presence. That hadn't shocked her, though. She wasn't his biggest fan, and he knew it. And until Amelia gave him what he wanted, he didn't plan to give her any information.

But what he wanted wasn't in Amelia's power to give. He wanted his son, Gregory.

When the airship was being built and Adrien had needed more power for it, Elon had tethered his own child to it, sucking the power—and the life—directly out of his son to fuel the airship. Gregory had been betrayed by his own father and there was no fixing that, but it didn't stop Elon from trying to use Gregory as a bargaining chip.

He wanted to beg his son for forgiveness.

Elon refused to believe that Gregory was no longer in the city. He'd left with Hannah, Parker, and the Founder to go on another quest. There were bigger things at stake now, and Gregory wanted to be a part of them, and there was little left for him in Arcadia.

No matter how much Amelia wished she could give Elon what he wanted so she could get the answers that she so desperately needed, there was no way for her to make that happen.

And when she'd gone to see him just after Cathillian was attacked, after making sure he was settled and safe at home, she was pissed. She wasn't taking no for an answer this time.

"I didn't come here for me this time," Amelia began. "This time, I'm here for someone else."

"Is that so?" Elon asked incredulously. It was obvious that he still didn't care. "And do you have Gregory? Because if you don't, I don't give a damn who you're here for."

Amelia had exhaled heavily. The past couple weeks of irritation had already brought her rage to the front. Rubbing the bridge of her nose, she took a moment to steel herself, knowing that it would take patience to get anything at all out of him.

"I know you don't care. I'm just hoping that somewhere in the blackened heart that was capable of trying to murder his own son for nothing more than a moment of appreciation from the monster he served I will find even the tiniest shred of humanity. I doubt I will, but I have to try. For her."

"Her who?" he asked, stopping his pacing for a moment.

"Her name is Arryn. Ten years ago, she fled the city with her mother on horseback. Two Hunters chased her into the woods to the west as they rode for the Dark Forest. Her mother was killed, but Arryn made it the rest of the way to the Dark Forest, where she was raised with the druids. Now she's back, and she wants answers."

Amelia watched as his face turned from disgusted confusion in the beginning of her statement to donning realization at the end of it.

He knew who she was.

"Christopher and Elayne," was all he said.

Amelia's eyes narrowed as she looked at him. That was the first bit of information she'd ever been able to get out of him. Slowly, she nodded her head. "Yes. Christopher and Elayne."

Elon sighed as he sat down on his bed. Staring at the floor, he began to wring his hands as he shook his head.

Amelia shifted her weight from one foot to the other, debating on taking a step closer to the cell. "If I didn't know any better, I'd almost think you were feeling something other than disdain. It almost looks like guilt or sadness."

Elon looked up then, his eyes suddenly glassy as though he might start crying at any moment. "Arryn is alive? She's here?"

Amelia cleared her throat, realizing that not only had she discovered the perfect person for Arryn to talk to, he also knew much more than she had expected. The tone in his voice when asking about Arryn had sounded almost concerned. Worried.

"Yes, she is. She came back because she wanted answers. In reality, she wanted to come back and destroy Adrien, but that had already been done."

Elon had laughed, but it wasn't amused. It seemed to hold more disbelief than humor. He leaned back against the wall, his eyes staring at the ceiling as his hands clasped over his torso. "You know, if it had been her instead of the Boulevard girl, I would've helped. I would have destroyed everything."

That was news.

Amelia couldn't help the shock that crossed her face. "What? Are you serious? I know that you and I aren't exactly the best of friends, but I'm gonna need you to tell me what the hell happened. Why would you betray Adrien for Arryn but not for Hannah? What happened to turn you from hating him to worshipping him?"

Elon took a deep breath before releasing it in a heavy sigh. "Christopher was my best friend. In fact, Arryn and Gregory use to play together often, though I doubt she would remember. She was too young back then. Christopher was one of those rare men who would lay down his life for anyone he called friend, and his wife wasn't any different. Hell, I actually saw Arryn punch a kid straight in the face when he stole one of Gregory's toys and made him cry. I knew right then that Arryn was gonna be just like them."

There was a pause as he stared into nothing. Finally, he looked at Amelia and asked, "Is she? Is she like them?"

Amelia swallowed, shocked at what she was hearing. "Y-yes," she stammered, clearing her throat once again. "Yes, she is. Like I said, she spent ten years in the Dark Forest training for the day she could come back to the city, destroy Adrien, and reclaim everyone's freedom in her parents' name. I'd say from the description you just gave me, she's a hell of a lot like them."

A slow smile spread across his face as a single tear rolled down his cheek. He quickly wiped it away and looked back at the ceiling before continuing with the story.

"I don't know where, because Adrien never trusted me much. Even when I was building that damn ship for him, he still didn't trust me. So, I don't know where the warning came from, but somehow or another he found out there was a group of people trying to dethrone him. Traitors to the city, he called them. Of course, I was concerned. While I saw the issues rising in our city, I wholeheartedly believed everything Adrien told me, just like the majority of us did. Just like you did."

Amelia grabbed a chair and pulled it up next to the bars to sit. Somehow, even though Elon had done all that he had, at that moment she could feel his grief, and it didn't seem right to stand over him.

Elon continued, "Christopher came to me and told me that he needed my help. It was at that moment I realized my best friend was one of the people trying to take Adrien out. Back then Adrien wasn't quite so crazy. He was just a dick. I thought if I talked to him, he might be able to neutralize the situation by talking to Chris, trying to make him see what he did, what he made me see."

"And what was that?" Amelia asked. "What was it that you saw?"

Elon shrugged. "I guess the same thing that you did. I saw a man who was trying to keep the city safe. The Boulevard people were supposed to lack magical promise. If they tried to use it, they could hurt themselves and hurt others. I saw our fearless leader trying to keep our people safe. But I also saw my best friend not seeing that future, so I thought Adrien might be able to help him. I never in a million years thought that Adrien would do what he did."

A knock at Amelia's door startled her, bringing her out of her memories and back to her office, her desk, and that box sitting in front of her. She took a deep breath, hand over her chest as though it would help slow her jumpy heart.

"Yes! Come in!" Amelia shouted.

Marie walked in, her smile fading as she saw Amelia's expression. "You okay? I'm sorry if I interrupted something."

Amelia shook her head, pushing her chair back from her desk and standing. "No, no, you're fine. I need to go through this box again. It seems that I'm looking for something a little bit more specific now, but it can wait. What brings you in here?"

Marie took a step forward and smiled again. "It's the factory. It appears that the few men working inside have finished. They wanted you to come down and do a walk-through. The factory is now ready to be opened to the public for work as soon as you sign off on it."

Amelia took one last look at the box, realizing that she needed to have a long talk with Arryn about Elon and the things she had found out. It had been weighing on her since the day Cathillian had been injured, but she knew talking to Arryn while things were so hectic at home wouldn't be the best idea.

She sighed. *Don't wait too long, Amelia,* she thought to herself. *You don't want her to hate you for keeping it from her.*

"Okay, let's do this. Let's get our city back on track," Amelia told Marie as she followed her out of the room.

IT TOOK Talia a full day to get to the Madlands while teleporting Scarlett along with her. It required quite a bit of energy to make any kind of jump alone, but carrying someone else made it much worse.

She had to stop mid-way for rest, and then again at the border. She wanted to be fully restored before she attempted to confront the remnant. If she showed even an ounce of weakness, she would be killed and everything would be wasted.

Talia and Scarlett stood at the edge of the mountains looking down into what was known as the Madlands, the desolate wasteland that was home to the destructive and murderous remnant.

They didn't build anything, though they were more than happy to set up camp in whatever was already there.

All they were good at was destroying, which was why their homes were dug into the sides of the mountains or in the ruins of old buildings that had fallen and crumbled away since before the Age of Madness.

Talia would need to locate the leader and get his attention without being killed in the process.

If she pulled *this* off, nothing could stand in her way.

Talia and Scarlett began making their way down the mountain into the remnant territory. Talia had no idea how her companion felt, but Talia was rather sure of herself.

She was nothing if not confident. Sometimes a little too confident, but it hadn't bitten her in the ass yet, so she didn't see any reason to let it start that day.

Once they neared the bottom, however, Talia began to feel slightly apprehensive.

"Don't you find it strange that we haven't been confronted yet?" Talia asked.

"What do you mean?" Scarlett asked. "Did you expect a welcoming party?"

Talia laughed. "Actually, yes, I did. Remnant are extremely territorial. If they sense even a footstep too close to their borders, they go into a frenzy. We not only made it to the border, we crossed it. We are inside the Madlands, and still no remnant. Either they're completely clueless that we're here, or more likely, they know and are strategizing."

Scarlett was about to say something, but was interrupted when Talia threw her hands out in front of her, a barrier exploding around both of them to deflect a battle axe just before it would have cleaved one of them in two.

"What the *fuck*?" Scarlett asked, clearly startled by the change of events.

Talia lowered her hands, though her barrier stayed in place. She turned with a dark smile on her face and gazed back at where they had just been. There, toward the top of a large hill in the mountainside, stood a couple dozen or more remnant looking down at them.

"That's one hell of a way to welcome a lady!" Talia shouted.

One by one, the remnant jumped from the edge of the hill, landing the twenty or so feet below. They rolled as they landed, quickly coming back to a standing position, and descended the side of the mountain with death on their faces as they approached the two women standing on their land.

Talia couldn't help but admire how agile and coordinated they were given that they were known to be stupid, mindless beasts.

There was one remnant larger than the rest standing at the front as they approached. He walked straight up to the edge of

Talia's barrier and smiled, his red eyes staring directly into hers as his jagged, broken teeth showed through his dangerous grin.

"It ain't very often that dinner comes to me," he commented, his voice guttural and terrifying to a normal person—though Talia found it rather exciting.

It was an adrenaline rush for her to stand there in remnant territory, staring one of them down. It was like facing death head-on with only a thin barrier separating them.

Talia laughed, the darkness of it catching even the remnant off-guard. "Oh, I assure you that dinner hasn't delivered itself today either. I came to speak to you, woman to beast. Now, are you the one in charge around here, or do I need to take your head to the one who is?"

There was a pause as the remnant studied her before he threw his head back and gave a loud laugh. The other remnant behind him followed suit, chortling right along with their leader.

He reached out and touched the barrier with the tip of his finger, the power of it burning his skin. Talia could smell the charred flesh and see the smoke rolling off it as his cold eyes stared into hers. He didn't flinch as he allowed himself to burn for a moment before finally pulling away.

"You're a little stronger than I gave you credit for. I bet that means you taste better, too," he told her, licking his lips.

The beast made her sick, but not because she was afraid of him. She knew that she would never physically stand a chance against him, but she knew without a doubt that she was much stronger in other ways. She felt offended that he would think she would so easily be taken as prey.

Keeping her focus on her barrier, she took a step forward. "Promises, promises. All the boys say that, but they always seem to let me down. Which is why I'm not going to give you the chance. Now, if you're done flirting, we can get down to business."

Talia could almost feel Scarlett's apprehension as the woman shifted her weight back and forth before stepping right behind her. Talia didn't care. She could handle herself; her companion was only there for backup if needed.

"Those are strong words coming from a scared little girl in a shield," he sneered. "Why don't you drop it and let me flirt with you out here?"

Talia smiled, cocking her head to the side a little as she maintained constant eye contact. "Oh, sweetheart. You think I'm afraid of you. That's cute."

Talia reached behind her with both hands, placing them on Scarlett's hips as she took a few steps back to guide her companion to take a few steps back as well. Once there were several feet between them and the remnant, Talia removed her hands and stepped just outside of the barrier.

The remnant crossed his large arms over his chest as he watched Talia. She slowly took one step, and then another, each movement controlled and confident as she strolled up to the beast.

She stopped when there was no more than a foot or so between them. "Is this better? Can you hear me now?" she asked.

The remnant shook his head. "I ain't sure if you're brave, or if you're fuckin' stupid."

"I believe the one that you're looking for is confident. I'm very confident."

The remnant was fast, but Talia's reflexes were faster. As his arms unfolded and darted for her, she threw her own hands out, sending him flying several feet back onto the ground. Without wasting a single moment, she arced her hands over her chest, conjuring two large fireballs before throwing them next to him on the ground.

She controlled the flames, encircling him as the dead brush around him caught fire.

The other remnant quickly ran forward, and Talia was equally fast to react. She pulled two daggers from sheaths on her lower back and threw them, each one hitting a different remnant in the chest and dropping them.

Three more came at her, and she turned, throwing her hands out in front of her and letting a burst of energy blow forward, sending them back into another approaching remnant.

She quickly extended her hands to her sides, flexing her entire body as she pulled downward, extracting what little water there was in the air around her to create ice shards.

"Stop!" the remnant leader shouted.

A few listened, but most continued charging for Talia. With the flick of her wrist, shards of ice cut through the air, impaling several in the chest and face, ending them before a single extra step had been taken.

The leader was fast to intervene, snatching another of his men by the arm before he could advance farther. He threw him to the ground, standing on his throat.

"I said *STOP!*" he yelled, his voice booming out over everything.

The rest of the men and women immediately halted, some even taking a few steps back. Talia's eyes locked on the leader's as he stood inside the thick flames. Talia didn't stir, and she didn't drop the remaining ice she had created.

She stood there, watching his every move as he took a step forward, briefly standing in the flames before walking the rest of the way across.

She realized at that moment that her fire had done nothing to him; he'd allowed her to hold him there. His skin burned, but he didn't care. He was clearly curious about what she could do.

He took several steps forward, slowly approaching her. There was a dark smile on his face, telling her that he was clearly amused by her.

"Impressive," the remnant told her. "I think that you might have actually taken every one of them by yourself had I not intervened."

Talia smiled. "Good boy. I was starting to think I was gonna have to kill everyone before I got you to listen to reason. And people say you guys have no brains!" She laughed. "Certainly, smart enough not to let me kill all your men. Now, that business I mentioned?"

He nodded and pointed to the ice shards in her hands. "You can drop those now. You'll have no need for them. I promise to be a good boy... For now."

Slowly Talia dropped her hands and allowed the ice to fall to the ground. It almost immediately melted, the dry earth soaking it up.

"What the hell are you doing?" Scarlett whispered from behind her. Scarlett had stepped out of the barrier and came to stand behind her once again. "You'll get yourself killed."

Talia scoffed. "This was partly your idea, remember? I'm *so* glad I brought back-up. You were almost completely useless. Now, shut up and let me work. You've proven yourself to be no better than a damn ornament. Piss me off again and I'll feed you to them as a peace offering."

Scarlett glared at Talia, but wisely didn't say anything. Talia turned her focus back to the remnant in front of her. His eyes were narrowed as he smiled down at her, the very image of it horrifying to the normal person. She was undeterred.

"So, what did you have in mind?" he inquired.

"I'm glad you asked," Talia replied, smiling. "I have one hell of a deal to make with you, the prize at the finish line being Arcadia."

CHAPTER FOURTEEN

L eaving Cathillian that morning had been rather difficult. Arryn hadn't been sure he was feeling more like himself, though he certainly acted that way.

Days ago, Arryn had made a promise to Amelia that she would have a one-on-one discussion with Talia. It wasn't something she was looking forward to, but given the idea that Jenna could be snooping around and getting ready to cause trouble, she needed to know sooner rather than later if Talia was the one they were looking for.

Arryn hated herself for being so obsessed, but with Doyle's warning and her terrible gut feeling, she couldn't just let it go. At the very least, Amelia understood that, even if she didn't quite believe that Talia was the one.

As Arryn approached the hallway leading upstairs to Talia's office, she saw Jackson making his way down it. He looked up and jumped as he saw her, but quickly regained his composure.

"Arryn!" he exclaimed. "What are you doing?"

Arryn laughed. "I'm the teacher, I should be asking you that. But I assume you were just leaving from talking to Talia, right?"

Jackson looked back down the hallway, then returned his

focus to Arryn. "Uh, no. She's gone. She had to leave for a couple of days because her mom is sick. I had to drop something off."

Sick mom, Arryn thought. *Likely story*.

"Ah, I see. Well, that ruins my plans. I was actually planning to go talk to her," Arryn told him.

Jackson nodded, nervously looking around. Arryn thought he was acting very strangely, but she knew he'd recently had a run-in with some Boulevard boys, so she wasn't exactly surprised by his fidgety behavior. Still, she couldn't just let it go, either.

"Yeah, I guess we both wasted our time. Anyway, it's nice to see you again." He waved before walking away.

Arryn paused, staring down the hallway that led to Talia's office. She heard the footsteps stop, but she still debated moving forward.

"Arryn?" Jackson called, catching her attention. When she turned to face him, he was looking at her with a curious expression. He nodded toward the opposite end of the hallway. "Shouldn't you be heading back to class, too?"

Arryn clearly heard the warning in his suggestion. He may have thought he came off as smooth, but it was obvious to Arryn that his tone, combined with the question and his earlier nervous behavior, conveyed apprehension at her being anywhere near Talia's office while she was gone.

Arryn smiled and nodded. "Of course. I do need to get back. I just needed to talk to her, but I guess that since she's not here, I'll try to catch her again tomorrow."

Arryn walked forward, making her way back down the hall toward her own classroom as she listened for his footsteps to head downstairs. As soon as she heard the click of his steps descending to the first floor, she slowly turned to risk a look.

Satisfied that he wasn't standing right there, she quickly made her way back to the corner, slowly peeking over the railing to see that he had made it all the way downstairs. Jackson was completely out of sight before she turned to look back down the hall toward Talia's office.

Taking a deep breath, Arryn quickly walked back down the hall, up the stairs, and rushed into the Dean's office before closing the door behind her.

Arryn sighed in relief as she leaned against the door, catching her breath. Once she felt more comfortable, she turned her attention to Talia's desk. On it, she found an envelope that she couldn't help but investigate.

She quietly crossed the room, looking toward the door before picking up the envelope. It wasn't sealed, though it was tucked closed. Flipping it open, she pulled the contents free and read them. It was from Jackson, and he'd written her a note of some sort.

Talia,

I've done as you asked. I start Fundamentals of Nature Magic *tomorrow. I'll get close to her and find out why she's here. I don't know if you plan to see the druid again or not, but let me know if you find out anything else that can help from him. Just don't get too close. You mean a lot to me. You won't have anything to worry about with me around. You're taking care of all of us, and it's time we take care of you.*

Jackson

As Arryn reread the letter for the third time, certain that the *she* Jackson was referring to was Arryn herself, she could sense someone coming down the hall. Jumping into action, Arryn quickly tucked the letter back into the envelope and laid it on the desk where she had found it.

Arryn spun around in a circle several times, looking for good place to hide but coming up empty. She knew damn good and well that whoever was coming would certainly find her.

Finally, her eyes landed on the window. She took a deep breath as she opened it and mentally prepared herself to drop two stories to the ground.

It was scary, but she had done it when she was a child, so she knew she could do it again, especially now that she had nature magic to heal herself if she were to break anything on the way down.

Arryn sat on the ledge and swung her legs out, making sure to look around to see if anyone noticed her. She pulled the curtains closed to prevent someone from seeing her from the office.

Taking another deep breath, Arryn dropped, fighting the instinct to scream on the way down.

The ground was coming very quickly, and her fear grabbed her, hands shooting out in front of her as she prepared for the collision with the earth below. But it never came.

Vines shot out of the ground, wrapping around her and catching her before lowering her safely the rest of the way. Arryn felt like crying for joy, but knew she had to be quiet. She silently thanked the Matriarch and Patriarch before running around the side of the building and flattening herself against the cold stone wall to catch her breath.

She needed to get home, to get to Cathillian. More than anything, she wanted to tell him about the letter she had found. He had to believe her then. Didn't he?

It was just past the middle of the day when Cathillian finally made his way into the kitchen. His strength was back and he felt fine, though he was still heavily fatigued. Jenna had done quite a lot, much more than he had believed her capable of.

"Aren't ye supposed ta be in bed?" Samuel asked.

Cathillian turned and saw the rearick standing a few feet behind him, having come over from the couch. Cathillian smiled, happy to see his friend.

"Samuel! You're still here. I wasn't expecting that. Then again, I guess I should have. Today's the first day I've woken up on my own, and I still slept most of it."

"Aye." Samuel nodded. "We figured ye should still have someone with ye while Arryn's in class. Lemme guess, hungry?"

Cathillian looked over his shoulder at the kitchen before turning back to Samuel. "I haven't eaten in three days. I'm starving."

Samuel was about to respond, but was interrupted by Arryn busting through the front door, quickly slamming it behind her before making her way across the living room.

She pointed at Cathillian, her brows furrowed. "Aren't you supposed to be in bed?"

Cathillian sighed and rolled his eyes, throwing his hands in the air before dropping them. "I'm hungry! Damn. Slip into a coma for three days, and everybody acts like you're dying."

Arryn looked at him incredulously before turning to Samuel. "You're a terrible babysitter, but it doesn't matter." She turned back to Cathillian before Samuel could respond. "This will save me time. I needed to talk to you. Like, now!"

It was obvious just how jumpy she was, maybe even scared or nervous. Cathillian put his sense of humor aside and nodded. "What is it? What's wrong?"

Arryn shifted her weight, nervously debating her words as she looked back and forth between Samuel and Cathillian. "I'm just gonna come out and say it. I know no one believes me, but Talia is up to something."

Cathillian exhaled a heavy sigh. "This again? Arryn, I was really worried about you when you came blowing in here like that."

"Talia…" Samuel began, confusion on his face as though he was trying to recall something. "Who is that?"

Arryn gave a sarcastic laugh. "Oh, *I'll* tell you who it is."

Cathillian threw his hands up in defeat again. "Great. Here we go. Good job, Samuel."

Arryn shook her head, clearly choosing to ignore Cathillian as she kept her focus on Samuel. "She's the Dean of the Academy, and she's up to something. Since the moment I met her, she's been giving me bad vibes, but no one listens! Well, today that changes."

Samuel clapped his hands together once before pointing a finger in the air in excitement. "There! I knew I knew that name. Ye ain't wrong, lass. That lady Dean has somethin' wicked in her. I don't trust her as far as I can throw her."

Arryn studied him with shock on her face. "Wait, you believe me?"

Cathillian took a few steps forward, also unable to take in what he just heard. "Yeah, you believe her? I mean, it's not that I don't, but it's more that she's had a vendetta against the Dean since she arrived, and the woman has done nothing to her. I've met her, and she seemed like a very nice woman."

Samuel snorted. "And I met that bastard Adrien, too. He seemed like a goodhearted, charismatic Chancellor with nothin' but the safety of the city in mind, but we all know how that turned out, now don't we? Just because someone ain't never done anythin' directly to ye don't mean they're good. After all, those remnant never did anything to Andrew before that night, right? But he still took 'em down with the best of us."

Cathillian had never thought of it in those terms before. Just then, he felt terrible for having dismissed Arryn's worries quite so harshly. Even if he didn't quite understand where they were coming from, he knew from personal experience that people weren't always what they seemed. It hadn't been fair of him to judge her.

"You're right. I hadn't really thought about it that way. Arryn, I'm sorry. Why is today different? What did you find out?" Cathillian asked, changing his expression from sarcastic to something sincerer.

Arryn took a step forward. "I went to Talia's office. Long story short, Amelia promised if I talked to her and tried to make another judgment, whether it be the same or not, she would show me how to guard my mind because someone is still looking at my thoughts. Anyway, I went there, and I ran into Jackson on the way."

"Jackson," Cathillian repeated. "Is that the kid that you told me is always attached to her at the hip?"

Arryn shook her head. "It's not that I see them together a lot. It's just when I *do* see them together, there's this look on his face. He's enamored with her, and it's not like she does anything to deter it. They stand way too close to each other, and she smiles at him in the most... I don't know how to explain it. It just creeps me out. But yes, that's Jackson."

Samuel shivered. "I saw 'er in the bar one night. That ain't weird, except why she goes. She either sits at the bar or in the corner and stares. She just watches. Even with that cloak of hers, I know 'er when I see 'er. That's a woman who stands out."

Arryn sighed, smile spreading on her face. "It feels so good to finally have someone listen. Anyway, when I ran into Jackson, he was acting weird. Kind of defensive over her office. He told me that she was gone to help her mom or something like that, but then he made sure I walked away before he went downstairs. What he didn't realize was that I waited for him to get all the way down before I went to the office anyway. He left her a note. That's why I'm freaking out."

Cathillian's brows furrowed as he crossed his arms. A note. He couldn't help but be curious to know what was inside. "What did it say?"

"It said something about him doing what she told him to. He said that he's enrolled in my class. I didn't know that, but I do remember Amelia mentioning that I was getting another student. It has to be him. He also talked about you."

"Me?" Cathillian asked. "What about me?"

"He didn't say your name specifically, but he mentioned *the druid*. He told her to let him know if she found out anything useful from the druid, and then he was so worried about the two of you that he also warned her not to get too close. As disturbing as that was, for many reasons, what was most disturbing was the end of the letter. He said, 'you take care of *us*,' then said, *'we* need to take care of you.'"

Samuel groaned as he nodded. "Sounds to me like there ain't just one person to worry about. Seems like there's a lot more. Better watch yer back, lass. She has it out for ye."

Cathillian swallowed hard, unable to believe what he was hearing. Not only had Arryn been right and he so very wrong, but he'd allowed Arryn to be placed in danger because of his refusal to trust her.

His own powers had failed him. He hadn't even sensed anything wrong with her.

The day Talia had come over she'd used him as an instrument against Arryn. She knew that her very presence would cause conflict between them. At that moment, Cathillian became pissed off. It far surpassed anger or even rage.

Taking another step forward, his expression revealing just how much hatred he felt, Cathillian said, "How do we take this bitch down?"

CHAPTER FIFTEEN

Over the next several days, Samuel and Cathillian set out to find guardsmen who wanted to learn extra skills. They'd started by going into the barracks, taking Arryn with them.

Amelia had given them free reign, so they wanted to see what they were working with.

With twenty men in that room alone, they decided to take their point—that the Guard was in no way, shape or form capable of protecting the city the way that it needed to be—and shove it right up their asses.

But with flair, as was their style.

They'd snuck in and triggered the magitech lighting, immediately alerting the men in the room that someone was with them.

It didn't take long for them to jump up and into action, doing their best to fight off the druids and rearick—but it didn't go well.

Arryn was easily able to breeze through them with her staff, tripping them and then hitting them in the stomach hard enough to force them into a ball, but not hard enough to actually hurt them.

Cathillian was a blur as he ducked and swung, avoiding faces as much as possible, but still finding ways to take them down to the ground.

Samuel was the funniest of them because he was the shortest. Nearly a foot shorter than most the men in the barracks, Samuel was able to move through with his hammer, using it to shove the men down to the ground while they tried to strategize attacking a man his size.

Within only moments, they were able to take down all twenty of them, though they were careful not to leave any lasting damage—only minor bumps and bruises.

Once it was over, Arryn had walked to the front, no fear on her face as she stared down the men who were supposed to be protecting her city.

Squaring her shoulders, she told them, "*You* are the ones responsible for keeping the city safe, and we were able to take you down easily. Your training is going slowly, and you're even slower. If you want *real* warrior training and the chance to learn how to use real weapons, and not just those magitech pieces of shit, then you'll find us at Lord Girard's house. We'll meet there at dawn before going to the training grounds."

Cathillian had stepped forward then. "In other words, if you want to be the ass-kickers instead of getting your asses kicked, then you need better training. We have the blessing of the Chancellor, so if you wanna learn, we are here to teach."

"Well…" Arryn started, "she knows we're teaching them. She just doesn't know we're ripping them out of their first session with their commanding officer to do it."

Cathillian turned back to the men on the floor. "Yeah! So, if she comes for us, Arryn here will be happy to take the fall for it."

She elbowed him in the side as Samuel stepped forward, taking the lead before they began to argue in front of their new recruits.

"We have a feelin' the city ain't done needin' ta be protected," Samuel had chimed in. "Especially with everythin' goin' on. So, get yer asses out there and get some skills *actually* worth learnin'."

When the fallen recruits began looking at one another and whispering amongst themselves, the trio had left them to their thoughts, hoping they would come to them. Because now more than ever, Arryn was certain Talia was the bad person Adrien had planted, and Cathillian and Samuel were right on board.

Today Arryn, Cathillian, and Samuel all stood outside the city wall on the eastern side near where Cathillian had been training the cadre in his nature magic. It was where he and Arryn trained every morning, and now it was where they would begin training the new Guard.

Cathillian and Samuel went to work with half the men, pairing them off and teaching them the stricter forms of close-quarter combat. It was obvious that Guard training had focused mostly on running and endurance with a secondary emphasis on magitech weapons.

The idea that these men couldn't even throw a knife properly didn't set well with Cathillian, while the fact that they couldn't even line their arms up correctly for a proper punch got under Samuel's skin.

All in all, it was as if their training was only beginning, when in reality, they had been training for weeks.

For the past few days Arryn and Cathillian had spent some time in the evening crafting bows. With nature magic on their side, it was quite an easy task, especially with Arryn being able to use her physical magic to heat the wood to curve them. Arryn had just finished passing out the newly crafted bows to her ten students when she heard a familiar voice.

"Well, good morning!" Amelia called, smiling as she casually strolled up to Arryn. Amelia didn't make eye contact as she scanned the new training ground. "This is quite the turnout."

Arryn's eyes were wide as she stared at Amelia, wondering just how pissed the Chancellor was that they had yanked the recruits away from their regularly scheduled exercises with the Guard.

Arryn sighed and decided to fully face her fate, crossing her arms defiantly as she turned. "I'm not sure if I should greet you or run for my life. While I'm pretty confident in my skills, you remind me a lot of Elysia. In other words, you're not someone I want to piss off."

Amelia laughed as she turned to face Arryn. "At first, I was a little annoyed, but the moment we finished talking about setting all this in motion, I knew damn good and well that you had no plans to wait—or follow schedules. I figured you'd get your men one way or another. After what happened to Cathillian and how easily those four guards at the gate were taken down, I realized whatever you guys had planned would be a good route to go." Amelia took a deep breath as she looked around again and smiled. "You definitely didn't disappoint."

That was news to Arryn. Good news, to be sure. It made her happy to know that Amelia now believed in her and wanted to let her help beyond just teaching students how to grow flowers.

Arryn pointed to Cathillian and Samuel in the distance, who were now sparring. Given there was two feet difference in height between them, it looked comical, but it was also quite impressive. What Samuel lacked in height he more than made up for in skill and fury.

"They're training in close-quarter combat. We snuck into the barracks the other night and beat the shit out of the Guard. You should've seen it. It was so easy that it was scary—and kind of hilarious. I don't know what they're training for down there, but I promise you it isn't fighting. If we train these guys hard enough, they'll get good really fast. Rotating groups would work best."

Amelia nodded. "I like that idea. It seems like you have the full barracks here. Give these men two weeks with you and then rotate. Have them go back and train an entirely different group while I send you more. At that rate, I think that we could train quite a lot of people in a short amount of time. What are you in charge of?"

Arryn smiled and held up the bow that Elysia had crafted for her. "What I do best. I'm teaching these men how to hunt their enemy with deadly accuracy."

Just at that moment, an arrow cut through the air toward them. Amelia lifted her hand, sending the arrow flying in a different direction when it nearly hit her, but other than that simple movement, neither she nor Arryn flinched.

The arrow hit the ground a few feet away, and the man responsible screamed his apologies, but Arryn's eyes stayed focused and unblinking on Amelia's, both women's faces blank as Arryn said, "Some additional training *may* be required."

Amelia nodded, clearly fighting back a smile. "*May?*"

Arryn shrugged. "I *did* say they were deadly."

With a laugh, Amelia rolled her eyes and waved at the man, who still stared at them with horror in his eyes. He was clearly terrified that he had nearly killed the Chancellor with a stray arrow, though he relaxed when Amelia waved him off.

"I'm glad things are going so well here, near-death experience aside. But…"

Arryn narrowed her eyes as she studied Amelia. All amusement drained from her face as she looked at her with concern.

"But what? You seem hesitant to talk," Arryn stated. "You should know by now that you should just blurt things out with me. It's easiest."

"I talked to Elon. It's been almost a week, and I should've come to you sooner, but with everything that happened to Cathillian, and with the dead guards, and more missing students, it took me a while to get around to it."

"More missing students?" Arryn asked.

Amelia sighed. "Yeah. It was a student named Dallas. He was a jerk from what I could tell. Hung out with a group of other

Boulevard students. Dallas was one of the group involved in beating the hell out of Jackson."

Arryn nodded, realization on her face. "Oooh. Okay. I know who you're talking about now. I see them walking around together all the time. Always in a pack."

"Yep, but not anymore. Dallas was found with his throat slit. It looks *exactly* like Amos' death. Blood drained and everything." Amelia sighed as she shook her head.

"Why didn't you come to get me?" Arryn asked. "I might have been able to help."

"It's not your problem," Amelia replied, a sad smile on her face. "Besides, with all this and everything else on your plate, you have enough to deal with. I'm handling it. No worries about that. I'll get all this figured out. But I didn't bring that up to worry you over it. I wanted to tell you about my conversation with Elon."

Amelia had talked to Elon...

Arryn's mind was swimming with possibilities. It bothered her that Amelia hadn't come to her sooner, but she understood. She wasn't sure if it was good or bad news, but if it wasn't what she expected to hear, with Cathillian down and Arryn struggling to take care of him, teach at the Academy, and dig up dirt on Talia, it would've been difficult to process. Arryn swallowed hard, preparing herself to receive what could be the end of whatever hope she had left when it came to finding her father.

Arryn gave a simple nod, signaling to Amelia that she was ready to hear whatever it was she had to say.

Amelia cautiously glanced at the group to make sure that no other stray arrows would come their way before turning back to Arryn. "It turns out that Elon was much easier to talk to than I thought he would be. He was best friends with your father."

Arryn's eyes widened, her brain automatically trying to search her memories for anything that might tell her who he was. "I'm trying to remember, but... I don't know. I can't seem to remember anything."

"He said that you were probably too young to remember him, but you might remember his son, Gregory."

Arryn gasped, her eyes widening as she nodded. "Yes! I remember Gregory! We used to play together when we were little. His mom was a piece of work, but his dad didn't seem so bad, though I barely remember anything about him."

Amelia nodded. "Elon said that by the time you were old enough to remember anything about him, he was already wedged up Adrien's ass, so he was gone all the time."

Arryn took a nervous step forward, excitement filling her, even though she knew Elon wasn't a good person. He couldn't have been, since he was close to Adrien, and now he sat in the prison, both for his involvement with Adrien and for nearly killing his son. The name hadn't been familiar to her when Amelia first told her about him, but now everything was clicking together, and she felt terrible for her old friend Gregory.

"Your father went to Elon for help. Elon was very close to Adrien, and Christopher thought that he could sort things out. Unfortunately, Elon got scared. He knew that Adrien was on the hunt for someone, but he had no idea who. Adrien knew someone was planning to take him down, and Elon didn't want to see anything bad happen to your parents. He thought that if Adrien knew that people misunderstood him, he might be able to change their opinion."

"So, he ratted my parents out? He was the one who basically sentenced us to that fate? You're telling me that the man who caused all of this is sitting in prison right now?" Arryn asked. Before she'd spoken, she'd felt confused. But by the end of her questions, Arryn was furious. She wanted Elon just as bad as she wanted Adrien.

"He did, yes. But from what I can tell, his action was born from good intentions. Obviously, he had a selfish reason for it— he was worried that if Christopher got caught the old-fashioned way, Elon, being his best friend, would be suspect, too. At least, that's the way that I see it, and he didn't do much to dissuade me. But all in all, I think he really believed he was trying to help your parents."

Arryn closed her eyes, silently shaking her head as she did her best to calm her rage. "So, what happened to him? What happened my father?"

"He said that your father was taken and held prisoner. He was questioned for quite some time to try to get any kind of information out of him they could. They didn't believe that he was working alone, and Elon knew it, too, but after everything that had happened, he was smart enough not to tell Adrien that. Elon said that once Adrien believed Christopher wouldn't give anything up willingly, Christopher was let go."

Arryn's eyes widened, her jaw opening in disbelief. "What? He was let go? Why didn't he come for me?"

Amelia nodded as she continued, "Yes, he was let go. Adrien believed he would get comfortable and lead him to whoever his accomplices were; he thought he would catch more of his enemies by allowing one of them to live. He figured your father, having lost everything, would run to them for comfort. Unfortunately, that plan didn't work out very well."

Amelia took a deep breath, pausing for a moment. Arryn wanted to shake the woman for not talking faster, but instead she used that moment to process everything that had been said so far.

"Elon said that it's been a long time, and he can't remember exactly when it happened, but a month or two after you fled from the city and your father was released, someone came for him."

"An ally? One of the people he was conspiring with?" Arryn asked, but was quickly met by a shake of Amelia's head.

No...

That didn't seem right to her at all. Who would've come for her father? Of all the people in the city, why in the hell would they have come for him?

Amelia continued, "I was in the Academy all the time, so I

have no way of proving this or disproving it, but Elon said that the reports were that someone killed the guards at the gate and came through the city. The thing is, no one saw them coming. There was only a path of dead bodies on the way. It was like they hunted him down, but they definitely came from outside of the city."

Arryn's brows furrowed, her eyes narrowing as she thought hard about what could've happened.

"What the hell does that even mean?" Arryn asked. "Who would've even known about my father being in trouble?"

"If Samuel hadn't told me the specifics of what happened to Cathillian when I crossed paths with him the other day, I never would've put the two together."

Oh, that didn't sound good. Bile was rising in her throat.

"You can't be serious. Are you saying there was a similarity with what happened to Cathillian?" Arryn asked.

Amelia nodded. "The guards who were killed throughout the city that night had no wounds. There were no bruises, and their weapons were still holstered. There was no evidence of any kind that anything had happened to them; it was like they had just dropped dead. When he told me about it, all I could think was, 'damn... It would take one hell of a subtle warrior to float through a city like the guards didn't exist and kill so quickly and easily that no one saw them coming.' No one heard them. And there was no evidence how it was done."

"You think the dark druids did this. Is that what you're saying?" Arryn asked.

"I know! It sounded crazy to me too, but think about it. They were able to kill in a way that left no marks. That dark druid did that to Cathillian and to the guards at the gate. There were no marks on any of them. Don't you think that that's too big of a coincidence?"

Arryn thought for a moment, putting together all the pieces that Amelia had given her, but then she realized that there had to be more. This had happened a month or two after Arryn had fled the city. Something else had happened along that timeline as well.

"Before I left the Dark Forest, Elysia, Cathillian's mom, told me about a man named Aeris. He was the older brother of Jenna, the dark druid who attacked Cathillian the other day. Apparently, he took my arrival in the Dark Forest so badly that he betrayed his people and left the Dark Forest to join the dark druids. That happened a month or two after I arrived, so it's not too hard to believe that he would've come to Arcadia to take my father. He knew that I believed he was still alive, so all he had to do was find him. The whole family is petty, so I wouldn't put it past him."

"It sounds like we have a pretty good lead. And Elon said that it looked like there was a fight and that Christopher was alive when he was taken from the city. So... I am happy that we found something to start with, but it looks like the journey to find your father will continue outside the city. I'm sorry, Arryn."

Arryn sighed as she looked from Amelia to the men who were training hard to learn how to protect the city. "I can't leave yet. Something is happening here, and I know it. Deep down, I think you know it, too. If I were to leave now and something happened to the city, not only would I never be able to forgive myself, but my father would never forgive me either. Right now, my responsibility and allegiance lies with the city. Once I know it's safe, I'll look for my father. Which brings me to my next point... I found an interesting letter on Talia's desk that I think you should know about."

CHAPTER SIXTEEN

On the way to class that morning, Arryn had a very interesting interaction. In fact, a lot of things had been strange. Singled out, they seemed normal, but now that they were happening more often, she was starting to get paranoid.

Walking through the halls, she'd caught a few students staring at her. Caydon and Camdon. They weren't in her nature magic class, but they were in her physical magic class with David, the teacher she'd seen standing with them when it happened.

She'd smiled and waved, and they each responded with what appeared to be uninterested smiles and flicks of their wrists— poor excuses for a greeting. Even after that, they stared at her, whispering to one another as she continued toward her class.

In physical magic the day before, Arryn was showing fast progress, having transformed a small wooden horse into glass before most of the other students had completed the task.

She'd been so proud of herself, but David had rolled his eyes and told her that her technique was sloppy and if she didn't work harder, he'd fail her.

Meanwhile, another girl damn near melted hers, and he'd smiled at her and praised her on her great effort.

At the time, she thought he might have been trying to use tough love as motivation. It was sometimes how the druids trained, so she found it motivating. But after how she'd seen him with other students, paired with receiving the stink eye every time she saw him outside of class, she was beginning to think he just didn't like her at all.

Was it because she was both? A student *and* a teacher? Was Talia involved?

She wasn't sure, but being in the Academy at all was beginning to weigh on her. Between all of those small occurrences and the daily buzzing in her mind, she couldn't help but wonder just how many people Talia had under her thumb.

…Or if she was simply going insane after all.

When Arryn got to class that morning after her run-in with David and the twins, everyone was chatting about the latest disappearance—Dallas.

The city was on the verge of something huge, and Arryn could feel it, but there was no way for her to protect against it. All that mattered to her at that moment was the fact that she now had her friends rallying behind her.

Almost immediately, the discussion of battle magic came up again, and it occurred to her that her role in Arcadia had become quite a bit like the more experienced and higher-ranking warriors in the druid community.

When new recruits began training, that was all they did from the moment they woke up until the time they went to bed.

Recently, Arryn's duties had been to wake up early, train hard with Cathillian as well as work with the guards, then go to the Academy and teach the students basic magic, and now it seemed like she would be taking on a new role as well.

But with the worry of everything going on, Arryn welcomed the challenge. Everyone deserved the opportunity to be able to protect themselves if the worst were to happen.

Things seemed to always be evolving. She and Amelia had

agreed that they needed to see each other less. If they were to draw Talia out naturally, Talia would have to be able to trust Amelia. She would need to think that Amelia's interest in Arryn was purely academic and nothing personal—no true friendship. Talia couldn't feel threatened, or she might act irrationally and cause more damage than originally planned.

And both Arryn and Amelia were unwilling to let anyone get caught in the crosshairs if they could help it.

But it was obvious to Arryn that Talia was already beginning to feel the pressure. Jackson's presence in her classroom was enough to tell her that.

He'd made sure to secure himself a seat right in front, and he continuously stared at her, even smiled several times. Each smile chilled her to the bone, but she reminded herself that she knew he was doing it for her, for Talia.

And Arryn planned to go right along with the show.

When class was dismissed, Arryn noticed Jackson looking around and fidgeting with things, purposely taking his sweet time. He obviously planned to stay after class, but Arryn wanted to get the jump on him.

"Jackson, would you mind staying after class? Since it's your first day, I thought it might be best if we got to know each other a little bit," Arryn requested with a smile.

She could almost feel a shift in his energy; the cool confidence he had exuded had become nervous. Nature magic allowed its users' senses to be like those of an animal. On top of being able to sense intentions, though that clearly had its limitations, they could also sense anger, apprehension, and danger, although they had to know what to look for.

Jackson gathered his things and left them on his desk in a neat pile, coming to stand in front of Arryn. "Yes? What did you want to talk about?"

Arryn pulled her long, black braid over her shoulder, playing with the loose hair that hung just below the tie. It was something she'd witnessed the other girls doing while flirting, and it made her feel awkward on their behalf.

It seemed weak, even insecure to act shy and timid around someone a girl was interested in. Why wouldn't they just be straight forward?

She hated insecurities, and she saw them all the time in the girls in Arcadia. Mostly the younger noble women. The girls from the Boulevard seemed stronger, like they didn't give a shit what anybody thought.

Arryn liked them. If things weren't quite so intense, she might have actually taken the time to make friends with some of them.

"Well, I had the time to stop and really talk to everyone else to find out about their intentions, but I don't know what yours are." Arryn gave another smile, and Jackson was quick to reciprocate.

"My intentions? What do you mean?" he asked, his voice and posture suddenly becoming rigid and apprehensive.

Arryn leaned back on her desk, looking at the floor for a moment before shrugging and turning her eyes back to his. "Some of the students in here want to learn nature magic because they never want to starve again. They want to be able to grow food no matter where they are. Others want to know how to heal. They want to make sure their families never get so sick that they die, or be sure that if they see another battle, they will know that they can save their friends and family. Nature magic means different things to everyone. What does it mean to you?"

Jackson visibly relaxed as he nodded slowly in understanding. "Oh, I see. Well, to me, it's new and exciting. I'm not the best physical magic user around here, so the opportunity to try something new that I might be better at is interesting to me."

There was a pause as Jackson looked at the floor, then back at Arryn. He bit his lower lip as he took a step forward. "Plus, I've seen you come out of one of the physical magic classes. You're so different. The way you dress is different. Your confidence is different. You seem so sure of yourself all the time. If you were another student I wouldn't have a problem saying this, but given that you're my teacher now, I probably shouldn't."

Arryn almost laughed. He was trying to seduce her, and she knew it. It was exactly as he had written in the letter; he would find out what he could from her, and he was just trying to use his charm to do it.

Unfortunately for him, Arryn didn't need the approval of a man to know that she could kick ass when she needed to.

She had learned that from a tribe full of strong, female druids for half her life.

Arryn decided to play the part he expected of her: the shy, naïve girl from the Forest that didn't know how to cope with the charm of a man.

Arryn leaned forward a bit on her desk, her eyes narrowing as she allowed a curious expression to grow. "You probably shouldn't say what?"

Jackson smiled, running his fingers through his hair. "I just... You're beautiful. I've never seen anyone like you. I know I shouldn't say that. We don't know each other, and you're my teacher now."

Arryn forced a giggle. "Yeah, because you found your way into my class. Remember? You requested to be here, so the restrictions between us are because you put us in this predicament."

Jackson stood taller, smiling a bit more. He seemed to be feeling a bit more confident after her response. "That's true, but... We're the same age, though, right? So, is it really like you're my teacher? It's unheard of for someone so young to be put in a position of power like this, I would assume for this very reason. But I can keep a secret if you can."

It took every ounce of Arryn's resolve not to reach out and punch him right in the throat. It was one thing to be cold and terrible like Adrien had been, but another to be devious and misleading like Jackson—to be willing to use someone for their own personal gain.

It disgusted her.

She did her best to keep him from seeing that. She smiled again. "I'm flattered, Jackson. But like you said, we don't even know each other. Maybe we should fix that."

Jackson nodded, his smile a bit too eager. "Yeah! I like that. When would you like to get together? I'd like to get to know you as soon as possible."

Clearly, the man hadn't spent nearly enough time with Talia, because he was terrible at this fact-finding crap. Way too eager, way too desperate. Even if Arryn wasn't aware of what he wanted, she certainly would've been suspicious.

"I don't know. I'll have to think about that. With training and everything, I have a lot to do throughout the day. But I'd like to find the time."

He nodded, exhaling heavily as if the conversation had greatly relieved him. "You have no idea how good that is to hear. I was so nervous. Everybody around here gets the wrong idea about me. I'm not so bad, and I was worried that you might think that I am. I'd really like to get to know you more, Anna."

Arryn bit her lip to hold back the tirade forming in the back of her mind. "Arryn."

He looked at her with a confused expression. "What?"

Arryn stood straight. "Arryn. My name is Arryn, not Anna."

He looked as if he wanted to curl up in a ball. His energy shifted once again. Confidence became nervousness and insecurity. "I'm sorry, I meant Arryn."

Arryn waved him off. "No worries. But I do need to get ready for my next class. I'm heading to physical magic, though I'm sure that you already knew that."

He nodded once before saying, "Yeah! Me, too. I have to go to physical magic, too."

Jackson quickly said his goodbyes before grabbing his things and escaping from the room. It was no surprise to Arryn to see him head down the hallway in the direction of Talia's office instead of back the other way to physical magic.

Arryn gave him a few minutes' head start before leaving the room herself. While she did need to go to her physical magic class, she also needed to get outside for a bit. She wanted to stand under the trees in the courtyard and feel the purity in them.

She knew it would calm her down just in case she ran into him again—or worse, Talia.

She made her way down the hall and jumped as she turned a corner and ran directly into not only Jackson but Talia and Scarlett as well.

Her eyes widened and her breath caught in her throat as she stared at them, knowing they had been discussing her and that they were also standing directly in the path of her exit.

Before she could speak, she felt that familiar buzz in her mind, vibrating through her head and telling her that somebody was in her thoughts. She immediately went on the defensive, thinking of anything and everything she possibly could to keep them distant.

"Hey!" Arryn exclaimed. "Sorry, I wanted to go outside and take a walk before class. It's beautiful outside. I didn't mean to interrupt."

Talia smiled, but it was disturbing. "No worries. We just ran into Jackson. I was on my way to my office, and Scarlett's on her way to her classroom. Are you all right? You seem... well, just not yourself."

Arryn couldn't keep the words *lying bitch* from crossing her mind as she faked a smile. She was about to speak when she saw Scarlett's eyes widen.

Shit! Arryn thought. *It's her, not Talia!* She scolded herself for thinking anything more in their presence before giving a smile.

"Anyway, it's nice to see you guys. Jackson, I'll see you tomorrow in class." Arryn waved and squeezed through them to get to the stairs.

TALIA STEPPED to the side and let Arryn go through, knowing full well it was in her power to crush her right there. Unfortunately, she needed to be posed as an enemy before she could even think of doing something like that. Otherwise, the people would turn on her and things would get a lot worse before she was ready. Everything had to stay on course.

"Well? Did you get anything out of her?" Talia asked Scarlett.

Scarlett's eyes still gazed after Arryn. Finally, she said, "She was definitely startled by seeing us, but all of the things running through her mind were pretty normal. She was thinking about her druid friend, about his attack. She is also thinking about her talk with Jackson. If what I saw is accurate, Jackson, you did an excellent job in the flirting department."

"Thanks!" Jackson said, a little too excited at the praise.

Talia rolled her eyes. "Jackson, thank you. You can go now. We'll meet later."

Jackson began to protest, but Talia's stern look shut him down quickly enough. With nothing more than a nod, he turned to walk down the stairs.

Scarlett watched his retreat. "You didn't have to be *SO* cold, did you?"

Talia shook her head, clearly annoyed. "Back on task, mystic. Was there anything else on her mind that we should know about? Because she seemed awfully jumpy."

Scarlett smiled. "Well, she did call you a lying bitch when you mentioned casually running into me. Other than that, she either doesn't have a clue or she's gotten very good at controlling her thoughts."

Talia rubbed the bridge of her nose. "That girl is gonna be the death of me if I don't get to her first."

Scarlett looked at Talia pointedly, raising her hands to her sides. "I keep telling you that you need to end her. Get her out of the way. But no, you *gotta* do this the hard way."

Talia sighed and looked at Scarlett with disdain. "Yes, I know. It looks like it's time to change things around here. We need to turn everyone against her—fast. We need to make sure Amelia doesn't trust her, or anyone else for that matter."

CHAPTER SEVENTEEN

After a long evening of training followed by a terrible night of sleep, Arryn wasn't in the best mood the following morning, and her trainees took notice.

She was very rough on them that morning, making them repeat shots over and over, one right after another until they hit their target dead-center. Only then would she allow them to change positions or switch out. Merely hitting the target wasn't good enough this morning; only perfect accuracy would do.

Not wanting to waste her time on anyone else, she took Maia out into the field and continued training from horseback. She'd gotten very good at shooting at moving targets, and she didn't want to slow down now.

When her trainees saw her in action, they realized why she was so hard on them. It was because she was good. *Very* good. If they were gonna have their asses kicked, they wanted it to be by somebody who knew what they were doing, not like the typical Guard training they received every day.

By the time Arryn got to the Academy, she was physically and mentally exhausted, and in no mood to deal with any shit. It was like the calm, peaceful place inside of her had broken and her ability to keep her mouth shut was long gone.

Arryn was sick and tired of playing by the rules. She was fed up with tiptoeing around while trying to figure things out. Arryn had never been one for backstabbing and lying. When she had a problem, she confronted it head-on, none of this sneaking around bullshit. She hated it.

And she planned to do something about it.

As she strolled into the Academy, up the stairs and down the hall toward Talia's office, she thought about how much her life had changed over the last few weeks. She thought about the good that was clouded by the bad.

The remnant attacks. The missing students. Doyle and his vague message. Elon and his stunning information. The only thing that she couldn't quite figure out was Talia. And that ended today.

Arryn didn't even bother knocking when she reached Talia's door, just opened it and walked inside, shutting it behind her before crossing the room and having a seat in front of her desk. Talia didn't say a word as she watched Arryn's every move.

Seeing Talia's shocked face, Arryn was fully aware of the shitty expression on her own, but she didn't care.

"Good morning, Arryn," Talia greeted her. "Please, come in and have a seat."

A half-smile spread across Arryn's lips at the Dean's sarcasm. While she couldn't stand her, she did appreciate a good sense of humor.

"Thanks. I think I will." There was a pause as Arryn sat there, studying Talia. She looked into her eyes to search for something redeemable, but she couldn't see anything, good *or* bad. More confusion. She didn't like it.

Arryn leaned forward and reached her hand across Talia's desk, palm-up, as if she expected Talia to lay something in it.

Talia looked down at Arryn's hand before meeting her eyes again. "What? I don't understand."

Arryn smiled. "I didn't either the first time a druid extended her hand to me, but I learned. Now, I'm extending *my* hand to *you*. I'm asking you to take it because I want to know who you are. I can't get a read on you. And I'm done with playing mind-fuck games. Either you're good and I owe you an apology, or you're a piece of shit and I need to rip your fucking head off. So, let's play, shall we?"

There was a moment of disbelief in Talia's expression before it changed to one of annoyance, or maybe even worse. Finally, Talia's eyes narrowed as she leaned forward on her desk.

"Those are pretty brave words coming from someone who has absolutely no idea who I am. If I'm as bad as you think, then what is stopping me from turning you to ash? What is it that keeps me from turning this entire building," she laughed then, lifting her hands and motioning to everything around her before returning them to her desk, "hell, this entire *city* into my own personal fire pit?"

Arryn pulled her hand back and relaxed into the chair, crossing her arms in front of her as she glared across the mahogany desktop between them. She shrugged.

"You know, I've been asking myself that for a while now. Kept going back and forth with it. Everyone around me said that I was crazy. Hell, *I* even started to believe that I was crazy. I mean, what person in their right mind meets someone and just automatically hates them?" Arryn asked.

Talia shook her head. "If anyone had asked me that before I met you, I would've said that I didn't know. But now that I've met you and developed quite a hatred for you, I would have to say you and I are a lot alike in that department."

Arryn laughed. "You and I are nothing alike. I know you'd like to think that. You have everyone else fooled, even Amelia. The woman who desperately wants to see the good in everyone. But you're the fool if you think that'll last forever. She's very gullible, but she's not an idiot."

Arryn knew damn good and well that Amelia was smarter than her words let on, but she wanted to place the idea that she and Amelia weren't as close as the Dean would choose to believe.

It was only a small thing, but Arryn didn't want anything to happen to Amelia while she was baiting Talia and hoping to out her.

A dark smile spread across Talia's lips. "And what would you say about that *delicious* friend of yours?"

Arryn's expression became amused as she realized Talia was trying to use Cathillian against her. "Well, he is certainly pretty to look at, but there's not a lot going on upstairs. So yes, I would call him gullible as well. Me? Not so much. You see, it took a long time, but I finally realized why I'm clinging to this feeling so hard."

"Is that so? Please, do tell."

"I'm so happy that you asked!" Arryn chirped. "When I came to the Dark Forest, Elysia, the daughter of the Chieftain, told me that she chose to trust me because of my potential for power. Not only physical, but with nature. She said that I was strong, pure. She once told me that I had likely been touched by nature magic all my life, but I didn't know it."

Talia rolled her eyes. "*Fascinating.*"

Arryn laughed again. "Thank you! I'm so glad you think so. Because here's where it truly gets fascinating. Of course, the last few days I've been thinking hard, and then even harder on top of that. And finally, I remembered something. I met Adrien once. I even shook his hand. The funny thing was, when he touched me, I felt cold. I felt empty. There was something about him that I just didn't like. I'd forgotten about it, but lately lots of memories have been coming back, including the one where my father told my mother that Adrien had a daughter."

Arryn paused, letting that sink in. Talia's eyes briefly widened before her stony mien returned.

After a few moments, Arryn continued, "Then I remembered something else. I remembered the initial reaction I got when I met you. I smiled, and I was happy to see you. I was excited about what the future might hold, and then I took your hand. And I felt cold. I felt empty. It reminded me very much of the way Adrien had made me feel. Now, I have no way to prove you're his daughter, but I do know that those memories are real, and so is the warning that Doyle gave. He told us that Adrien had someone inside the city. I have a feeling that was you."

Talia's eyes narrowed as she studied Arryn. It was obvious that she was weighing her words carefully. Finally, Talia said, "Again... If you are so sure that I'm bad, why the hell haven't I ended you? Why would I help rebuild a city I only planned to take down?"

Arryn shrugged again. "I don't know. Perhaps you don't want to be the Chancellor of a broken city. Perhaps you want to be Queen in your prosperous Queendom."

Nodding her head, Talia remarked, "Interesting theory. But like you said, there's no way to prove whether you are right or wrong, so I guess you'll just have to learn to trust me."

"Oh, I don't think so. Like I said, the only way I'm walking out of here trusting you is if you give me your hand. I might not be the mystic I think you have on your payroll who looks through my head all hours of the day—and yes, I *can* feel that—but nature magic is on my side, and that's all I need."

"And if you find something you don't like?" Talia asked, her voice low. Arryn heard the warning in it.

"I can't kill you today. I need to prove your guilt. I suspect that's the reason I'm still alive. Am I right? Amelia knows I don't like you. Amelia knows I don't trust you. If you kill me, you're the first person she'll start with. That's the only reason you haven't made a move on me yet. It's the same reason I haven't made a move on you. Because Amelia trusts you."

Talia stood, shoulders squared, and smiled down at Arryn. Taking the hint, Arryn also stood, mimicking Talia's confident stance.

As a dark smile spread across Talia's face, she extended her hand. Arryn took it, and that cold, empty, dead feeling almost immediately began rushing through her. It was only through sheer will that Arryn was able to hide it in her expression, but judging by the almost sadistic look on Talia's face, she knew.

Just before Arryn let go, Talia challenged her. "Let the games begin. And have fun trying to prove it."

Arryn smiled as she left the room, shutting the door behind her.

Now, I can really get to work. Time to do what I was meant to.

As soon as Arryn had left the room and the door was safely closed, Talia began pacing the room. She had no idea why she'd been so confrontational. It was the worst possible scenario, and she'd failed to act properly.

Nature magic was unfamiliar to her, so she had no idea how one's natural energy was any different than any other person's. She'd assumed it *was* no different, just heightened by the nature magic.

Still, she couldn't help but wonder, if she'd focused on positive intentions could she have fooled Arryn's test? Somehow, Talia was certain that if there was anyone in the city capable of taking her out, it was the Arcadian druid, but that couldn't happen.

Talia refused at all costs to let it.

As soon as she was sure Arryn was long gone, Talia made her way out of the office and down to Scarlett's classroom. Before

Talia had even reached the door, Scarlett was stepping outside, closing it and quickly striding toward Talia.

"You called?" Scarlett asked.

"How did you know?" Talia asked, her demeanor slightly off. She was well aware that she wasn't behaving the way that she normally would.

Scarlett looked at her incredulously. "Are you serious? I heard you mentally screaming my name all the way down the hall. What's going on?"

Talia shook her head, nervously looking around for anyone who might be listening—especially Arryn.

"Just..." Talia nodded as she pointed to her temple, tapping it twice.

A few moments later, Talia saw Scarlett's eyes turn white and then widen, as they stared into her own before returning to normal. "I think you just fucked up. A lot. What the hell were you thinking?"

"I don't know!" Talia said, her voice quiet, but her actions explosive as she turned her hands in the air. "She was sitting there, confident, challenging me. I've never had anyone get under my skin like that. I've never met anyone like her. I have always been able to keep my calm, no matter what, but that girl..." she growled. "I want her gone. Now. There's no more 'well maybe we can do this, or maybe we can do that.' Now. It has to happen now."

Scarlett nodded, gently running her hands down Talia's upper arms in an obvious attempt to soothe her. "Right. We can do this, but remember what you said. It has to be thought out, planned. It can't be random, it can't be what I would consider my way. I feel like in the condition that you're in, you'd be willing to walk right into her classroom and tomahawk her in the face, and we can't do that, now can we?"

Talia didn't much care for being talked to like a child, but hearing facts and logic from Scarlett in a soothing tone was proving surprisingly helpful. At that moment, her annoyance with her partner was lessened, and she felt grateful.

"Amelia went to talk to Elon recently," Scarlett told her. "I snaked that out of Arryn's mind. Amelia told her that he knew all about her father. Maybe we can…"

Talia smiled. "Yes. Elon was my father's engineer. He knows almost as much as Doyle did. I want you to sneak in and talk to him. Also we need to find out which students have any kind of attachment to Arryn, but I assume that we're looking for a noble. When we find the person, we will kill them, take their blood as we have been, and we'll make sure that Arryn gets caught."

Scarlett smiled in response. "Oh, I believe I can help with that."

CHAPTER EIGHTEEN

The past couple of days had been difficult for Amelia. Not only did she have everything inside the city to worry about, but the outside of the city was proving to be just as terrible.

Over the course of the past two nights, the remnant had destroyed two farmhouses and a small village. Nearly a hundred people were dead, in total. There had been only a single survivor, a man who had seen his entire family ripped apart by the beasts.

When he'd arrived at the gate, he'd been covered in blood and was almost hysterical. Nothing he'd said had made sense, and his words were slurred from the post-adrenalin fatigue and the sobbing. The guards had thought he was crazy and arrested him, believing he'd been the one to kill his family.

But Amelia knew better.

All the warnings she'd had were coming to fruition. She'd believed that the remnant would never come close to the city, but now she was worried it might happen sooner rather than later.

Given that they were getting braver and braver and the invasions seemed planned and organized, she was beginning to wonder if maybe there wasn't an outside source causing all this.

Regardless of what her worries or thoughts might have been, there was a lot of work to be done to keep the Arcadian people calm. They were beginning to fight in the streets over various plans, and Amelia was worried she might lose control of them.

The people were losing their restraint, something that she absolutely could not allow to happen. She couldn't lose control of the city no matter what.

A knock on the door startled her, and she reached up to wipe away the tears that she'd suddenly become aware of. Clearing her throat, she called for the person to enter. She almost immediately regretted it.

"Talia, nice to see you," Amelia said as Talia walked in, all smiles.

The Dean nodded and took a seat in front of Amelia's desk. "I'm sorry to bother you, but I was wondering if you had time to talk."

Amelia's heavy sigh turned into an unamused laugh. "Not really, unfortunately. I'm sure that you've heard there was another attack last night. Two, actually. This time, it wasn't just a farmhouse, it was an entire village. Luckily, it was a small one, but many were lost."

Talia's eyes widened as she sat back in her chair, shaking her head in disbelief. "When is this going to stop? There's so much violence."

In her grief for the dead, her frustration for the duties surrounding those deaths, and her sensitivity to the fears of her people, she found herself desperately wanting to get into Talia's head, no longer trusting her.

Unfortunately, Amelia knew that if she even tried, Talia would probably be aware of it. Especially if Arryn was right and Talia had mystical abilities, or had someone working with her who did.

That was a risk that she just wasn't willing to take.

"Something has to be done, that's for sure," Amelia agreed. "I haven't quite figured it out, but I'm working on it. With the attacks getting closer and the disappearances increasing, the city is falling apart. The only thing we have going for us right now is that the factory is up and running and the men are back to work. That being said, it also causes concerns for the women left at home. They're worried about break-ins and things of that nature, or an attack by the remnant while the men are away in the factory. At this point, I'm at a loss. So, I don't mean to sound rude, but whatever it is, just spit it out."

Talia slowly nodded. "Right. Um… Well, I came here to talk to you about Arryn."

Amelia knew that was why she'd come. Arryn had tried to tell her about something that happened between the two of them, but she hadn't had time to listen to it. With bodies being brought in, Amelia had no time at all. All she'd gotten was a warning that Talia might come to her.

"Okay, what is it?" Amelia asked as she changed positions, preparing for whatever story might be told.

Was Talia the evil monster Arryn believed her to be? Amelia had no way of knowing. All this time that Arryn had been coming to her, telling her how obsessed she was with Talia and how worried she was, and she'd blown Arryn off. She now understood just how crazy it could make a person feel.

With Adrien, everything had been straightforward. There was no requirement to figure it out, especially once he went crazy. It was easy to see that he was a dark man with terrible intentions.

Both Talia and Arryn had worked so hard to help build the city up. Was it possible that Talia really *was* the threat Doyle had warned her about?

"Chancellor?" Talia asked, her voice cutting through Amelia's distraction.

Amelia shook her head, trying to free herself of those intrusive thoughts. "Sorry about that. It's hard to focus. What about Arryn, now?"

"Again, I apologize for bringing this to you, but I feel as though it's worrisome, especially given all the other things happening around here. Arryn came to see me the other day, and she threatened me. She came barging into my office without a knock or appointment, sat down, and immediately began trying to intimidate me. I'm not exactly sure what this girl's problem is, but I feel as though she's a danger to herself and to the city."

Amelia sighed, doing her best not to roll her eyes. "I don't know what's going on between the two of you, but it's getting out of hand. She doesn't like you, you don't like her, and there's a conflict between the two of you. Clearly. There are bigger things in the city to worry about. Like the fact that Doyle, Adrien's right-hand man, informed me just before we took him out that Adrien had someone outside the city. Someone who is now *inside* the city. To me, that's a bigger worry than some squabble between the two of you."

Arryn and Amelia had agreed days ago that they would no longer see one another and would no longer stand up for one another. It had been Arryn's idea, but it had seemed like the best thing to do. Being indifferent to Arryn was an excellent tool to use if Talia was in fact the enemy.

"I completely understand, Chancellor, but I believe this goes deeper. She mentioned something about someone named Elon and getting vengeance on him and anyone who might've helped him. She's obsessed with her father and finding him. I don't know what's going on, but Elon and whoever was connected to her when she was a kid is in danger. I know a lot of people died in the Battle for Arcadia, but if they had anything to do with her father's disappearance, she's either coming for them, or she's coming for their kids. The same kids who go to our Academy. We can't let that happen."

Amelia narrowed her eyes.

"What do you want me to do?" Amelia asked.

Talia had leaned forward, ready to speak, when there was a

knock at the door. Amelia groaned and called for the person to come inside.

It was a young woman, Mikhaila. She was another of the nobles in the Academy, and one who regularly stood up for her Boulevard classmates.

"Dean, Chancellor, I'm really sorry to bother you, but I thought this shouldn't wait," she started, her voice shaky.

Amelia nodded. "All right, go ahead."

The girl took a few steps more into the office and fidgeted with the long sleeve of her dress. "I was several minutes early to class today, and I saw something that I don't think I was supposed to see."

That was certainly news. "Okay," Amelia prompted, "what did you see?"

The girl swallowed hard as she looked at the floor. "I went to see Talia, but she wasn't in her office. Someone said she was out for the day, so I just went to class. When I got there, I saw Arryn and Jackson talking, but they weren't just talking. They were standing very close. It was obvious that there was more there than just a teacher and her student. Even still, that wasn't what bothered me most..."

The girl paused she looked from Amelia to Talia and back again. Amelia took the opportunity to study Talia's face and saw that she looked completely confused. It seemed that Talia was just as shocked by the impromptu visit as she was.

Mikhaila continued, "I overheard Arryn say something about Amos just before she said someone else was going to die."

Talia's eyes widened, her jaw opened slightly as she sat there staring at the girl in shock. Amelia on the other hand, had no idea how she felt personally. Something wasn't right.

Arryn wasn't the killer, not in the sense that whoever took Amos had been. Arryn had never killed anyone, as far she knew, outside of the fight in which they'd taken Doyle down. And that had been self-defense, and in the defense of others.

"Are you sure about this?" Talia asked. "This is quite a statement."

"Mmmhmm," Amelia groaned. "Convenient, even, given our current conversation."

Talia looked at her in what appeared to be honest confusion, her eyes wide and her lips tight as she shook her head. "I had nothing to do with this. I know that you're confused and conflicted about who to trust right now, but that right there is evidence of everything I've been telling you."

The girl took another step forward, her hand rising slightly as she dared to speak again. "I don't have any idea what you guys have been talking about, but I know what I came in here to say. And I know it might seem difficult to believe, but if you've sat in her classes, you know she's obsessed with the defense of the city. She has been overly curious about all its weaknesses. She's constantly telling us that we need to push back and take what we want. That we should learn to fight for ourselves, because the city is weak."

Amelia knew that one was true, though the girl may have misunderstood the context. Arryn had come to her complaining that the city was weak, but why would she point out its weaknesses and even train men to get stronger if she wanted to take down the city? Why would she encourage the students to learn how to take care of themselves if she wanted to rise against it?

Something was definitely not right.

Amelia knew that Talia must have had no idea the girl would show up, much less say the things that she did. It was evident by the genuine shock on her face. But she also knew Talia was using it to her advantage.

Knowing that she needed to say something, Amelia decided to play along and sort it out later. "Thank you both. It seems that I have a lot to take care of. None of this conversation is to leave this room, is that understood?"

Both women nodded.

"Good. I'll put the Hunters on this. If there's something to find, they'll find it, trust me. Treason is the one thing I will not stand for in our great city," Amelia told them, her voice firm and final.

She thought she caught the faintest of smiles on Talia's face before it was replaced by something solemn, more appropriate to the conversation.

Amelia didn't believe any of this, but she couldn't let Talia know that. Until Amelia had all of the pieces, she couldn't trust anyone, though her gut was telling her Talia was rotten, and her gut didn't usually lead her astray.

TALIA HAD ONLY MADE it a few blocks away from the Capitol building when, in true Scarlett form, the woman leapt out and walked beside her. Talia almost jumped, but at this point, she was beginning to get used to it.

"It went really well in there," Scarlett chirped.

Talia's face was confused as she looked at Scarlett. "Were you spying?"

Scarlett gave an exaggerated smile. "Who do you think let the girl in? Let me tell you, the setup on that was absolutely brilliant. I would pat myself on the back if I didn't deserve to get it from you instead. *Dammit*, I'm a genius."

Talia stopped, unsure if she should be excited or apprehensive. "Why was it genius? Tell me everything."

Scarlett seemed all too happy to relate her tale of scheming. "First of all, Mikhaila wasn't the only one in Arryn's class today. Well... Obviously, there were others there, too." She waved her hands in the air as she shook her head. "I'm getting ahead of myself. Anyway, it was only Arryn and Jackson, and Mikhaila was walking in, so I just used my magic to make myself invisible.

Even Arryn bought it." She tapped the side of her temple and winked.

There was hope blossoming in Talia's chest as she listened. "You created an illusion?"

The mystic nodded. "Indeed, I did. But here's the thing: it went so beautifully that I couldn't have planned it all myself. I snuck in on Jackson talking to Arryn, hoping to hear or spy on something good. The door was open, so they didn't even hear me come in. I just stood there, listening. Jackson was doing a great job, laying it on thick, though I will say she did seem a little suspicious. But it worked out great. They did mention Amos, but not in the context that I led Mikhaila to believe. And Arryn did mention that someone would die again, but..."

Talia smiled and nodded. "But not in the context that Mikhaila was led to believe by you. Let me guess, Arryn was discussing something more along the lines of *worrying* that someone else was going to die."

With a finger pointing at the Dean, Scarlett exclaimed, "Yes! You are correct. They were discussing the disappearances, and Arryn was worried that someone else might die. Boy, was she right. But here's the best part... While you were chatting it up with the Chancellor, I was hanging out around the Capitol building, listening in. Amelia is doubtful of you both. That might sound bad, but it's actually a good thing. She has no idea who to believe, though she is having a hard time believing it's Arryn. Still, once Mikhaila came in there, Amelia seemed to shut down. It was hard to get anything out of her after that, but she seemed very convinced that something needed to be done."

Talia almost sighed in relief, though she didn't get that Amelia distrusted Arryn from her behavior. She might have doubts, but she seemed more annoyed than distrustful. Talia wondered how accurate the mystic's words were.

Instead of dwelling on it, she took the small victory. "That is great news. I don't need Amelia to completely trust me; I just need her to trust Arryn less. As long as I look better than her, things will be okay."

Scarlett giggled. "Oh, things are about to go a hell of a lot better than just okay. While I was in there, I killed two birds with one stone. I nosed around in Elon's head, and I found our victim. His name is James, and he is a mutual friend of Arryn and Elon's son, Gregory. James' father was the one who delivered the orders to the Hunters to take out her parents.

"Unfortunately for poor James, he's actually a good kid. Seems to do well in school, people like him, supports the Boulevard students, that kind of thing. Turns out he didn't much care for Daddy or his politics. But... That's not going to do much for him when *Arryn* gets a hold of him."

"This is fucking fantastic," Talia said, a little more excitement growing. "We're going to kill him in the same way as the others. Drain him dry and leave the knife. Not only do we want to make use of the blood, but we want to make sure that Arryn looks undeniably guilty for this one, putting doubt in their heads about the others. After all, she was the one who told them Amos was killed somewhere else when no one else had figured that out."

Scarlett nodded. "Exactly. So, here's the plan: we take James, kill him and drain the blood, and then we need to dump the body somewhere. Kind of like usual; hidden, but not too much. I'll use my magic to convince the group that his death was necessary because Arryn is planning to use her magic to do something crazy. It won't take much. They are already wrapped around your fingers. We just want to make sure they don't have a moment of doubt."

Talia continued walking down the street, looking around every so often make sure no one noticed them. "Good. I'll hide the knife in the lockbox that's in her desk. She doesn't use it, but it was there from the last teacher."

"We can even use the vines that are outside your office to bind him with. If we do that, it will be an obvious sign of nature magic. Once they find the body and start pointing fingers, I'll work my magic on a few of the students. All I have to do is convince them that they saw Arryn put something in her desk before class. Convince a couple others that Arryn's up to no good. Those nobles are pathetic. News like that will spread like wildfire. Soon, Amelia will have no other choice but to arrest her on suspicion. Even if she doesn't believe it, she'll still do it."

Talia nodded. "Yes, she will, because she's losing control. With the remnant attacks and bodies piling up, people are losing their faith in her. She will arrest Arryn for no other reason than to make people happy, to make them feel more comfortable and safe. Then, all we have to do is seal her fate. Do something huge that will prove Arryn is the evil the city has been fighting all along."

Scarlett laughed. "I assume you are referring to Doyle. I heard that bit, and I sensed your shock. I know that he was the one who had brought you the news of your father, so it would be quite disturbing to hear he had been found and had warned Amelia that someone was in town. We just need to make damn sure that person is Arryn."

There was silence as Talia looked at the sky for a few moments. Finally, she said, "Only a few hours, then we get to work. Oh, and by the way, I think I know the perfect place to hide the body."

SCARLETT HAD WAITED all day for this. It was finally time for her to really put her talents to use, and she couldn't be happier. Not only were her mystical powers strong, but manipulation and planning were also powerful talents of hers, even without using magic.

As she walked around the living room of Arryn's childhood home, looking at the entire life that had been abandoned in a single night, she smiled to herself as she thought how perfect the plan had been.

At first, Talia had wanted to hide the body in Arryn's old house, but Scarlett was quick to intervene.

Had they placed the body there, it would have been too obvious. It would've looked like a setup. So instead, they decided to kill James there, bleeding him out while only spilling a bit that looked accidental before taking his body somewhere else and dumping it.

The best part had been that anyone who looked out the window that night would have seen Arryn walking toward that side of town.

Scarlett had used her powers of illusion along with her mental magic to make herself look like Arryn as she'd walked beside James. They had been in the same Academy, but they hadn't actually run into each other recently, so James had been very happy to accompany her.

Scarlett couldn't help but think how warm and fuzzy Arryn would have been made to feel by how much James had missed her and thought of her in her absence. Now, as she looked at his body, his head hanging over the edge of the couch as he bled out into the last jar he would be able to fill, she felt even more pride in her plan.

Once the jar was full, she placed it in a bag along with the rest and slung it over her shoulder. Then, she reached out with her mind to Talia, letting her know that it had been done, and it was safe to teleport in and take the body elsewhere.

Within moments a loud crack sounded in the room as Talia's magic exploded, bringing her with it.

"I would recommend hiding him in the corner of the park by the wall. We used the park the last time. Let's stick with the theme here," Scarlett suggested.

Talia nodded. "Things are really moving forward now. I can't believe it. Finally, I'm on my way to getting the revenge I've needed for so long."

"Don't get too excited yet," Scarlett warned. "Arryn has been waiting for revenge for a decade. She has a lot to lose, too. She won't go down easily; we certainly have the upper hand. Just don't get too cocky. That's when people fail."

Talia's movements were calm and fluid as she slowly and threateningly moved across the living room, her eyes never leaving Scarlett's. "I don't need you to remind me of that. Remember, I'm the one who usually keeps *you* in control."

Scarlett decided not to respond, knowing it would do no good. Besides, Talia had no idea what she was in for, and Scarlett didn't care to elaborate. Pride goeth before the fall.

Talia reached down and grasped James' lifeless hand before her eyes turned black and a cloud of magic exploded around her again, both of them disappearing from the room.

CHAPTER NINETEEN

The next morning, Arryn had only barely finished breakfast when Celine came bursting through the door, screaming for Arryn. She quickly dropped her plate in the sink and ran into the living room.

"What's wrong?" Arryn asked, her eyes wide with concern.

Celine was nearly doubled over, her chest heaving as she quickly took breath after breath. After a few moments, she swallowed hard and finally found her voice.

"You know that I check the house every day. Well... I used to. After you came back, I haven't had much need to go back as often. It's been a while since I've checked in to make sure that no one is messing with it," Celine started.

Arryn nodded. "Okay, calm down a bit. Did something happen?"

Celine took another deep breath before continuing. "About a week and a half ago, maybe longer, maybe shorter, I don't really remember, I went to check on the house and the furniture looked like it had been sat on. The sheet had been rumpled up a bit, though it was still in place, and the dust had been wiped off a couple of things. Not like someone had cleaned them, but more like their hand had touched the surface briefly and wiped it away."

Arryn shrugged. "Well, I'm not exactly surprised. It *is* an abandoned house, and there are still some homeless people around the city who refuse to live in the noble houses. Maybe someone put their pride aside and squatted in my old house. There might be people in some of those other houses, too."

Celine shook her head. "I thought of that, too, but then I checked the other houses. None of them have been tampered with, only yours. But that's not why I came running in here. Like I said, that happened a week or two ago, and I just dismissed it. I figured if that was all the damage they did—and nothing important was missing—then it wasn't that big of a deal."

Arryn's brows furrowed with worry. "This doesn't sound good." Her voice sounded almost hopeless. She knew that look of fear and worry on Celine's face. It was the look people gave her when they had very bad news for her.

"I went to check today, and the living room was covered in blood. Well, maybe not covered, but the far end of the couch is soaked, and there are a few puddles on the floor. Arryn, it's still wet." Celine's expression was both concerned terrified, and Arryn couldn't blame her.

"We have to go to Amelia," Arryn urged.

"Like hell you do," Cathillian snarled, stepping into the room. She wasn't even aware that he was awake yet. "Whatever happened, happened in your old house. Don't you find that a little suspicious?"

Arryn laughed. "Are you serious? Of course, I find it suspicious! I would like to think that someone cleaned an animal while using my couch as a table and cooked it in the fireplace directly across from it, but I think we all know that's not what happened. Too many people have gone missing. If we sit around, it's only going to make me look guiltier. I have to confront this head-on. Amelia has to know."

Cathillian sighed, running his fingers through his long hair but stopping to clutch the sides of his head. "You've given me a headache. But fine, let's go see Amelia."

As the group made their way across the city toward Amelia's house, they passed several men who were heading to their house to meet before traveling outside the city for early-morning training.

Cathillian stopped long enough to tell them to begin practice, but he would be late. He instructed them to tell Samuel that he needed to speak with Amelia right away, but Samuel was to continue training as usual.

Other than that, no one said anything. Only the sounds of Echo calling out every so often as she played in the sky accompanied them on their journey across town.

When Amelia opened the door just before six, she wiped her eyes and brushed her hair back with her fingers. It was obvious that she'd just climbed out of bed. Arryn felt badly for waking her so early, but she needed to talk to her now.

After having invited everyone inside, Amelia took a seat on the couch, and Arryn, Celine, and Cathillian explained what had happened.

Arryn had no idea what to expect from the Chancellor, because her eyes and her expression revealed nothing. She looked completely disconnected and exhausted. With everything she'd had to deal with since coming into her position, Arryn couldn't begin to fathom what hearing something like this would mean to her.

After several awkward, silent moments, Amelia finally took a deep breath and let it out. "There is blood in Arryn's childhood home, it looks consistent with murder, and you are coming to me because you think this screams *setup*.

With only slight hesitation, Arryn nodded. "I'm coming to you with this because if Celine is right, someone else has been taken. Worse than that, they've been killed. I'm coming to you because I need you to know that I didn't do this. *I did not do this*, and I will do whatever it takes to help you find who did, though I have a damn good place to start."

Amelia laughed as she leaned back into the couch and covered her face with her hands, but it sounded exasperated and almost maniacal. She pulled her hands away and looked Arryn in the eyes.

"I don't know what's going on in this damned city, and it's pissing me off."

Arryn sighed as she took a step forward. "What does your gut tell you? I'm not going to stress you out more by trying to convince you of anything. Just ask yourself... What is your gut telling you?"

Amelia stood, pacing back and forth for a moment as she chewed on her lower lip. She stopped and turned to face Arryn once again. "For days now, Talia has been off. Something is going on with her, and I have the worst feeling. But then I think about how much she's done for the city, and I can't help but wonder if I'm wrong. Then I think, Adrien had a lot of people fooled, too. Even me. So, maybe she had me fooled, too."

"At the risk of sounding pushy," Arryn told her. "I'm going to take the stress off you. I have never doubted my own instincts. You may have had bad judgment in the past, but you've been through hell and back since. You've learned a lot. If your gut is telling you that Talia isn't who she says she is, then go with it. Your instincts are telling you Talia's bad. Get off your ass and prove it."

A brief smile crossed Amelia's face and she looked at Arryn. "Is that what you've been doing? Getting off your ass and proving it?"

Arryn's brows rose as she nodded. "Uh, *yeah*. Why do you think that I'm pretty sure that it was Talia who did this? I pissed her off the other day. I tried telling you about it before, but you were too busy with the remnant attack. Sorry... attacks. She actually said the words, 'let the games begin,' so I'm pretty sure she's trying to set me up. She needs me to be the villain before she can get rid of me. Otherwise I'm the poor, pathetic orphan who fled the city for her life only to come back post-Adrienocalypse and start over."

Amelia stared at the floor for a few moments before nodding. "You realize that I have to investigate this murder, right?"

Arryn nodded. "Yep."

"And you realize that if the evidence says that it was you, or if it looks like it was you, I'm going to have no choice but to arrest you until I can find proof that it wasn't, right?" Amelia asked.

Once again, Arryn nodded. "Yep."

Amelia sighed. "I'm going to trust you. I have since you came to the city, and you've given me no reason not to. But if you're right and this is her, then I can promise you she's done a good job of setting you up. The city will be convinced that it was you, because I can promise that she's going to work her magic turning everyone against you. Especially if she has a mystic on her side."

"You can't let the city lose faith in you, Chancellor. If the evidence points to me and word spreads, you *have* to arrest me. If the city loses faith in *you*, Talia gets what she wants. She can take the city. As long as a strong leader is in place, Talia can't win. That's the game she's been playing this whole time by gaining everyone's trust. She wants to win by default, not by force. That's why she's setting all these little things up. If it all points to me, she will believe she's won."

For the first time, Cathillian spoke. "Arryn's right. If she continues to go free even after all of the evidence points to her, the people will turn against you, then Talia can rise up and say she will do something about it. Or it could be much worse. If Talia believed that you were on Arryn's side completely, she could lose her patience and change tactics entirely. She's used subtlety up to this point, even though there have been deaths. We have no idea how big a group she has, so if she is challenged too harshly—Arryn, that means you—then she could decide to use extreme violence. She could start another war."

Amelia clapped her hands together. "Good, then it's settled. I'm going to do as I promised Talia and have the Hunters investigate Arryn, and I'm going to get the Guard together while we search the city for a body. Arryn, stay in the open. Do everything normally. Train this morning, go to the Academy; don't change anything. I'm almost positive I know how this is going to go, so more than likely, you can expect us within the next day or two."

Arryn nodded, a smile on her face. "Great. I look forward to it. By then, I should have my evidence, or I'll have a plan to get it. In the words of Talia, 'let the games begin.'"

THE FIRST DAY after Arryn's meeting with Amelia went fine. Training proceeded as usual, the students were as attentive and curious as they normally were, and there were no visits from Amelia or any guards.

Celine assured Arryn that no news was good news, but Arryn wasn't so sure; it was driving her crazy not knowing what was going on. She wasn't a sit-around-and-wait kind of person. She liked to know exactly what to expect and when to expect it.

The second day, however, Arryn realized just how right Celine had been.

Only half the students showed up to her class, and those who did were whispering and commenting to one another. When no one dared to look her in the eye, she realized there was much more going on than just distracted students.

Arryn had finally had enough, so she decided to do what she did best: confront the situation head-on.

"So..." Arryn began, pausing briefly as she walked around to sit on the front of her desk as she did often, "tell me. What happened to the other half of the class? And why are you all so distracted? Usually I can't get you to shut up about battle magic, battle strategy in fighting, the Dark Forest, and whatever else pops into your head, but today you haven't said a single word to me. I find that strange."

The students nervously looked at one another before facing forward, but finally a new girl in the back stood. Her name was Maddie, and she had blue eyes and blonde curls that stretched down her back. She was noble, judging by her dress.

"Since no one else here has any guts, I'll be the one to say it. You seem nice, and you've always been very straightforward with us, so I don't exactly believe the things that are being said. Unfortunately, many of our fellow students do. There was another body found, this time in what will be the Boulevard park, and everyone thinks it was you."

Arryn nodded, her eyes never leaving Maddie's. "I see. Let me ask all of you this... Why exactly are these things being said? What proves that I did it or even gives you an *idea* that I did it? More than that, why would I go out of my way to train you guys how to heal yourselves, give you details on battle strategy, and encourage all of you to take care of yourselves, and train some of the Guard every morning before I come into this classroom, if I wanted to kill someone? Doesn't that sound strange to you?"

None of the class answered, though they whispered to one another. Maddie was right; they were all cowards. They were willing to say things behind her back, but not her face.

"Maddie, I suppose that since no one else in here has any intention of answering, that question is for you."

"Most of the people here are Boulevard students, and that means they never had the displeasure of meeting Adrien. In other words, they've never met true evil. It's easier to point fingers and gossip than it is to actually search for the truth."

Arryn nodded, intrigued by the young woman. She looked to be about fifteen or sixteen, but she was very smart and strong-willed. Arryn liked her.

"And what is the truth? At least, what do you think it is?" Arryn asked.

Maddie shrugged, her eyes never leaving Arryn's. "I have no idea what the truth is, but I've met evil. I know evil. You're not."

Arryn looked around the room, suddenly disgusted with the peers she'd not only taught, but studied with. She remembered the things her father and mother had told her about the city. Nothing became notable unless it was interesting enough. Apparently, being a good, honest person wasn't an interesting enough story.

Only being a traitor was.

Arryn waved her hand in the air. "Class dismissed. Not a single one of you is paying any attention to what I say anyway, so there's no point in wasting my breath. Just so you know, I *do* know what's happening out there. I know who did this, and more than that, I'm trying to stop them."

Arryn took a deep breath, her nostrils flaring as she struggled to keep her rage under control. "Here's a little history lesson for you. I kept my past hidden from all of you because I had no idea who I could trust. I had no idea who among you might still secretly side with Adrien. The truth is, my parents—at least my mother—died helping me flee the city. They'd been planning a way to save the city from Adrien, but they were caught. The father of my best friend, Gregory, the person who fought alongside Hannah and all of you in the Battle for Arcadia, turned my father in, leading to my father's capture and my mother's death while trying to get me to safety."

Arryn stood and took a few steps toward the desks in front of her, her eyes moving from student to student.

"The druids took me in because my mother had saved the grandson of the Chieftain from being killed by a lycanthrope only a week before her death. The grandson's name was Cathillian, and he accompanied me back here to the city. I was raised among the druids. I learned their ways, learned their values, and learned how to fight. I needed to know how to fight so I could come back here and kill Adrien. But I didn't make it in time; I missed that opportunity, the opportunity that all of you had. To fight for your city."

The students looked at one another again, but stayed deathly silent as they turned back to her.

"When I heard what had happened, I came back immediately. The fight was over, but the requirement to continue protecting the city continued. I came back here to make sure that the Guard was well-trained after largely being replaced, and guess what, it's getting there! Every morning Cathillian and I train them. I came back here to make sure that the new Chancellor wasn't a tyrant. She isn't.

"My mother is dead, and I still haven't learned the fate of my father, something I'm still searching for. So, before you decide to believe the rumors, remember everything I've taught you. Remember everything I've said. Because no matter what you decide, I'm still working to make sure that the person responsible will pay. And I *will* die to protect you if it comes to that. Can you say the same?"

Arryn saw guilt and mixed emotions on their faces as they glanced at one another for support. They shifted uncomfortably in their seats, obviously uncertain how they felt given the story she just told.

Finally, Arryn spoke again. "As I said, class is dismissed for today. If I'm not in prison for a murder that I clearly didn't commit tomorrow, I'll see you then."

Arryn shook her head and walked behind her desk, taking a seat in her chair as she watched everyone leave the room. Well, everyone except for Maddie.

Once the rest of the students had departed, the young woman came to stand in front of Arryn's desk. "Nice speech."

Arryn nodded. "Thanks. Glad you liked it."

"Like Amelia, I fought beside Hannah in the battle. In fact, we spent a lot of time in Girard's house training and planning before anything ever happened."

Arryn laughed. "Yeah, about that. Funny that it should be the headquarters for yet another bad storm brewing here."

Maddie nodded as she studied Arryn. " I've only been in your class for a few days, but I've gotten to know who you are as a person, even though I knew nothing of your past until today. I don't think you had anything to do with James' murder, but I believe you when you say you know who did."

"Yeah? Would you believe me if I told you it was the almighty Dean of Students? Because I kind of assume not many people would," Arryn's voice was sarcastic, though her words were honest.

Maddie thought for a moment before nodding again. "Considering the fact that one of the students in here, Jackson, is disturbingly close to her and told some of these students about the murder in the first place, yeah, I believe it."

Arryn sighed as she sat back in her chair. "Jackson. I'm pretty sure Talia sent him into this class to distract me and get information, but I'm a little too smart for that. I know honest flirting from that of a shit like him trying to use me for his own ends. And, I saw a rather intimate letter from him to Talia. He only has the hots for her. Gross."

"So, what's the plan?" Maddie asked.

Arryn smiled. "I don't know a damn thing *about* you, but I like you. And it doesn't matter what I say or whether I'm going along with it or not, my fate is sealed, so I guess it won't matter if I tell you that Amelia and the Hunters absolutely *will* find evidence that it was me. I can promise you that. As far as this city is concerned, I *am* the killer. And when the evidence is presented, I'll be arrested."

Maddie laughed. "Well, good luck with that. It sounds like you have it all figured out, but that leaves a huge problem. If you're right about who did it, Talia would be on the wrong side of those bars. If you want a little advice, I would suggest constructing your escape plan now. Get out and use the illusion that you're locked away and out of her hair as the opportunity to get whatever evidence you need."

With that, Maddie gave her a reassuring smile and walked out of the class, leaving Arryn to her thoughts. It was obvious what was about to happen. Like Maddie said, she needed to plan her escape.

CHAPTER TWENTY

Two days had passed since James' body had been found in the Boulevard, and things were moving along nicely. So far, everything had gone to plan. The first day, Scarlett had put a lot of effort into using her mental magic to convince students that Arryn might have killed James.

They decided her suggestions should be subtle in the beginning. Everything was new, and people would be struggling with the loss of another life as well as developing their own opinions, so it made sense to keep everything simple.

The following day, however, Scarlett fed them more. She began filling them with doubt and suspicion: maybe Arryn was completely twisted? Maybe she'd tainted the Chancellor? After all, Amelia had been very close to Arryn since the moment she'd arrived.

Scarlett had done a very good job creating chaos and fear around Arryn, and just enough fear regarding the Chancellor that it would force Amelia to do things she might not want to do, if for no other reason than to keep peace.

Talia couldn't be happier with the direction in which their plan was moving. To keep everyone informed, Talia decided to hold a meeting with her group. It was broad daylight, so there was only one option—her special place in the basement of the Academy.

Talia looked from face to face; the group of supporters was sitting there, all eyes on her. They were enamored with her, just as she'd hoped they would be. They had done everything she'd asked of them, and had never doubted her.

Still, it didn't hurt to use Scarlett's influence to cement their loyalty.

"We have to stop her!" Victoria shouted. "We cannot allow her to undo all we've worked for. If she succeeds, it's hard to say what will happen."

Talia nodded. "Trust me, I know. This is what I've been trying to prevent. We've worked much too hard to push Amelia to the edge and let the city see her weaknesses. If Arryn manages to prove it was me and take me out of the equation, you all will fall shortly afterward, and then where will the city be?"

Shocked and disgruntled whispers broke out among them. It was obvious to Talia that everyone was just as worried as she was, but for far different reasons.

They were afraid of losing their savior, and Talia was afraid of missing out on her revenge. Something needed to be done fast while the city was up in arms, and Arryn was falling from her pedestal.

Bernice—another teacher—stood, taking a confident step forward to command the floor. Talia didn't intervene when the woman began to speak.

"Talia's right. Something needs to happen, and I think I know what." She paused for a moment as everyone quieted down. "We need to make Talia the hero, and ensure that Arryn is the one who looks like a traitor. If we can accomplish that, it'll seal Arryn's fate."

"What exactly did you have in mind?" Talia asked.

Bernice turned to Talia. "It will be both easy and difficult to plan, but if we can pull it off, it will mark you as the hero of the city and prove Arryn as a cold-blooded killer without a shadow of doubt."

Talia smiled, loving the idea already, though she hadn't even heard any of the details yet. But until it was finalized, Talia had her own plan to put into action. No matter what, at this point in the game, there couldn't be any downtime. Amelia had to fall, but Arryn had to fall first.

THE GOVERNOR of Cella had just settled down for lunch when the warning bells rang to signal an attack on the city. He rushed from his office, heading toward the barracks in hopes of finding someone who might know what was happening.

When he stepped outside, he was met with chaos—the entire city was in disarray. Everyone was running around screaming, then rushing into their homes and bolting the doors.

The guard ran out of the watchtower, meeting him just outside the door. "Governor, remnant have been spotted in the southeast. I don't have an exact count, but it's a horde. It's the biggest group I've ever heard of attacking all at once."

The governor was caught between the urge to flee for his own life and the need to get everything in order for his people. He knew that without him the guards would fail, and his city would fall. His citizens would be hunted and lost. Men, women, and children would be torn apart and killed, and some might even be eaten alive.

Taking a deep breath, the governor reassured himself that he could be everything the city needed; that was the entire reason he was in place. He wouldn't allow the city to fall, not on his watch.

"I'm going to need a magitech rifle. Find the guards. Gather the citizens trained in magic and get them on top of the walls. The rest I want inside the gates. We will take as many down as we can from up high, and we will do our best to keep the rest out with our gates. But if anything comes through, unleash hell."

The man nodded before running off toward the gates. The governor wasted no time taking action.

He ran as fast as he could to the first house he could see, beating on the door as soon as he reached it. When it opened, he was relieved.

"Governor?" the man asked. "What is this? What's happening?"

The governor shook his head, waving his hands in front of him. "There's no time. Are you magically trained?"

The man nodded. "My wife and I both attended the Arcadian Academy."

"Then we need you. The remnant are attacking, and we need all the magic users we can get. If you have children, send them to the city building. They'll be safe in there. It's the deepest part of the city, and we're not going to let anything get that far, right?" the governor asked, not really giving the man an option to say no.

"You're damn right," a female voice interjected from behind the man. A woman roughly the same age as the man stepped out; the governor assumed it was the man's wife. "You'll need more than just us. You wrangle your guard, and we'll get all the magicians assembled."

The governor smiled, realizing then that there were good, strong people in his city. People he was more grateful for at that moment than at any other time. He'd only just begun defending, and he couldn't help but wonder how the Arcadian people had felt when fighting their war against Adrien. It wasn't the remnant, but they'd sure as hell had something to fight against.

When the governor went down the street to a large group of guards, he found his son standing there. "Nathaniel, what are you doing here?"

Nathaniel turned, his bright blue eyes seeming fiercer than usual. "I'm helping. I knew you'd disagree, but I've been learning how to fight. I don't know magic, so this the best I can offer."

The governor wanted to argue, but the look on his son's face told him his words would be lost; his son would find a way to fight no matter what. Instead of arguing, the governor pulled his son into a hug, patting him hard on the back before releasing him.

"I'm proud of you. Don't end up dead, otherwise, that deal I brokered to get you into the Arcadian Academy will have been wasted," the Governor told him, allowing his smile to grow for a moment.

His son reached behind him and pulled out a magitech rifle that had been leaning against the wall, which he handed to his father. "You're going to need this. The gates are closed, but they're coming. They'll be here soon. I'm going up to the wall. Turns out I'm one of the best shots in the city, but you'll just have to see that for yourself."

The governor forced a smile. "I have no doubt about it, son. Please, just make sure you come back to me. We need to save our city, but I don't want to lose you in the process."

The sounds of magitech rifles being fired and remnant growling and screaming from the other side of the wall echoed down the main street, reaching them even a quarter mile away.

Nathaniel looked toward the wall before turning back to his father. "It's begun. I have to go now. Get as many magic users as you can to the wall, and have them form as many fireballs as possible. We need to kill all we can before they burst through the gate."

The governor nodded as his son ran toward the wall. He looked down at his magitech rifle momentarily before scanning the frightened city around him. His son was a brave man; he'd somehow raised him that way. Taking another deep breath, he convinced himself that he could be just as heroic as he ran back to the houses to enlist magic users to help save the city.

AMELIA SAT IN HER OFFICE, hands shaking as she held the letter from governor of Cella in her hand. The city had been completely overrun by a horde of remnant. The body count was uncertain as he'd written the letter, but it had been enough to tear the city apart.

He warned her to take precautions in case the worst should happen. His army had been small in comparison to Arcadia's, but his had been well trained. They'd managed to kill them and keep their city standing, but only barely.

Tears ran down her face as she read the governor's account of what had happened.

There had been much blood and carnage, but the city had prevailed in the end. They had managed to kill most of the remnant, while the last of them fled for their lives.

It was everything Arryn and Samuel had worried about. Everything they'd *all* worried about.

Amelia had lost her own family to the remnant, so she knew just how dangerous and terrifying they could be. Just reading the letter brought back those memories.

She could hear their screams and cries, and she could remember how terrified she was while she hid, praying they wouldn't find her. Putting the letter face-down on her desk, Amelia wiped her tears away and pushed herself back in her chair, looking anywhere but at the parchment.

So much death. So much loss, and she needed to stop it. At this point, she was ready to give up looking like a hero—as long as her people were safe.

Sure, they wouldn't understand it when she began arresting seemingly innocent people, but they would come to understand she done it for a reason. All she had to do was gather proof, but she was beginning to feel like she had no other choice but to arrest now and ask questions later.

Students were dying, and the remnant were attacking. Something about the way it was all happening and the timeframe made

Amelia suspicious. It all seemed a bit too coordinated and convenient for her liking.

Sitting in her chair, thinking about the young people whose parents she had to give terrible news to and answering their questions when she had no answers made her feel numb. She felt as though her mind could no longer carry the burden of walking the fine line.

She thought of Hannah then, wondering what the girl might do. Hannah was an act-first-and-ask-questions-later kind of girl, though she had certainly learned a lot of patience from hanging around with the Founder.

If Hannah had been Chancellor, Amelia couldn't help but think that she would've kicked Talia's ass by now. Who cared if she had proof? Like Arryn, Hannah would have ignored what was right and wrong; she would've stopped at nothing to save the lives of everyone in the city.

And that's what Amelia planned to do.

Amelia needed to talk to Arryn right away. She would need to get Talia into her office so she could be arrested quietly and taken to jail without the city knowing.

She'd taken enough vacations that it would be easy enough to say she'd left for a few days, and then Amelia could use that time to gather the proof she needed.

She was worried about what she would do if Talia turned out to be innocent, but deep down, she knew something was very wrong, especially now that the city was becoming more and more convinced of Arryn's guilt. There was only one way that could've taken root as hard and as fast as it did—mental magic.

Amelia stood, ready to tell Marie that she needed to see Arryn immediately, but she heard shouting outside as Talia burst through the door.

"The Chancellor is busy, and you need to allow me to introduce you properly," Marie scolded. Amelia was quite impressed with her secretary's fierce expression and forceful voice—the woman meant business. "I sit at this desk for a reason, you know. Amelia, do you want me to get rid of her?"

Talia turned and looked at the woman, clearly offended. "Get rid of me? I'd like to see you try, *mouse*. Trust me, I'm not someone you want to fuck with." Talia's voice was low enough that she believed Talia was trying to hide her words from anyone other than Marie, but Amelia heard them loud and clear. Talia turned to Amelia. "Not when there's an emergency. Chancellor, I think your life is in danger. I came as quick as I could."

Amelia couldn't help but think how convenient it was for Talia to show up when she had just decided to arrest her. Unfortunately, she didn't have guards ready to take her, and taking her on alone would be loud and messy. It would alert the city to something happening, and Amelia wanted to keep it as quiet as possible.

"What are you talking about?" Amelia asked.

Talia took a few steps forward. "It's Arryn. I've had several people come to me and say that Arryn was talking about confronting you. She said she's not going to spend her life rotting in a cell when she needs to find her father, and she'll take care of you if she has to."

Amelia had heard enough. This was beyond desperate.

She was about to respond when an explosion went off on the far side of the building. Talia and Amelia both fell to the floor from the vibrations, Amelia hitting her head on the corner of her desk as she went down.

Her eyes fluttered a few times as she tried to focus, but everything quickly turned black as her consciousness faded.

CHAPTER TWENTY-ONE

Arryn was on her way to see Amelia to find out exactly what was happening with the potential murder charges when she was stopped in her tracks by a loud explosion.

A few seconds passed before another sounded out.

Vibrations shook the ground even where she stood several blocks away. Suddenly, Arryn was filled with fear as she realized that the explosion had come from the direction of the Capitol building.

Wasting no more time, Arryn ran as fast as she possibly could, sprinting toward Amelia. As she rounded the corner of the last building on the last block, nothing standing between her and the Capitol building that was engulfed in flames on the west side, Arryn spotted three people on the left, fireballs forming in their hands.

Rage overtook her as she saw them pull back, ready to fire again. They were planning to take the whole building down, not just part of it.

Arryn knew just by looking at the condition of the west side that several people must have died in the initial explosion, but she refused to allow anyone else to succumb to their evil, especially Amelia and Marie.

"Hey, guys!" Arryn screamed, catching the attention of the three people terrorizing Arryn's city. "Damn! You're redecorating and you didn't even invite me? I *love* the color green. We should discuss curtains."

The trio moved closer toward her, stepping out of the shadows in the process. She immediately recognize their faces. Two of them were teachers that she worked with—Victoria and David—one of them being her own physical magic teacher, and the other was a student named Hugh.

She hadn't seen much out of Hugh at all, and only knew him by other students talking about him. Unfortunately, it seemed like he knew her more than plenty.

Arryn swallowed hard, realizing that she would more than likely have to kill them. She definitely didn't *want* to, but she would have to in order to protect the people inside.

Voices began to fill the area, and Arryn became painfully aware that she had an audience now—even more people she would have to protect.

Victoria stepped forward. "We won't let you get any closer! You've done enough damage to the city!"

Confusion crossed Arryn's face, unclear what the hell she was talking about.

From the whispers behind her, Arryn understood that people thought she was the one who had blown up the building. She was about to ask what had made them think that when Victoria spoke again.

"The Chancellor has betrayed her city! Her friendship with you and every moment she protects you is another betrayal."

Arryn took a step forward, fists clenching at her sides. She was done with this. She didn't feel comfortable attacking the rebels in front of so many other people, especially with the allegations that were going around, but it had to end.

She needed to get inside to see if she could help. She couldn't waste any more time.

"I don't know what the hell you're talking about, but there are people hurt inside. I need to help them." Arryn took another step forward, but was halted by a fireball exploding close to her feet.

Her physical magic teacher, David, had thrown it, and now took a step forward. "If you take one more step, I promise you I won't miss again. You're not going near anyone in there. You've hurt enough people already. Why did you do this? How many have to die before the Chancellor finally sees what the rest of us do?"

Arryn could hear screams inside the building, screams from people who were burning, people who were dying.

Refusing to back down, Arryn took another step forward, her magic licking her palms. All three magicians had created fireballs, so Arryn immediately threw a shield up behind her to protect the growing crowd as she seized her opportunity.

"Everyone stay back! I had nothing to do with this, but I sure as hell plan to fix it," Arryn told them.

She jumped forward, landing on her hands and tumbling over once before planting her feet, narrowly missing the fireballs that were thrown at her. She swung her hand as though she were smacking someone in the face, and large chunks of stone broke from the street and hit the three in front of her.

Arryn only barely sensed the magic approaching in time to flex her entire body, a magical shield jumping into existence around her as a fireball hit her from behind.

Arryn turned and saw several citizens wielding magic, planning to use it against her.

But that wasn't the only thing that she saw.

There in the crowd was Scarlett, controlling what everyone saw. There was no hiding her bright white eyes, though no one else seemed to notice.

It made sense now why her colleagues and fellow students

had decided to make such random accusations—it was because Scarlett was inserting those words and convincing the crowd of their truth.

Arryn was a cold-blooded killer.

Arryn had blown up the Capitol building.

Arryn was in a fight with three *innocent* bystanders, and was threatening to *kill* them.

As she realized what she was up against, Arryn began to fear the outcome more than ever. If she let them go, they would do far worse, but if she killed them, there would be no going back. They would see her as a murderer, and it would take quite a lot to convince them otherwise.

Arryn heard a deep laugh, and she turned to see David. "You should have left Talia alone," he declared, his voice only loud enough for Arryn to hear. "You should have left the city alone. It's ours, and we *will* restore it to the way that it should be."

More screams erupted from the building, and Arryn realized she could wait no longer. It didn't matter what people thought of her, only that they were safe.

Arryn turned to David and smiled. "Then I guess this is *really* gonna suck for you guys. Turns out, I was raised by the druids not to give a shit what other people think, but to always protect them from shitheads like you. Bye, now!"

Arryn's eyes turned jet-black as she arced her hands over her chest, pulling them away to reveal two bright blue fireballs. She threw the first to the ground at the rebels' feet, the tiny explosion throwing them back on their asses.

Arryn could hear the roar of the crowd behind her as they prepared to approach. Extinguishing the other fireball, she turned and allowed her fear for the lives surrounding her to guide her hand.

She thrust her hands out and wind exploded around her, tumbling all the men and women back, though not harming anyone.

She turned back to her fight to see Hugh running, and she quickly threw her hand out, a thin, weak vine breaking free of the ground and wrapping itself around his feet to slam him to the ground.

David threw another fireball and Arryn thrust her hand out, pitching it directly back to strike him in the chest. He screamed as he hit the ground, rolling and struggling to put the fire out.

Victoria ran to Arryn to engage her in hand-to-hand combat, and at that moment, Arryn was struck in the back of the head by another citizen who was innocent, but still in the way.

She was worried that he would get hurt if he continued, so she did the only thing she could.

Arryn kicked him inside of the leg, buckling his knee and bringing him down before punching him hard in the temple. He fell to the ground, unconscious, and Arryn turned back just in time to block a strike from the other teacher.

Victoria wrapped her hand in Arryn's hair and yanked her head back, lifting a knife in her other hand to bring it down on Arryn's throat. Her eyes widened as she saw the steel glinting in the sunlight.

She grabbed the hand in her hair and spun, twisting Victoria's arm before dropping to the ground and throwing the woman over her back. The teacher landed hard on her side, air exploding from her lungs.

Arryn dove for the knife, but the other woman recovered more quickly than she had anticipated. There was a brief struggle before Victoria grasped the dagger and swung, slicing Arryn's face as she did.

Without hesitation, Arryn kicked her hard in the stomach, the woman falling flat on her back as she once again struggled to breathe. Climbing on top of her, Arryn punched her hard in the face, disorienting her before grabbing knife and driving it through the woman's heart.

David shouted as he charged. Arryn quickly pulled the knife

from the dead teacher's chest and lightly tossed it in the air to catch it by the tip of the blade before turning and throwing it as hard as she could, hitting him in the chest.

Arryn stood, stumbling a bit as she struggled to catch her breath. Her head swam from the adrenalin and the hard hit she had received. She glanced around at the looks on the faces of the crowd. They were terrified.

Since she'd managed to subdue all of them with a gust of wind, they were too frightened to approach. Only one man had summoned his courage to do so, and she'd laid him out in two hits.

She saw herself through their eyes, and her heart broke. She had just murdered two people in cold blood as far as they were concerned, but she couldn't let that stop her. There was no more time to be wasted when there were lives at stake inside.

As she turned to head into the building, she saw something that she hadn't expected.

Talia walked out of the building with Amelia's arm wrapped around her shoulders and several other people behind her. They were all filthy, covered in ash and coughing terribly with every step.

She gently lowered Amelia to the ground before turning toward the building with her hands outstretched. Within seconds, several people came to stand next to her as they manipulated and controlled the fire.

In only a couple of minutes, the flames were completely gone, and all that was left of the west side of the building was charred and crumbled wood and stone.

Once the fire was out, Talia looked around, her jaw dropping as her hands rose to cover her mouth. Arryn was caught between wanting to rip her head off and laughing.

It was certainly one hell of a performance, and the crowd was eating it up.

Had Arryn been smart, she would have fought the crowd to get to Scarlett. Because of her, Talia had everything she wanted in that moment.

"What happened?" Talia asked as she looked at the two bodies on the ground. Hugh was shackled by vines, but alive.

Shouts and accusations began to fly from the crowd; men, women and children screaming Arryn's name. "She did this! The outsider!" one man cried.

"It's her! She blew up the building. She tried to kill the Chancellor! I bet she killed Amos, Dallas, and James, too!" a woman shouted.

Talia's expression was a truly convincing cross between horror and shock. "Arryn?" Her voice was barely a whisper, but Arryn could hear it just fine. "This can't be true. You? You did this? Why? Amelia was your friend. *I* was your friend."

Arryn looked at Amelia, who was struggling to stand. There was blood pouring down her face and arms.

Arryn, I know it wasn't you, but I can hear their thoughts. Scarlett's in their heads, Amelia sent telepathically.

Fighting the urge to nod, Arryn responded, *I knew the outcome the moment I realized the crowd was building. They set me up. They set you up. This is Talia's challenge to you. You have to remain in power.*

I can't do this alone. I need you. We need to take her down together, Amelia told her.

If you don't arrest me right now, Scarlett will turn the crowd on you. Talia will have full control, and there will be a coup. You and I will both end up in jail, and Talia will have the entire Guard at her command. Do it. Do it now.

Arryn saw Amelia's eyes close briefly, and she knew right then that Amelia was as much part of her family as Celine, Cathillian, Elysia, and even Samuel.

Amelia stepped forward, using every bit of the strength she had left after fighting her way through fire to save the people who were behind her. As she raised her hand, the crowd quieted. Their accusations quieted. Their shouts for action quieted.

Amelia took a deep breath and prepared to speak, but she had one last thing to say to Arryn.

I'm sorry, Amelia said to Arryn.

Amelia, make it good, or you haven't even begun to be sorry, Arryn replied.

"Guard!" Amelia shouted.

She began to topple a little, and Talia was quick to catch her. Arryn quirked a smile as she saw Amelia hold on to the Dean for support. Several guards approached and stopped, awaiting instructions.

"Killer! Murderer! Monster!" came from the crowd, everyone shouting different things as newcomers were filled in by others as to what had transpired.

"Kill her just like she killed the others!" someone yelled.

Amelia held her hands up again, the noise of the crowd dying to a dull roar. "Arryn, for your crimes against Arcadia, against our great city, you are under arrest. The Guard will take you immediately to the prison, which we are very blessed wasn't destroyed in the blast. You will remain there until an investigation has been completed and we have what we need to try you for treason."

Tears ran down Arryn's face, and every one of them was as real as they could get.

She'd come back to Arcadia to fight for it, to be its hero, and now she was seen as a monster trying to destroy it.

"Do you accept these charges?" Amelia asked, taking a strong step forward, her eyes turning black as she did. "Or will we have to take you by force?" As Amelia issued her threat a fireball appeared in her hand, one that was not only large, but intensely hot. It seemed she'd taken Arryn's advice and decided to make a good show of it.

Arryn slowly dropped to her knees, signaling her surrender as she lowered her head. The Guard seized Arryn, tying her hands behind her back and carrying her to the east side of the Capitol building, which had not been destroyed and contained the jail.

Sit tight, Amelia sent. *I'll stop at nothing to get the proof we need, and I'll get you out of there.*

I appreciate that, but I don't plan to wait that long.

CHAPTER TWENTY-TWO

Cathillian, Celine, and Samuel all sat on the couch, listening to the terrifying description of why Arryn wouldn't be home. Amelia had to wait until well after dark before she could sneak away, but she knew they would be worried.

Cathillian shook his head, fists clenched hard and rage dominating his expression. "If I'd only believed her. It wasn't that I didn't believe her, I was just worried. She was obsessed. When the bitch came here I was convinced she was an innocent bystander to Arryn's irrational anger."

Amelia nodded slowly. "Yeah, well... I have a theory about that. Scarlett is a mystic. I don't have any hard proof, but Arryn believes it and call me crazy, but I'm sure as hell not going to brush away any more of her theories. They've all been right so far. It's possible that Scarlett was messing with your head to convince you that Talia was perfect so it would cause problems."

"Aye," Samuel added. "Livin' in the Heights, I've seen more than me fair share of those brain jockeys. Granted, I ain't never met a bad one, but I've seen what the good ones can do. I can only imagine what the bad ones are like."

Celine leaned forward, placing her elbows on her knees and

clasping her hands together. "So, what exactly did you arrest her for? How do we get her out of there?"

Amelia took a seat on the floor in front of the fireplace, folding her legs in. "It's very complicated, but I'll explain what I know. Students have been going missing for weeks, and they all show up murdered in the same way—throat slit, blood drained. Recently, there has been two murders. The last one was a boy named James. From the looks of it, he was the one killed in Arryn's old house.

"We found a knife by the body of this one. That was a little back story for you so you can see just how long this has been going on. When I had Arryn arrested today, it was because she had gotten into an altercation with three people, killing two of them and subduing a third in front of a crowd of people."

Shock crossed Cathillian's face. "What? That can't be accurate."

Amelia nodded. "It is. There was an explosion at the Capitol building. It was during the time you were outside the city walls teaching nature magic, so I can understand why you didn't hear it. That said, I'm pretty sure Arryn found them attacking the building. By the time she got involved, Scarlett had arrived with a crowd of people that she was controlling. I haven't had a chance to talk to Arryn, but I saw Scarlett, and I saw her eyes. I don't know if she realized that I saw her, but I did. She was using far too much magic and was spread so thin that it didn't have any effect on me."

"Okay, so Arryn killed the people involved. What then?" Celine asked.

"It was a mess. There were shouts about her being a traitor and telling me to sentence her to death. It was horrible. The crowd saw Talia lead me and the rest of the survivors out of the building safely. That along with Scarlett's magic set in stone that Talia was a hero, and they had seen Arryn kill two people—so she was the obvious threat. I had no choice, and Arryn knew it. She told me to arrest her. I had to do it to stay in control."

Amelia took a deep breath, brushing her hair back. It was obvious to Cathillian that she was fighting back tears. He couldn't exactly say that he blamed her given all she'd been through, all she was currently going through, and all that would still happen.

"I arrested her to safeguard my title and keep Talia out of the Chancellor's chair. I promised an investigation, and I immediately initiated it. Unfortunately, during the fight, Arryn stabbed both people in the chest. The knife she used was the very one that had been in my office; one that had gone missing, and I hadn't even realized it. I didn't know until I got back to my office after Arryn was taken to the jail. It was the same knife we think all the other people had been killed with, which only added to the evidence against her. But that's not the worst of it."

Cathillian sighed, his eyes closing as he rubbed the bridge of his nose. "It gets worse than that? Seriously?"

Amelia continued. "There were several people who told me they saw Arryn throw the fireballs that caused the explosion. Obviously, this was Scarlett's work, but other people heard it. I had no choice but to take it under advisement. Not only that, but along with the blood that was found in her childhood home, the people who saw her walking to her old house that night, and Dallas' friend who identified a cloaked woman with long dark hair, Arryn isn't just *one* of the choices. She's *the* choice."

Samuel sat back on the couch, popping his knuckles as he made a fist over and over. "What do we do? How do we get our girl outta there?"

Amelia smiled. "That's the best part. Or, I guess I should say the only *good* part. I don't think we have to worry about that. You see, I put Arryn in the cell next to Elon, who was best friends with Arryn's father, Christopher. He harbors great guilt about what happened, so I have a feeling that Arryn won't be in there for long."

Samuel laughed. "Is that so? Is that why Elon is still in there after all this time? Seems like he's not gonna be much help at all."

"Elon was the Chief Engineer. I doubt there's anyone in the city smarter than he is. Believe me, that man could've gotten out of that jail a long time ago if he wanted to. The only thing that holds him there is guilt. He won't allow Arryn to suffer. He made a few mistakes that he can't take ever back, not only with his son, but years ago with Arryn and her family. He can't make things right with his son, Gregory. I have faith that he's going to do everything he can to help Arryn. Keep an eye peeled—she'll more than likely be here before the night's out, but I can't know anything about it."

Celine nodded. "That's smart. If the mystic finds her way into your head, she'll know Arryn is gone."

Cathillian's expression had slowly turned from worry and rage to amusement. "Fantastic. Now, all we have to do is wait for Arryn to lose her temper and break out of jail. Thinking back, I have no idea why I was worried. That shouldn't take more than ten minutes or so."

ARRYN HAD DONE her best to heal herself with the limited energy she had available. She wasn't the best healer anyway, but exhausted by magic use and fighting, she was even less effective.

Her face had been injured the worst, the knife having sliced her from her temple down the side of her face and across her cheek and chin.

She was lucky the knife had missed her eye. Healing abilities or not, that shit would've hurt.

"Arryn?" a masculine voice called from the cell beside her.

She was just waking up, but she found the energy to respond. "Yeah? Who the hell wants to know?"

There was a pause before he spoke again. "I don't know if you remember me, but you were great friends with my son, Gregory. My name is Elon. You look so different, I never would've recognized you had they not said your name when they carried you in."

Arryn sighed. "Ah... You're the one who set our downfall in motion. I wonder, had you not opened your big mouth, would my parents have succeeded? Would you and I be sitting at a large banquet table, Gregory at my side like my parents always teased me about? Or would I have found myself an orphan in the Dark Forest anyway?"

"I suppose that I deserved that. I deserve a lot of things. Least of all, forgiveness from you or my son. I don't give a damn about anything else."

Arryn gave a sarcastic, unamused laugh. She wasn't exactly sure what to say, or if she wanted to say anything. She'd had a thousand questions for that man, but just at that moment, lying on that crappy bed and staring at the ceiling seemed like a better way to spend her time.

"What landed you in here?" Elon asked.

Arryn almost laughed again. Where the hell should she start? Her story was long, and one she didn't exactly feel like telling at that moment.

"I'm rather enjoying my quiet time, so I'm gonna keep this short and sweet. Your favorite person in the world had a daughter. Did you know that? Because I didn't. Not until recently. Turns out, that's what my father discovered about Adrien that led him to be killed."

"I did know that. He told me himself, but I spent many years pretending I didn't know. It was very important that no one— including me—was aware of her. And why do you think your father's dead? I told Amelia he was *taken*. Far as I know, he's still alive out there. If anyone in this world could survive, it would be Christopher. It's hard to kill a heart that pure."

Arryn laughed, but it was angry. "That's a funny story ya got there Elon. Almost as funny as how they gutted my mom. She had a pure heart, and they ripped it out pretty easily, wouldn't you say? So, don't dare lecture me on my parents or pure hearts."

She sighed, settling into the hard bed as best as she could. "As for the rest of it, I don't know what to believe, though I have hope. Hope that I'm not going to share with anyone—outside of this conversation, of course. I only say it to you because you actually knew my father, and I want you to know exactly what I go through every day *because* of you. I go back and forth between thinking he's alive and thinking he's dead, whatever drives me most that moment."

There was another pause. "But in your heart, you know you'll find him, don't you? You'll never stop until you do."

Arryn shook her head, even though she knew he couldn't see it. "No, I will never stop. Only getting answers or my own death will stop me."

"Yet, you let yourself be taken. Why?" Elon asked.

"Not that it's any of your business, and you wouldn't understand loyalty anyway, but I did it to protect Amelia. I did it to keep the city safe from Talia. If I'd fought, it's hard to say what would've happened. I wasn't about to put my own life above theirs."

Arryn heard the clang of bars. She couldn't see him, but she could sense his energy by his cell door. She imagined him standing there, gripping the steel bars.

"And Talia? You plan to stop her?" he asked.

Arryn sighed, rolling her eyes. "What is this, an interview? A game? Are you writing a book, or taking notes? Damn, man. Trying to be arrested in peace over here. Yes. Talia *must* be stopped. She's far worse than her father, if you can imagine that. I didn't think it was possible. Clearly, the rotten piece of shit didn't fall too far from the monkey in the tree."

"You can't stop her from in here, you know."

Arryn's arms fell to her sides with a thud as she gave a heavy sigh. "You know, I hadn't thought about that. Amelia wasn't joking. You really are the smartest man in the world! Thank you for that earthshattering advice. I'll never forget it. I really hope you *did* take some notes over there. I can't wait to read the book. Educational stuff there."

Arryn heard a familiar creak and she jackknifed to a sitting position with a start. Elon stood in the open door to her cell. As soon as she saw his face, she was flooded with memories of her childhood.

She did remember him.

He had seemed so happy when she was a child, so fatherly. She didn't understand then, but once he started disappearing more and more for work, he began to change. He no longer seemed proud of Gregory, just annoyed by him.

Arryn wasn't around him much after that, but she remembered him from before, and the look in his eyes told her that the earlier man stood before her now.

He took slow, careful steps across the room before sitting on the end of her bed. "I know you don't trust me. You're smart not to, but though I'm only the shell of the man I used to be, I would never hurt you. Still, you're wise not to believe it. However, I have great regret. The decisions I made about your family set me on the path that made me capable of trying to kill my own son for a man who was more than happy to let me do it."

Arryn looked at the door and at Elon. "If you had the ability to escape this entire time, why didn't you? Why have you stayed?"

He smiled sadly. "I belong here. The moment I was arrested and paraded through a room full of rebels..." He shook his head as he trailed off. "That room full of children, teenagers, adults, and our elders that had fled something I made... Something I crafted because I wanted to save the city in *Adrien's* honor... I thought what I was doing was right, but when I walked into that room and saw my son sitting among them alive and well because of them, I realized I was the monster. I wasn't given the opportunity to speak to him, and I didn't deserve it at the time."

"And you think you do now?" Arryn asked.

He shook his head. "No, probably not. But like you, I haven't given up hope. Amelia tells me that he's on some grand adventure to save the city with Hannah, the girl from the Boulevard. I have no way of knowing if that's true or not, but I kind of hope it is. I kept him under my thumb the way that Adrien kept me. He deserves adventure. He deserves a life. He deserves to be happy. I will wait here and serve my time until my son comes home. If I die before that happens, that's fine, too."

Arryn swallowed, forcing back her mixed emotions. She fully believed Elon deserved to be locked away for life for what he done, but the man who sat before her now was the man she remembered from when she was child. Humble. Kind.

At the very least, she was happy he could serve his time, however long it would be, as the old him.

"How do you plan to do it?" Elon asked.

Arryn looked down at her bed, pulling a loose string on her sheets before meeting his gaze again. She shook her head. "I have no idea. Things are dangerous with Scarlett involved. She's a mystic. She controls the minds of others, convincing them I'm a monster and Amelia isn't much better. I don't exactly know what I plan to do, but it has to be me."

He smiled, seeming to be moderately amused. "You're going to need to do better than that. I know, more sage wisdom. But you do, and I think I can help."

"How?"

"There's a basement under the Academy. I'm not sure how many people remembered that it existed, but Adrien had it sealed off. Well, that's what he told everyone. In reality, he had the entrance rerouted to his office. I'm betting that if you go into Adrien's old office in the Academy tower, you'll find whatever evidence you need. That being said, no one can know that you're missing. You cannot be seen."

Arryn sighed heavily, closing her eyes. "That must be where she's been killing them. The Hunters have been tearing the city apart, and they have found nothing. The victims have been killed somewhere else and taken to wherever they were found dumped. The only exception was a student who was killed in my childhood home. That was when the framing began."

Elon nodded. "Then that's where I would start. I'm not positive, but I'm pretty sure that's where you'll find what you need. Also, there was once a lockbox that Adrien commissioned me to make years ago. It was rather feminine for something he would want, so I imagined it to be a gift, though for the life of me, I couldn't figure out who he would give it to, though now I'm betting it was Talia. Find that lockbox. I would imagine the lockbox's contents and that basement will give you absolutely everything you need."

"I would assume there's a magitech lock on the box, correct?"

"That was the best part. I was actually quite proud of myself. He said that the key needed to be hidden but accessible, so I crafted a pendant, a necklace. It had eyelets on either side to keep it from turning over, and carefully tucked away in the hollow back is a key attached by a tiny hinge. The pendant is silver and has a blue gem in it. It's really quite beautiful."

Once again Arryn rolled her eyes. "You mean like the one Talia wears? Fuck me! All of this was right in front of my face the entire time. I don't believe it."

"You don't have to believe it, you just have to prove it's true. You can't get the key since she's probably wearing it, but if you get the box, you can bring it to me and I'll get it open for you. It should be dark now, and if I were you, I wouldn't waste any more time. You should get going while the city sleeps, but be careful.

Adrien obviously wasn't a stupid man, and no offspring of his will be either."

Arryn nodded, taking a deep breath as she stood facing the open cell door.

I'm coming for you, Talia, Arryn thought.

CHAPTER TWENTY-THREE

Arryn hid out for two days, avoiding her home at all costs. To keep Cathillian from worrying, she'd used chipmunks and other creatures to send messages to him, but in true Arryn fashion, she'd been doing it in the most annoying way possible.

A raven brought Cathillian the first letter, and it was kind enough to shit on his head as it flew over and dropped the note from its talons. When he opened it to read after cleaning himself up, Arryn told him that she hoped he had enjoyed her gift since that was the only way she could personalize it for him.

The next day he woke when several mice who scurried under his bedsheets and tugged his thin blonde leg hair hard enough to be painful. One of them had a note strapped to its back, and it started with "Hahaha," so once again he knew she was fine.

Today he was greeted by a chipmunk with its cheeks full of peanuts. It made its way into the house, scurried up his leg, and used its tiny hands to push the contents of its cheeks into his lap. When he pulled the small note from the creature's back, he was once again greeted with Arryn's not-so-subtle sense of humor.

"Dearest Cathillian,
I know you must be losing your mind. You must be scared. I'm the

braver of the two of us, and I am stuck in hiding. But I sent Chippy here to keep you safe. As you can see, his nuts are also bigger than yours."

Samuel seemed to like that one the best. "They're gettin' better," he told the druid. "I'm kinda hopin' she don't come back for a while. I get excited every time I see a new varmint come in."

Later that night, Cathillian, Samuel, and Celine were alerted by the sound of the back door opening. As they piled into the kitchen, they saw Arryn holding her little chipmunk friend.

"He felt bad." Arryn held her hands out, the chipmunk resting comfortably in them. "He said you got a little jealous when the two of you started discussing endowments. I told him it was okay, that you were used to it."

Cathillian laughed and crossed the room to pull her into a hug. "I knew you had a natural connection to animals that was better than the rest of ours, but I didn't realize that it was quite that thorough. It certainly made for an interesting few days."

"I had kind of missed hanging out with the forest creatures. We've just been having a jolly old time fixing each other's hair and talking about boys—it's been great. So, what have you asshats been up to?"

Cathillian smiled. "Is that a joke? We've been waiting for you. Amelia said you'd probably break out, but we had no idea when. Given that you've been sending me notes since the night you were arrested, I'm gonna go out on a limb and say you broke out then."

"You got that right," Arryn declared. "Well, it's more that I walked out than broke out. Shockingly, Elon helped me. I just came by to show you guys I'm alive and okay, but tonight's the night."

Cathillian and Celine looked at each other for a moment before both focused on her. "What do you mean, 'tonight's the night'?" Celine asked.

Arryn walked over to the sink and set her furry friend on the counter while she got a glass of water, chugging it before refilling it. "I've been stalking the Academy for a couple days. The Guard is surrounding it, and I'm pretty sure there are teachers inside, but I didn't sense Talia's energy so I'm gonna break into her office."

Cathillian's eyes widened. "Hell, no! You've been gone for three days because you were *arrested,* and there is no way we are just gonna stay here while you break into the Academy. At the very least, you're not going alone."

Arryn checked on Chippy before stepping forward and poking a finger into Cathillian's chest. "Here's the thing, big boy. I don't need your permission. I appreciate everything you do and have done for me, and I appreciate your counsel. I know you care, but I don't have a choice. Scarlett can't keep this compulsion up forever, and we need to be there with proof when she fails.

"I don't know how strong Talia is, but she has a group of people willing to fight and die at her side. We don't know how many there are or how dangerous they are. We've turned people against her, so she no longer has an army. She's weaker. So, sorry, but I'm not asking permission. This is going to happen my way."

Cathillian's brows rose as he looked at her with concern. He could tell by the expression on her face and the strength in her voice that she really wouldn't allow anyone to stop her.

Sighing, Cathillian said, "Then we'll help you. What do you need from us?"

ARRYN STOOD at the corner of the building, doing her best to stay out of the guards' sight while remaining close enough to watch them. When Cathillian offered to help, she had the perfect job for him.

She sent him a couple blocks down to approach from the south, putting him in a great position to cause some noise. It was

Samuel she heard first, screaming at Cathillian before stumbling onto the street in the bright moonlight.

"Yer mum must be some piece of work ta have created a piece of ssshit like ye!" Samuel slurred.

Arryn rolled her eyes, realizing their master plan was to pretend to be drunker than hell and in a fight.

"I'd say that your mother was a hideous bitch, but I know for a fact she isn't since I was with her all last night," Cathillian snapped back.

Arryn saw the guards by the Academy laughing as they took in the two drunkards arguing in the street.

"Bastard!" Samuel yelled. "Take it back, ya pointy-eared pansy!"

Cathillian laughed before leaning over and putting his face directly into Samuel's. "I don't have to. Your mom was busy taking it back all night long."

Samuel roared with anger. "That doesn't even make sense!"

"It doesn't have to! I fucked your mom!" Cathillian shouted back.

Arryn had to bite her lip. Those two dumbasses were too much to handle, and the guards were watching with excitement, not moving to do anything about the argument. They seemed completely harmless, minus their terrible insults.

If they didn't pick it up, they would have to work extra hard to keep attention off her.

Arryn heard a loud pop and turned back to see that Samuel had punched Cathillian right in the face. *There you go!* Arryn thought.

Now that things had gotten physical the guards jumped into action, running down the street toward her loud friends. Arryn quickly made her way across the cobblestone road to the side of the Academy, careful to make sure her footsteps didn't fall too loudly.

Within moments Arryn was out of anyone's line of sight,

careful not to alert any of the other guards surrounding the building.

She found herself wishing she'd learned how to teleport, knowing how helpful it would have been at that moment. It would be loud, but she would be inside and no one would have seen her enter the building.

Unfortunately, only the best magicians were capable of such a feat, and Arryn was still only mediocre at best. Her skills played more to her physical capabilities than her magical ones.

Taking that into consideration, Arryn carefully began scaling the stone wall, grateful she'd chosen to go barefoot—just like back in the forest.

As she climbed, she did her best to keep an eye out for any onlookers. Shadows fell on this part of the building in such a way that her body, which was clad in black leather, remained easily hidden.

Within moments she reached her classroom's window, having used her strength, agility, and minimal nature magic to break off tiny pieces of stone so her hands and feet could fit in the resulting gaps.

The last time she'd been in class she'd made it a point to unlock her window. It was something no one else would have noticed, but it would allow her to get back in if she needed to. She had no idea things would happen as they had, so she was doubly grateful for her foresight.

She pushed the glass up and it opened just as she'd expected. Quietly sliding through and dropping her bare feet on the cold floor, she turned to close the window and the curtains.

Arryn made her way down the hall, moving on the balls of her feet so her steps were very quiet. She passed Talia's office, which was up the stairs and toward the end of the hall on the right.

She was surprised that she hadn't run into anyone, but she couldn't rest just yet—she needed to stay on high alert.

Arryn ascended to the next floor, entering the tower where

Adrien's office had been. Following Elon's directions, she found the secret door. The pupils of her eyes turned green as the corneas clouded with darkness. She focused her mind as she pulled water from the damp night air and placed her hand against the magitech lock.

She pushed the water inside and froze it, droplets expanding beyond what the lock could accommodate and drastic temperatures shorting the magitech core. The entire lock broke apart as she turned her hand, pulled it free, and quietly dropped it to the floor.

Arryn quickly looked over her shoulder, checking the area make sure she was still alone. Satisfied, she opened the door and made her way down a set of stairs, magitech lighting switching on as she passed each sconce.

Arryn soon came to a massive room capable of holding dozens of people. It was dimly lit, and its rich dark colors made the room feel creepy and cold.

Her eyes wandered around the room, taking in everything. If nothing else, Amelia would be able to examine her thoughts to find out what she had seen.

Chains hung from the ceiling, and there was blood crusted inside the cuffs that dangled from the bottom. Though its lively energy was long gone, Arryn was able to tell the blood had belonged to Amos, the first victim she'd had contact with.

On further search, she found a large stain on the floor not far from the cuffs. A thick, loadbearing pole stood almost in the middle of the room, and at the bottom on the hardwood floor was a massive black spot. Leaning down, she brushed it with her fingertips and knew that it, too, had belonged to Amos.

Anger clenched her throat as she stood and examined the room further. Across the room on a table against the wall, she found several jars. When she reached the table, she opened one of them, nose almost immediately assaulted by the scent of blood.

This is a room of death, she thought. She couldn't help but wonder how many people had died down here. She could only sense Amos' blood, but she knew what was in the jars was someone else's. She imagined several people had fallen victim to Talia in that room.

Arryn took one of the smaller jars and made her way back upstairs, satisfied that she wouldn't find anything personal of Talia's down there.

When she reached the door to Adrien's office, she carefully peeked to make sure no one was around. She'd been lucky so far, and she hoped her luck would continue.

Assuming she knew Talia, anything personal she had would be kept in Adrien's office. Not only because he was her father, but also because she would believe that no one would want to go into his office.

Even after his death, his office carried a certain level of respect and fear. Not even Amelia herself had wanted that office, and had avoided it at all costs. No other teacher, and especially no student, would dare nose around in there.

Her office, however, the office of a sweet, kind Dean, would not be off-limits and thus would be at risk from nosy people, including young Jackson.

No, if Arryn knew anything at all about her enemy, it was that she would hide her most important belongings in Adrien's office where no one would enter.

She searched the desk, knowing it more than likely held the very item she was looking for. The bottom right drawer was sealed with another magitech lock, but like the one on the entrance to the basement, it was no match for Arryn's skills.

Within moments, she pulled the drawer open and stared into the space, empty save for a single box. She pulled it free and saw the same designs she'd seen on a blueprint in the box of Adrien's things Amelia had given her. It was identical.

Unfortunately, Arryn didn't have the key, but she knew that if she took it to Elon he would be able to open it without one, or he would just make another one.

Arryn smiled as she clutched the box to her chest before closing the drawer and standing, crossing the room. She had what she came for and was confident that all the evidence she needed would be hidden inside.

Arryn had almost reached the door when she heard the handle move.

Shit! she thought, realizing at that moment that she hadn't kept her guard up. The one lesson Elysia and Cathillian had always reinforced for her, and she had failed! In her excitement, she had forgotten to sense for anyone who might be approaching or was already inside.

She realized that she was at the highest point of the building when she looked out the window. If her magic failed when she fell out the window this time, she more than likely wouldn't survive the fall.

Planning wouldn't matter anyway, because she'd run out of time. The door was opening right at that moment, so Arryn decided to fight instead of hide.

Once the door was wide, another student, Leon, stepped inside, and he smiled as he locked eyes with Arryn.

"Wow, I'm surprised it took you this long. We've been waiting for you to show up, though we figured it would've been a lot sooner than now," Leon told her.

Arryn smiled sarcastically. "Well, I'm all for surprises. I feel like it really makes a person feel special to get the unexpected. For instance, I'm going to kill you, so *if* you happened to survive, it would be totally unexpected and seem like a *real* treat, now wouldn't it?"

He shook his head, his smile never fading as he took another step and shut the door behind him. "Are you always so incessantly sarcastic?"

Arryn shrugged. "I really feel like a good sense of humor is the key to any situation, even bad ones. Take yours, for instance."

"My situation? I think you should probably be worrying more about yours. We have more power than ever thanks to Talia and Scarlett. With their help, we've been able to use the blood of others to grow and complete ourselves. We're unstoppable, and once you're gone, we're going to restore the city to the way it was, the way it should be."

Arryn looked at him incredulously. "See what I'm talking about, Leon? You clearly have a wild sense of humor if you believe any of that crap you just spouted. And you have no more power now than you did the day you met Talia. I don't know if you've been bathing in the blood or drinking it or what the hell you been doing, but I promise you it doesn't work that way."

He laughed. "Well, I think you'll come to understand once I show you just how strong I am. You're not walking out of here alive."

"Funny, because I sure as hell didn't plan to *walk* out of here *dead*. Obviously, because I mean, how would that even be possible? Am I right? Who even came up with that saying? He was an idiot, and you're another one for using it. I'm bored—you're boring. Did I mention that I have attention issues?"

While stalling, Arryn sensed that he was the only one present just then. No one was in the halls, and no one was below them outside, though she couldn't tell if anyone was on the lower floors.

If she wanted to get out, the best way to do it would be to go out the window.

Leon looked at her in confusion. He'd obviously expected her to quiver in fear at his presence, but she hadn't given him what he'd sought. "Okay, I'm done stalling now. You don't have any friends around, so let's get this over with. I have shit I need to do, like take down that bitch friend of yours."

"Stalling?" He seemed angry, his entire body going rigid as his fists clenched. When he realized he'd been had and she hadn't even touched him, his face grew angrier.

He threw his arms straight out, creating a blast of telekinetic energy that sent Arryn backward toward the wall. She managed to tumble in mid-air so her feet hit first, forcing her into a crouch on the wall before she pushed off, somersaulted across the floor, and rolled to her feet.

She smiled. "My turn!"

Echoing his own move, she threw her arms straight out, creating her own blast of energy to send him backward into the door. Leon wasn't nearly as agile as she was, slamming hard against the wood and grunting.

Releasing her energy, her eyes turned black as she arced her hands over her chest and created two fireballs. Just as she was about to throw them, she saw his hand move, but didn't see the object until it was too late.

The jar of blood she'd brought from the basement smashed into her face, breaking on contact, and shards of glass sliced her face and embedded themselves into her eyes. Completely unable to see, she couldn't brace for his attack.

His fists slammed into the side of her head, easily taking her to the ground because of the amount of pain she was already in. Wrapping her hair in his fingers, he slammed his knee into her face several times before dropping her head to the floor.

"You know, I helped with the setup. It wasn't difficult. We already had the murders in place, and Talia had been to the Madlands. The remnant are under our control, the Chancellor is under our control, the entire fucking *city* is under our control, and you want to say that Talia hasn't given us more power? That we aren't more powerful?" He laughed as he stepped in front of her. "You're about to understand just how wrong you are, and I can't wait to see what I get for delivering your fucking head to Talia."

Arryn was completely blind, since the little bastard had

fought dirty. Not just dirty, but *dirty dirty*. She was covered in her own blood as well as someone else's, someone innocent whom she should've been able to protect.

The very thought of that pissed her off more than she could have imagined. Arryn used her power to sense around her, pinpointing her position in relation to the rest of the room. By her calculations, the window was somewhere behind her target.

His hand once again wrapped around her hair as he snapped her head back, the angle causing incredible pain in her neck and head. But instead of giving him the satisfaction of knowing he was causing her any discomfort at all, she smiled.

"You know, I think there might be something to this blood thing. I suddenly feel very powerful," she told him, hoping to invoke even the slightest bit of fear in him.

At that moment, she called on all her rage to save her as she thrust her hands into his chest, her magic blasting in all directions. Arryn was thrown backwards, her body smashing into the desk before flying backwards over it and into the wall.

There'd been an explosion across the room, and she could feel air coming in from outside, though she had no way of knowing what had happened to her opponent.

Taking a deep breath, Arryn used a little of what was left of her energy as she covered her face with her hands, making sure to keep her eyes opened as she slowly and carefully pulled her hands away. She used her nature magic to sense her own anatomy and physical magic to pull anything that didn't belong there from flesh and eyes.

She blinked, sighing in relief since the broken glass was removed. She once again covered her face as she used her magic to heal herself, wiping the blood from her eyes as she did.

Everything was cloudy at first when she opened them, but it quickly cleared and she took in the damage. Her body had somehow smashed the desk in half before landing on the floor behind it. She had no idea how she hadn't crushed her spine, but it was something she certainly didn't take lightly.

Across the room, the entire wall and a good portion of the floor were missing, flames licking the wood where she'd used both telekinesis and a large amount of fire to blow her attacker into oblivion.

She couldn't help but wonder if Leon actually made it outside and onto the ground below, or if he'd disintegrated in the blast.

Either way, she didn't give a damn. All that mattered was that he had been a cold-blooded killer and now he was dead. He'd never hurt anyone else.

Arryn could hardly move as she searched for the box. She sighed as she found the object she'd literally gone through hell to find to her left. Feeling unconsciousness approaching, she scooted across the floor and grabbed the box, pulling it to her.

Footsteps sounded inside the room, and Arryn's entire body stiffened as her eyes widened.

"Arryn!" Cathillian's voice called to her over the roar of the flames.

She sighed in relief, thanking the Matriarch that it was her friend and not another enemy.

"Over here," she croaked.

"Celine is causing a distraction," Cathillian said. "Come on, I have vines ready to lower us to the ground. Pretty sure everyone's gonna know it was you, though. So much for subtlety."

Arryn smiled, her head falling back as he lifted her into his arms. She took a breath, willing the words to come. "Well, you know me—I like to make an entrance. Or in this case, an exit."

Wrapping her arm around the box, Arryn fainted.

CHAPTER TWENTY-FOUR

E lysia stood in the trees, overlooking the barrier to the other side. A *Schatten* shadow warrior had retrieved her and told her what had happened.

Ever since the battle training, Elysia and the Chieftain had ordered the *Schatten* to fan out around the border, hide in the trees, and watch for anything out of the ordinary. They were to stay well inside the border so as not to be seen, heard, or sensed, and they were not to engage unless attempts were made to cross the border.

Even with her precautions, somehow the dark druids had been stealthier than the shadow warriors had been able to detect.

As Elysia looked down at body after body, she imagined the hundreds of animals that had been sacrificed for this incursion. Deer, raccoons, birds, and everything in between surrounded the Dark Forest border.

The tree she stood in began to creak, and she looked down to see her father using a root to elevate himself to the branch his daughter stood on.

"I don't understand," Elysia murmured, looking at the lifeless bodies decaying around their walls. "Ryel said the other walls weren't as heavily affected. It seems the southern wall is the worst, but they strung the dead out around our entire perimeter."

"I can't pretend to understand what's going on here," the Chieftain muttered. "And while I don't like admitting it, at this point I can't help but believe they are more than capable of coming through our barriers. They can apparently come in anytime they want, so I'm not sure why they're waiting."

Elysia shook her head, unable to take her eyes away from the beautiful buck on the other side. He was one of the biggest deer she'd ever seen. It was early spring and there had been many births in the forest, but not even the young had been spared in their latest assault.

"I'm beginning to wonder if this has anything to do with Arryn and Cathillian," Elysia mused.

The Chieftain turned to look at her quizzically. "Why would you think that?"

Elysia took several steps back, leaning against the tree trunk before sliding down to sit on the thick branch. A small squirrel ran onto her shoulder and hid inside her cloak. Smiling, she took a moment to pull him free and cradled him in her hands, gently stroking the side of his face with the pad of her thumb.

She could sense the fear in the little one, and she took a moment to push her magic, reassuring him that as long as he remained in the Dark Forest, they would keep him safe. Within moments, the little guy had curled into a ball in her hands and closed his eyes, falling asleep.

The Chieftain never said a word as he watched their interaction, giving Elysia a few moments to rest her mind and reassure herself as well as her new little friend.

Finally, he spoke. "Why do you think this concerns Cathillian and Arryn?"

"None of it started until they left. When Cathillian sent word, he told me that Jenna had shown up at the Arcadian gate and killed several guards. She's lost. Whatever redeemable qualities she may have had are gone. There is no saving her now that she has taken innocent life."

"They're safe though, right?" the Chieftain asked. " I hope Jenna hasn't made any more moves."

Elysia shook her head. "That's all he said. He said he tried to stop her, but she fled. He didn't give any more detail than that, but I feel like I'm missing a large piece of the story. Still, I can't exactly leave to hunt them down and find out what's going on, not with our own borders being threatened so often. I have no choice but to believe him and trust they're safe."

The Chieftain nodded. "They are safe there. If anything terrible were to happen, they know where we are. They would send Echo for help if they needed it. And while I couldn't invest myself in a war against Adrien because of how much we stood to lose, nothing would stand in my way if we had to go to Arcadia now. I would move the very heavens to save them and any who stood with them. You should trust them. They know what they're doing."

Elysia nodded. "I suppose you're right, but I can't seem to shake this feeling. It's like a black cloud is hanging over all of us, like death and doom are in the air, breathing down on all of us. I'm afraid for them. I don't think it's limited to us here; I feel it for Cat and Arryn, too. Jenna wouldn't have stopped at Arcadia for no reason. There's a message there."

The Chieftain laughed. "Are you blind? Have you seen my grandson? He's the spitting image of his grandfather! The ladies love him."

Elysia laughed, far harder than she meant to. "Is that so? He apparently got his narcissism from you."

"That he did. But Jenna always seemed jealous of Arryn. I don't think it was limited to the fact that Arryn showed more promise both magically and physically. I think it was because of how close she and Cathillian were."

"Cathillian never liked Jenna. Even as a child, he only had eyes for Arryn. I'm no fool... I've seen how the other girls look at him. We raised our children to be confident, forward, and never to back down from something they wanted. Cathillian is no stranger to women, but he's never shown much *real* interest in anyone except Arryn. Jenna was always jealous of that.

"I kept my mouth shut because I hoped she would use it as fuel make herself better and stronger. The need to impress someone else, while annoying when they don't notice you, certainly goes a long way when you're doing things to make yourself stronger."

The Chieftain shook his head. "No, it only made her angrier. She worked so hard to try to get his attention, and failed at every turn. Arryn worked, too, but it wasn't for Cathillian's attention. It was for honor. Because Arryn never cared about love or *other* things, Jenna hated her for the way Cat took to her. She never saw how hard Arryn worked when she wasn't around Cathillian. She busted her ass every session and between them until she got the hang of whatever it was she was being taught to do. Cathillian always took notice of that."

He leapt to the branch Elysia sat on and knelt in front of her. "Like his mother, he admires strength. The day Arryn came here, she had just lost everything, but she'd still fought her way through a dangerous forest to come to us. Arryn is a survivor, and he's always been drawn to that. I don't know if your gut is right. I don't know if the same cloud that hangs over us hangs over them, but I do know they are strong."

"If I'm right, we need to keep them from the Dark Forest as long as possible. If Jenna is trying to lure Cathillian back, then we need to make sure they believe everything is safe here. That's why I lied when I sent Echo back. I wrote that everything was fine here, but that I would heed the warning. I'm just grateful that Echo didn't witness anything like this." She gestured with her free hand over the border to the sacrifices. "Jenna and Aeris are after something, and somehow Aeris has the most control. I have a feeling that if Arryn and Cathillian come back, war *will* find us."

The Chieftain reached out, placing his hand on his daughter's knee. "I trust your judgment, and we will do what we can to keep them away. When the time comes, when the children come back to us, if war does find us, we will meet it as we have done everything else. As a family."

Elysia shook her head. "I can't lose Cathillian like I lost his father. I can't do that. I don't care how long I have to deal with the crude warnings. I will do all I can to keep Cat and Arryn away from the Forest, and I will find a way to end Aeris myself."

TALIA WAS PLEASED. Things had escalated quickly. After Arryn had escaped from jail, hid out for a few days before breaking into the school, killed another student, and blown the entire side of the tower away, her fate had been sealed. Even with the evidence in the box she had managed to steal, there was no way anyone would believe her.

Now, all that was left to do was to seal the fate of the entire city. It was necessary for Amelia to die, and Talia to be recognized as the hero. The further into the game she got, the more Talia saw the allure of power. She finally understood what Scarlett had been talking about.

At some point, her motives had turned from simple revenge to creating a legacy. The city would be hers.

As expected, Scarlett made her way into Talia's office. She had a large smile on her face as she sauntered across the room and sat on the front of Talia's desk, crossing her legs.

"So, when should I have your crown made?" Scarlett asked, playfully running her finger across the smooth wood of the desk. "And how should I present it?"

Talia sighed, pausing in the task of writing a letter. "Do you ever stop?"

Scarlett shrugged. "I keep hoping you'll come around, but you're such a prude." She winked.

"I assure you that I'm no prude. I just strongly doubt you could handle my interests. As for the metaphorical crown, it's almost time." She folded the letter and placed it in an envelope, sealing it with wax. "I'm sending this with you. The remnant won't eat you alive if they know what's good for them, and I know you understand that you have to ride there as fast as possible. If you get there quickly enough, in a day's time we could have ourselves a celebration. I even put in an order with a rearick for a barrel of mystics' brew for the occasion."

Scarlett took the letter, letting her fingers brush Talia's as she did. "Is this what I think it is? The grand finale?"

Talia smiled. "It most certainly is. You deliver that and the remnant will come and take the city."

Scarlett nodded slowly, turning the envelope over in her fingers. "You *do* know the remnant can't read… right?"

There was a pause as both women stared at one another. Talia felt a little embarrassed at the mishap, but she didn't plan to let Scarlett know that.

"Exactly. Which is why *you're* going to read it to them. I don't trust you to tell them word for word what I need said. There… It's all written down and nicely packaged for you so it can't be fucked up."

Scarlett nodded again. "Mmmhmm. If you say so."

Rolling her eyes, Talia said, "Anyway—back to business. The Guard will fall for the most part, and I will do my best to help them. Amelia will be pulled in too many directions. It'll be my time to really shine, to solidify myself as the better leader, especially when I turn on the remnant and kill them myself."

Scarlett inspected the envelope for a moment and leaned across the desk. "How many do you think you'll need? We have a large army, but they're idiots. Have you seen them? If one of them so much as passes gas, they fall over." She rolled her eyes as she further laid across Talia's desk, her face only a few inches from the Dean's. "It's rather pathetic."

"You'll see. It's all there in the letter. They have numbers, so I asked for no less than a couple hundred remnant. They should be excited—this is the war they've been waiting for. I need few enough that we can rebuff them, but enough that we lose half or more of our army. Amelia will absolutely need to die. Of course, I'm certain you can be of help there. Amelia won't stand down from the battle. She *will* fight. All you have to do is overwhelm her so she blanks out for a few moments. That should be enough time for some remnant to run her through."

Scarlett nodded. "What about Arryn? We both know she's hiding out somewhere, and she's going to come back with a vengeance. Two days is more than enough time for her to rest. As long as she doesn't have any other heroics planned, she'll be charged and ready to go for the battle."

Talia smiled, the very darkness of it seeming to chill the room as she leaned closer to Scarlett, pressing the tip of her nose against the mystic's. "That's the best part. I've already discussed this with the other teachers. If Arryn comes—and she will—I want you to lure her away from the crowd. Once she is out of sight, we'll take her out. I think chilling out in the Frozen North would do her some good."

Scarlett swallowed hard, her eyes locked on Talia's. "The... The North?"

"Mmmhmm," Talia murmured. "Yep. I want her to suffer. Killing her is too fast. I want it to be slow and painful. We take her down, bleed her out a little so she wears herself out healing, then take her north and drop her in the frozen wasteland. She'll have no clothing, no supplies. Using magic will only weaken her further. Even if she manages to warm herself enough to stay alive, she'll start to die.

"Not even nature magic would allow her to grow food there. Well, not at her level, anyway. She'll either freeze to death or starve. Either way, she'll be gone, and will have had a lot of time to wonder exactly what's happening here in her city. Her last moments on Irth will be filled with worry, desperation, and an *extreme* sense of failure."

Talia pulled back quickly, tapping her desk once before standing and pointing at the letter in Scarlett's hand. "See to it that gets delivered tonight."

Scarlett grumbled a bit as she reluctantly stood and walked out of the room. Just before crossing the threshold, she looked back and said, "You're a real tease, you know that?"

Talia only waved her away.

HAVING BEEN LARGELY invisible to everyone else, Celine was the best choice to send toward the Capitol building. The only person who had seen her and knew her identity was Amelia. The rest of the city wouldn't care less and had long forgotten her relation to Elayne, Christopher, and Arryn.

When she arrived at the Capitol building, she saw several men working to clear the area that had been blown apart. The death toll stood at ten now. Several bodies had been pulled free that night, but it had taken clearing to find more. It was a tragic loss, and one the city would not soon forget.

As Celine made her way to Amelia's office, she was surprised to see how largely unaffected this side of the building had been. It was incredibly obvious to anyone with a brain that it had been a setup. Someone had deliberately avoided attacking Amelia directly.

But because of Scarlett's involvement, the panic in the city was widespread and only getting worse. She had only needed to affect the first group. After that, the misinformation was securely sown, and each of those people spread it like wildfire.

Celine didn't know a lot about mental magic, but she knew enough to understand that all Scarlett had to do was come into contact with someone for a suggestion to be planted in their mind that would solidify the allegations against Arryn.

Amelia's role was once again being called into question as a result of Scarlett's machinations. It was obvious to everyone in Girard's house that Amelia's life was in danger, but she was desperate to restore her reputation with the people.

Arryn's escape had made Amelia look suspicious. The city was quickly coming to believe that Amelia had released Arryn under the guise of an escape, and they thought she was no longer fit for her position.

It was only a matter of time before Talia would be able to fully take power.

Celine's job now was to convince Amelia to keep herself safe while they made a plan to rescue the city. A dead Amelia would do no one any good.

"Celine! Please close the door," Amelia quickly exclaimed.

The woman did as instructed before turning back to the Chancellor and crossing the room. "I'm sorry to bother you, Chancellor, but as I'm sure you're aware, this is rather pressing."

Amelia's expression softened, her shoulders falling a little. "How is she? How's Arryn?"

Celine nodded. "She's fine. She nearly died in that last fight, but she held it together until we got there. Cathillian and Samuel pulled her out of the building, and we got her home in time to heal her. All of us have been on the run since."

Amelia gestured to Celine with an open hand. "Not all of you, it would seem. I'm glad that at least one of you can walk freely in the city."

"That's why I'm here. With me being the only voice for us, I had to talk to you immediately. During the fight that Arryn was in, that student told her they had control of the remnant. I wish there was a better way for me to tell you, but there's no time. You know there was a recent attack on Cella. The only logical path to take now is to attack Arcadia."

Amelia sighed, dropping into her chair. "Logical indeed. *Fuck*. If I was that heinous bitch, that's what I'd do, too. The city is weaker now than it ever has been, even after Adrien first lost control. We are on our way back, but if the remnant attack, the city will fall. We haven't had enough time to fully train the Guard, although because of Arryn, Cathillian, and Samuel's training, they are better prepared now than we could've hoped before."

Celine nodded again. "You have done all you can here. We know you want to stay and find a way to save them, but you can't. You can try to snap those people out of their daze, but you have no idea what damage you will do to them in the long term. Mental magic is very tricky, and compulsion is something we don't know a lot about."

"Damn it!" Amelia exclaimed. "If Julianne were here, this wouldn't be a question. But there's no time to get messages to her in the south. Not now. She's taught me a lot, so I know that if I tried to break Scarlett's hold I might damage their minds. Even if I killed her, severing that bond could hurt them. I'd love to just get Arryn and overtake Talia and Scarlett. Do you know how easy it would be to just rush out there and kill them? Sure, it would be a fight. Hell, we might even die in the process, but we could do it."

Celine's expression turned thoughtful, sympathetic. "But you can't."

Amelia nodded. "Right. We can't. This is going to take strategy and a war. You guys have a plan?"

"One of the guards who is still loyal to Arryn told us that Scarlett rode out last night. The funny thing is, the guards at the gate don't recall seeing her. The only reason he remembered was because he was on his way for shift change and not close enough to be affected."

Amelia smiled. "She compelled them to forget. Or hell, maybe they never saw her in the first place. That means she's up to something. Do you think she's going to warn the remnant?"

"Samuel thinks that's possible. If she rides fast, we have a few days. Maybe more, maybe less, but we need to prepare. The thing is, Talia can't know we're preparing. We should stay in hiding, and you should, too. You can't stay here and risk your life. You're worth far more alive than dead and as you said, we need to make a plan. I think you should come with us, hide out with us."

Silence filled the room as Amelia's eyes stayed focused on Celine's. After several moments' thought, Amelia finally asked, "You said there are Guard who are still loyal to Arryn?"

Celine nodded. "It seems that the men she and Cathillian have been training are still capable of thinking for themselves. They know Arryn would never have done what's being said about her."

"Good. We're gonna need them. Them and anyone else they know for certain is still free of the mystic's influence. Tell Arryn to meet me where Doyle died. I want her and anyone she trusts there with her. I'll look into their heads and make sure we can trust them. I might not be as strong as Scarlett in the mystical arts but I am strong enough to see the abnormalities if there is any compulsion present. Talia and Scarlett have no idea where we took Doyle down, so it's a place Arryn and I both know, and we should all be safe there for now."

With those instructions, Celine said her goodbyes and excused herself. She had no idea what was about to happen, but she prayed Arryn knew what she was doing. She'd only just gotten her back, and she couldn't bear the thought of losing her again.

CHAPTER TWENTY-FIVE

Arryn stared at the large tree that had somehow survived the fire that had engulfed the house surrounding it. She remembered the day she and Cathillian had worked together to force the large group of Doyle and Adrien's loyalists into the open.

They'd essentially split the house with the tree, but the house had later been set on fire by a wayward fireball. Somehow, the tree still stood, and she imagined it had everything to do with the magic that had been used to create it.

The sound of horses' hooves filled the air, and Arryn turned to see Amelia and Marie riding toward them. It warmed her heart to have someone like Amelia on her side; she knew that together they could accomplish anything.

"Hello, everyone." Amelia dismounted. Looking at the group of nearly twenty men dressed in Arcadian armor, she stated, "I'm glad you could make it. There are more of you than I actually expected."

"Aye. We picked the best group. They seemed stronger than the rest. Not sure how those mental magicians work, but I imagine it's harder to do it to someone with a strong will," Samuel told her.

Amelia nodded. "For someone like Scarlett, it shouldn't be a big deal. However, because she's using magic on so many different people at once, she'd need to use a lot more to affect those with stronger personalities and will. Having said that, I do intend to verify that all of you are exactly who you say you are. I don't trust many people right now."

Much to Arryn's surprise, no one objected to Amelia's plan. While she trusted the men she had brought with her to be honest, she didn't expect them to be excited about someone delving into their mind. But they'd allowed it.

It took quite a while, but once Amelia was satisfied with the outcome, she pulled Arryn and Cathillian to the side. Celine and Samuel quickly followed.

"They're all clean," Amelia told them, "but a few of them definitely had their minds wiped at least once. I saw memories of Talia pulling a body into the new Boulevard park. Another one saw Scarlett heading down the street toward your old house. It seems she's been keeping a closer eye on everyone than we knew. While they retain those memories, they have no recollection of them. When I asked them about the incidents they had no idea what I was talking about, and I could tell they were being honest."

"What does that mean for them?" Arryn asked.

"I truly have no idea. I'm worried that it will take someone a lot stronger than me to undo the compulsions. It's going to be this way with everyone in the city at this point. Well, at the very least, the ones Scarlett has planted thoughts in. We can't just walk up to them and beat the thoughts out of their heads. We can't force them to accept reality. If we do, we could break them. We have to make sure we have solid proof of what Talia's been doing.

"When they see the proof and are confronted with truth, they'll decide which makes more sense, and they'll come around.

We can't simply tell them that Talia is the psychotic daughter of their past Chancellor and that Scarlett is an insane mystic. Not many people even understand how mystical magic works, let alone believing one of their own is a mystic."

Cathillian stepped forward. "I think we can all agree that our biggest obstacle right now is the possibility of a remnant invasion. If they come, the city will be overrun. None of us have a clue what Talia and Scarlett have planned. We have to assume they want to destroy everything, or why else would they use the remnant?"

Amelia shook her head. "Again, I have no idea. I don't understand why these kinds of people do anything that they do. The city is weak, so I suppose it is the perfect opportunity. What's the plan? Do we have one yet?"

"We sure do, lass. We're gonna use the guards as plants. We send them back in and have them spread word throughout the Guard of the potential remnant attack. We have to make sure the city knows," Samuel explained.

"That will cause widespread panic," Amelia mused. "Is that part of the plan?"

Arryn nodded. "Obviously, anything we do will have completely unpredictable effects. All we have are what-ifs and possibilities. We think that if we put the Guard on high alert and citizens begin finding out about the impending attack, everyone will look to you for support. If they are looking to you for support, your life should be safe. Talia cannot make a move against you if you are in power, or she'll lose."

"At that point," Cathillian added, "you should be able to move back to the city without worry. Give the Guard orders, tell them what they need to do. Make yourself a hero. Show the people that you are the one in control, and you are the one who's going to save our city. No one else. Do not let them turn to her for help."

Amelia sighed. "So basically, we're playing her game. We're

using widespread panic and manipulation tactics to put me in control of the city that I'm already in control of and make myself look good in front of the people?"

Arryn shrugged. "Unfortunately, that's the world she's created for us. Did you think I enjoyed trying to be friends with her for a few weeks while hiding my utter disdain? No! But we have to do what's necessary."

Amelia shook her head and smiled. "Oh, no, you misunderstand. I have no arguments, mostly because I have no better ideas. Everything you've said has made perfect sense, and your plan will help me save the city and its citizens and make sure that I don't lose control. I can't exactly dispute those objectives."

Cathillian nodded. "If everything works as we expect, Scarlett should arrive back in the city tonight. If she rode to the Madlands, we'll know it when she returns. At that point, we just need to keep ourselves out of sight until the shit goes down and the people need direction. We will position our men at the gate so we can enter without any problems."

Amelia took a deep breath and smiled. "Great! We have a few hours before we need to get the guards back to see if Scarlett does enter the city in the expected timeframe. I think we should use this time wisely."

Arryn smiled. "Battle training?"

Amelia nodded. "Yep. Battle training."

As EXPECTED, Scarlett rode back into the city that night just after sundown. Once again, the guards at the gate had no idea that she had passed through, which told Amelia's group that her trip had certainly been a sensitive one. That was enough evidence for them.

Amelia sent her guards in and set them on their path of

planting doubt in the minds of the other Guard. When someone asked the inevitable question "How do you know the remnant are coming?" they were to answer that Amelia had gotten word from Cella that it could happen. They were on orders to alert the rest of the Guard of an impending attack.

Some of the Guard would question things, in which case they would come looking for Amelia. Others would become worried and begin talking about it, some telling their loved ones who would then tell others, and soon the city would need answers. Plans. Reassurance.

And Amelia planned to deliver all of it.

Around four in the morning, Amelia snuck into the city, avoiding the Guard and making her way back to her house. She instructed one of the men who had been trained by the druids to stand guard in her home, making certain no one came inside.

Not surprisingly, when Amelia arrived home, she found a dead student in her living room and char marks on the couch.

"I don't know if you noticed, but you made a bit of a mess of my living room," Amelia joked as she stepped into the room.

While a dead body on the floor was nothing to joke about, she could tell by looking at her friend that he needed to release some tension.

The moment she had walked in the door, she'd seen the look on his face and looked into his mind.

When the student came through the door, the Guard was ready, sword out. The student became enraged at seeing the Guard instead of Amelia, and began throwing fireballs. The first hit the Guard in the chest, but his armor protected him. The second hit her couch, and once he had ended the student's threat, he was quick to take care of the flames.

The Guard opened his mouth to explain, but Amelia put her hand up to quiet him. "Don't worry about it. I looked into your head the moment I saw your face. I know what happened. Thank you. Had you not been here, this man would possibly have killed me."

Confusion fell across the man's face, and he shook his head. "I don't understand. It seems counterproductive to kill you like this."

"What do you mean?" Amelia asked.

"Well, think about it. If you're killed in your own home and Talia tries to take over the city, it's gonna be obvious what happened. Maybe he wasn't planning to kill you. Don't take me wrong, he certainly wasn't here for anything good. His face showed hatred and he started throwing fireballs before he even asked any questions. He didn't mean you any good, but I don't think he was here to kill you."

Amelia nodded, her expression turning thoughtful. "Good to know. Now, if things go well—"

"They are," he interrupted. "In fact, everything is going a little bit too close to our plan. We're all kind of waiting for the other shoe to drop. The guards outside our group are freaking out. There was a lot of arguing in the barracks tonight when they were informed about the remnant. Some didn't believe it, and others were ready to march toward the Madlands right then."

"Good. Soon, they'll come to me for orders." Amelia sighed, momentarily placing her hands on the sides of her face as she shook her head. Dropping them back down, she told him, "We have to be ready. And when things really start to go down, we need to make sure Arryn is on that wall protecting the city. She needs to be seen."

The Guard nodded his head once. "Understood."

It wasn't much later when they heard loud voices coming down the street just before the pounding on her door started. Looking outside, they could see it was a mix of the Guard and citizens, all of whom wanted answers.

Amelia turned to him and smiled. "Here we go."

SEVERAL OF ARRYN'S trusted Guard students found her outside the city in the tallest branches of one of the trees Cathillian had grown with his nature magic students—students who had been tossed aside during all of this, though it was obvious they still worked every day to grow the mighty oaks.

"Amelia is giving orders. Everything is falling into place," one of them reported.

Arryn quickly made her way down the tree with Cathillian close behind her. "We've been watching the east and we've seen a couple of scouts from the remnant, so this is definitely happening. If anything, we've learned something. They use scouts, and they are far more battle-conscious than we knew. This will be one hell of a fight."

The Guard paused, his eyes widening as he took in her words. "Did you engage?"

Cathillian shook his head. "If we engaged, they would know that we knew they were coming. Then they might try something subtler, and we could lose more men. Samuel says that if they believe we are completely unsuspecting, they will use their normal tactics. They will attack head-on with a horde, and we want that if we want to take out large numbers at once. They didn't get close enough to the city to warrant us giving our plan up."

The Guard nodded. "Understood. We know Amelia is giving orders to the rest of the Guard, but we need to know what you want us to do."

Arryn smiled. "I'm gonna need my staff, bow, and quiver from the house. You guys should get your bows and quivers as well. I want all of you on the eastern wall before the sun rises."

The men looked at one another, all of them nodding and smiling as they turned back to Arryn. "Yes, ma'am," their captain said.

The men headed back into the city. With their own men positioned at the gate, they would all be able to walk in and out freely. The shift change wouldn't happen until well after the sun broke over the horizon, which was more than plenty of time. By that point, Arryn felt certain the remnant would already be there.

CHAPTER TWENTY-SIX

"Archers, hold!" Arryn shouted.

Her voice was the only sound that could be heard other than the gentle shifting of feet and the slight creak of bows as they were pulled tight.

The early spring temperatures were still frigid in the mornings; Arryn could see her breath in the cold air. A light fog had descended upon the area that morning, creating the illusion that everything was calm. Peaceful.

But with the obvious threat of a remnant incursion, it was anything but.

Hundreds of guards stood ready on the ground and several more stood on the wall with Arryn, bows in hand, as she tried to remind herself to breathe.

The possibility of a remnant invasion of the city had become reality.

Thinking back on everything that had led her there, she realized that even with all the problems that lay below her, she was happy to be right where she was. Defending the city as she should be.

That morning, she had ditched her normal garb and wore

something in the black and red colors of the city, even using one of the Guard's cloaks to conceal her on the wall. Until the remnant came, she wanted to keep her face hidden from anyone who might cause her trouble.

As it was, no one cared too much about the archers on the wall. They believed their true strength lay with what was essentially their infantry.

Arryn stood on top of the wall that separated Arcadia from the rest of the world and stared outward into the fog as she tried to see anything coming their way.

"Hey, bitches," Arryn called, holding her bow tightly and taking aim at what seemed like nothingness. "How lucky are ya feeling today?"

She heard a laugh from one of her archers beside her. "Lucky enough not to fall off the wall and on my ass. Anything else, ask me later."

A smile crossed her face. "Fair enough. Let's just hope Cathillian doesn't get hit on by one of their chicks. They might be ugly, but Cathillian can't deny a girl that thinks he's prettier than she is."

They were getting closer; Arryn could feel it. Any moment, the remnant would shout to announce themselves and the battle would begin. Her anxiety began to climb as she began to silently pray to anyone who could hear her for the safety of her men and the safety of the city.

She couldn't see anything, which caused her fear to grow.

But just as Samuel and Ren had told her, there wasn't a person on that wall or inside those locked gates who needed to see the enemy first. The remnant always made themselves known. It was their primary tactic—strike fear into the hearts of their enemies, get under their skin, and then rip them apart.

But Arryn had no plans to let them win today, no plans to allow them to succeed.

Loud gravel-voiced screams ripped through the air, chilling

Arryn to the bone. She looked at the men beside her, only to see them glancing at one another with fear on their faces. They turned to Arryn for direction, afraid of what was about to happen.

She knew how they felt. It was up to her to be their backbone.

"Archers, aim!" Arryn ordered. She heard wings behind her before she saw the large golden eagle who was Cathillian's familiar fly overhead. "Echo, warn Cathillian that the remnant are here. Oh! And that the ladies will eat him alive, and not in the good way."

"Did ye hear that, laddies?" Ren asked. "Sounds like we're on the wrong side of the city."

Cathillian and Samuel shared a look just before Echo's screech pierced the skies.

"They're coming from the east," Cathillian stated. "We need to get on the ground and prepare. Arryn will have the eastern wall covered, but they'll need us at the gate."

As Cathillian and the rearick avoided running through a crowd on the ground, making their way across the wall toward Arryn, he sent Echo to point the other Guard toward the gates and along the walls.

Cathillian ran as fast as he could, knowing the rearick would catch up soon enough. As he got closer to Arryn, he heard the familiar sound of bowstrings snapping. The remnant cried out as arrow after arrow pierced them.

Before Cathillian had even reached her, he saw Arryn staring at the remnant, her eyes never leaving them and her face fierce. She looked strong, like she was built to lead in battle. She lowered her bow and stood before shouting, "Archers! Move south toward the gate!"

Arryn ran and her men followed, stopping every fifty feet or so to loose another barrage of arrows into the horde moving southeast toward the gate.

It was obvious that the remnant had had no idea the city had archers, which was why they had approached the eastern wall directly before moving south. It gave them the best opportunity for a sneak attack. Coming directly toward the south gate, they'd have been seen a long way off.

But they weren't prepared for Arryn.

As Arryn and her group stopped again and took aim, Cathillian turned and raised his hands, causing vines to shoot from the ground and snatch a dozen or more by the throat. He roughly yanked his hands downward, and the vines pulled the remnant to the ground, breaking their necks.

He couldn't summon so much magic very often, so he decided to only do it once more and to save the rest for the battle on the ground.

"Cathillian!" Arryn called. "Glad to see you join us."

They ran another seventy-five feet down the wall before Arryn stopped the group again and loosed another barrage of arrows. It seemed strange, but her tactic was working well and thinning them out as they charged toward the gate.

Her men weren't the best archers, but they were able to hit their targets. Whether it was in the legs, arms, or something vital in a few cases, their arrows found the enemy.

Once again, Cathillian used his magic to take out some of the horde. With more than a hundred and fifty of them, it was the largest group he'd ever heard of.

"What's the plan once they hit the front gates?" Cathillian shouted.

Arryn pointed toward the southern wall as they drew closer. Magicians stood on the walls raining fireballs down on the remnant.

"It looks like Amelia has already begun!" she shouted back.

Right then, a gust of wind blew through, pushing the hood of

Arryn's cloak back to reveal her face. A few Guard on the ground took notice and began shouting her name and pointed her out to the rest.

"It's her! It's the murderer. She's come back!" one of them shouted loudly enough for Cathillian to hear.

The moment he heard it, Cathillian became enraged. His hand whipped out to his side and a vine burst from the ground and snatched the man up to bring him face-to-face with Cathillian.

His eyes revealed just how angry it made him to see Arryn defending the city she'd dreamed of coming back to for so long, only to be treated so harshly.

"She's no murderer. She's defending the city. Defending *you*. In case you hadn't noticed, she managed to take out several of the remnant before they have even come around the front of the city. Why don't you spread *that*? Because she's about to be your fucking hero."

The man's eyes were wide, and Cathillian didn't give him a chance to respond before lowering him down far enough that the remaining drop wouldn't hurt him. At that point, the vines released him and dumped him on his ass, giving Cathillian a small amount of joy.

He ran hard to catch Arryn, the woman who was strong enough to put her life on the line to save the city after being framed for murder and ostracized. At that moment, he wished more than anything that her parents could see her. He knew they would be proud.

"ALL RIGHT, YA SKINNY LITTLE BASTARDS," Samuel shouted at the Guard as he made his way through. "Lots of ye are about ta get yer arses handed ta ye, but ye can prevent that if ye keep your eyes open and fight with yer head."

Samuel had never seen most of these men before, so he had

no idea what their skill level was, but he hoped it was higher than beginner. He watched the men glancing at one another before nodding and focusing on him.

"You're a rearick," one of them said. "I'm sure you've fought them before. What do we do?"

"Stay low. Stay outta the reach of their weapons, and go fer the legs. The legs might be big, but that's the weak spot. They use their upper body more than anythin'—it's why they prefer weapons. Make no mistake, they're fast and they're strong, but if ye keep yer eyes open ye'll survive ta tell the tale."

"Rearick must be pretty crafty to go against them, little as they are," one of the men told him. "Not to mention weird-looking."

Samuel laughed. "Ye'll find there's beauty in bein' short and ugly. Fer instance, that pretty face o' yers is gonna be the first thing they notice. I'm bettin' the remnant will find ye pretty appetizin'. If I was you, I'd rub some dirt on that face."

The smartass turned pale as he quickly ran to the side and began packing dirt all over him. The rest of the Guard laughed at their fellow soldier before it was cut off short by the scream of the remnant at their gates.

Samuel headed toward the front gate, motioning for the men to follow. There were already dozens of men waiting directly in front, but Samuel wanted to bring up more.

As he got closer, he saw Amelia standing on top of the wall, giving the orders for the magicians to fire. The sounds of explosions rang out from the other side of the wall as hellfire rained down on the remnant bastards.

"Brace for impact!" Amelia shouted just before twisting her body to the side and leaning back, narrowly avoiding a spear thrown in her direction.

It sounded like thunder hit the gate as the remnant crashed into it, but as Amelia had told them, the Guard on the other side were ready.

Again and again, the remnant bombarded the gate, the sound

of splintering wood echoing throughout the immediate area. Several magicians on the wall had been hit with spears, axes, and other weapons that could be used as projectiles, but Amelia continued to fight.

Arryn soon joined the fray with her archers, firing arrow after arrow.

"Hey, short and handsome," Cathillian said, finally making his way to the front lines. "How's it going up here?"

Samuel gestured back to the men behind him. "This lot likes ta think they're funny. Pickin' on a short, old man. I'll show 'em."

"That's not nice. Bastards."

"Thanks, lad. Appreciate it," Samuel responded with a nod.

"Yeah! No problem. Making fun of you is *my* job," Cathillian said, turning back a moment to size up the men. "Talk about lack of job security."

The wood began to crack, the sound echoing out around them. It wouldn't be long.

"Brace yerselves, lads!" Samuel shouted. "The remnant are coming."

"From what I've heard," Cathillian told him with a wink before looking back at the men, "that's not necessarily inaccurate. I hear they like to have *fun* with their new toys after all."

"Wh-what?" a scared Guard behind Samuel stuttered. "When you say *fun...*"

The rearick had heard him make nasty remarks about his people at some point or another. So, he was happy to have Cathillian's quick humor at his side right then.

Samuel pointedly looked the man up and down, raising his eyebrows. "*Yeesh.* Lad, I'd suggest maybe ye should rub some dirt on that face of yers, too. Better safe than sorry and all that."

Cathillian couldn't hold back his laughter, enjoying the rearick's ability to give people a hard time no matter what the situation.

AMELIA'S CHEST grew tight as she watched as the remnant succeeded in smashing through Arcadia's gate from her perch on the wall.

Her instinct told her to throw fireball after fireball, but at this point, her people were mixed with theirs. She couldn't risk hurting anyone, and using that much magic this early in the game was a bad idea anyway.

"I'm out of arrows," Arryn reported. "I'm out of arrows, and I'm not as good with the vines as Cathillian is. Mine are wimpy. Tell him that, and I'll smack you myself. I'm gonna have to get down on the ground."

Arryn turned to leave, but Amelia grabbed her by the wrist. "Can you call a storm like you did the last time? A few lightning bolts could thin out their ranks. Look!"

Amelia and Arryn both turned to the horde of remnant threatening the city. Arryn and her men had killed fifty or so, but there were still more than a hundred about to crash the gate.

"I can't call on magic that big without a surge of emotion—you know how it works. I might be angry right now, but I'm sure as hell not blindly raging. That, and I don't know if it would be wise to use that much magic this early," Arryn told her.

Amelia knew she was right, but she also knew Arryn was right about something she'd said a long time ago. The Guard wasn't ready, not for this. A dozen or so of the bastards, sure. Maybe even fifty. But there was no way in hell they would survive an onslaught by more than a hundred remnant, even with hundreds of their own men.

The city would fall.

"You're right," Amelia replied, "but we can't let them take the city. You know as well as I do—even *better* than I do—that the Guard aren't ready. You don't have to call it for long. Focus on the lives that are about to be lost. Use it. Think about the fact that

Talia and Scarlett are sitting somewhere safe right now, watching this unfold."

Judging by the look on Arryn's face, that was the nerve Amelia had needed to strike. With only a single nod, Arryn took a deep breath, her eyes now a vibrant green while the corneas had turned the deepest obsidian she had ever seen.

Arryn slowly gazed toward the horde, the wind suddenly whipping around her as she did. The thinning fog began to thicken as it rose into the sky, joining the other clouds that were turning black.

The remnant slowed their attack as they looked at the sky. It was the distraction that her people needed, but as she glanced around Amelia could see they were just as intrigued.

Arryn's arms were raised at her sides as lightning webbed across the sky. Rain began to fall both inside and out of the city—on their side, though it was an absolute downpour.

Amelia's eyes were wide as she watched the girl work. She could only imagine how much magic and strength Arryn was using right then, but it was working.

"Amelia!" Cathillian shouted.

THE MOMENT CATHILLIAN felt the wind, he knew what was happening. He could sense the change in air and the magic that was being used. He swung his sword relentlessly, slicing through remnant after remnant. Although he was covered in blood, both the enemies' and some of their own men's, he continued to fight.

He looked toward the wall and saw Amelia standing next to Arryn, who was casting with outstretched arms. It began to rain, but it was nothing like the deluge that was pouring down on the other side of the gates.

As he saw the lightning snake across the sky, he knew what was about to happen.

"Amelia!" Cathillian shouted.

Amelia looked down, her eyes meeting his.

"She's too strong, and her aim is bad! She can't control the direction of lightning! It's raining over here, too. If she calls down lightning, it could fry everyone!" Cathillian yelled before tearing into another remnant who had run for him.

He kicked the remnant's chest hard, sending him backward before swiping upward with his sword and effectively cutting the beast in two. There was a tap on his shoulder, and he turned to attack, but it was Amelia. She'd climbed down from the wall.

"Use your magic to blow everyone outside the gate back. I'll put up a shield. Whatever remnant are inside will be protected, too, but we can't help it. I didn't expect her to conjure anything that big."

Cathillian laughed. "Have you *met* her? She doesn't do anything small." He rolled his eyes. "I hate serious moments. I keep missing out on good jokes. That was prime opportunity. Look... She's strong, but she doesn't have the skill to control it yet. She can't help herself—it's all or nothing. She's winding up right now, but I should be able to help guide her. I'm going to the wall, so get your shield ready."

A limb from a nearby tree broke free to lift Cathillian onto the wall. He could sense the shift in Arryn's magic as the lightning increased.

Cathillian's eyes turned dark green as he brought his arms out to the side, focusing on the remnant below. He thrust his hands forward, and a large gust of wind threw them back several feet.

Pulling his arms back, he hit them with another blast, making sure they were far away from the gate.

Grabbing Arryn's hand, Cathillian allowed her to lead. He helped guide her magic as they reached to the sky. As they did, lightning rained down into the field before the gates.

The plan was working, but not as well as Amelia had hoped.

By that point Arryn's magic had already begun to weaken and

as a result, the lightning was weak as well. Judging by the number of bodies on the ground, Cathillian calculated that about half of them had been killed, but the rest were once again running at the gates.

He shook Arryn, and her eyes quickly faded to their normal dark brown. "Are you okay?" he asked.

She nodded. "A little weak. I didn't mean to go that hard."

Cathillian smiled. "I'm gonna let that go because we're in the middle of the battle and you need healing. Dammit, I let one of Amelia's go, too. I don't like war. It makes my jokes inappropriate."

"Your jokes are *always* inappropriate." Arryn snorted. "Now, hurry up and heal me. We have to get down to the ground."

ARRYN WANTED to jump down outside the wall and run straight into the horde more than anything, but she knew it would be a bad idea. She was glad she'd been able to take out as many as she had, though she regretted using that much magic that early. Even after being healed by Cathillian, she could still feel the fatigue pressing down on her.

But that didn't stop her from swinging her staff with fury.

The battle had begun to fan out through the city, which allowed everyone to move more freely. It also meant that more remnant were able to enter through the gate now that it wasn't so congested.

Someone on the wall began screaming that a second horde was approaching, though it was much smaller than the first, around fifty or so.

It was obvious at that moment that had Arryn had not taken the measures she did, the city would have been overrun in minutes. While they were still in danger of falling, they also stood a chance at surviving.

When a large group attacked her, she used only enough magic to blow them backward, allowing her to take them down with her staff. It may not have been sharp, but it was stronger than any of their weapons, and it was more than capable of smashing skulls.

Arryn heard a loud scream, and she turned to see two remnant dragging a woman into an alley. Arryn growled as she ran, staff in one hand and newly crafted fireball in the other. As soon as she was concealed in the alley, she threw the fireball at one while striking the other in the head before kicking him backward.

She looked up, ready to help the woman to safety, but immediately regretted her actions. It was not a helpless woman she saw, but the smiling face of Scarlett. Behind her were several people with confident expressions and a few remnant, and Arryn turned to see even more remnant piling into the alley.

"Fuck—me." Arryn sighed, shaking her head.

Scarlett's laugh echoed through the alley. "I would *love* to, gorgeous, but I don't think we have enough time, and Talia might get mad at me. She's never been respectful of my... *needs*."

Arryn turned to Scarlett. "Judging by the excited look on your face, I'm gonna go out on a limb and say these remnant are yours."

"You have no idea how right you are about that. So, are you ready to have some fun?" Scarlett asked, her expression growing even more excited.

Without warning, Arryn spun backward, throwing her hands out as she did. Telekinetic energy exploded forward and pushed the remnant behind her out into the street. Arryn surrounded herself with a barrier before running toward the light.

While she was very confident of her abilities, she knew she'd made a mistake by weakening herself to the point that she had no hope of standing against so many magicians in such close quarters.

Before she made it into the open, the buzzing in her mind came back, and then it became painful. Sharp, searing agony shot through her brain, bringing her to her knees. She was unable even to scream as she clutched the side of her head.

Arryn was only vaguely aware of someone lifting her head, the pain easing just enough for her to see Scarlett nose to nose with her, smiling.

"I'm sorry. I didn't mean to give you the illusion that this meeting was voluntary. Attendance is mandatory, I'm afraid."

Scarlett got even closer, placing her lips by Arryn's ear. Arryn desperately wanted to move, but her body was useless. Scarlet had far too much power.

"Between us girls," Scarlett whispered, "it's really me who needs you out of the way. You distract Talia too much, and if she's to do what I need her to, you have to vanish. It's a shame, though. It would've been nice to have fun with you first. But Talia has plans, and for now, I need to entertain them."

Arryn swallowed, regaining only the smallest amount of control over her body. She tried to speak and failed, but Scarlett seemed to take notice. A fraction of the pain lifted again, allowing Arryn a bit more control over her mouth, but the rest of her body was still unable to move.

"It's been you all along." Arryn choked out.

Scarlett smiled again. "What can I say? We mystics are master illusionists. But it's time for you to go now. Good night!"

Pain once again tore through Arryn, her entire body tensing before she finally fell the rest of the way to the ground. The very last thing she saw before her eyes closed was Talia stepping into the alley with a smile on her face.

"Well done," Talia told Scarlett.

Scarlett's eyes never left Arryn's, allowing her to see the mystic wink one of her snow-white eyes in her direction. "Thanks, *boss.*"

And with that, unconsciousness took Arryn.

EPILOGUE

Cathillian found his way to Amelia, climbing over several bodies as he went. Luckily, most of them had been remnant, but several of their own had been lost as well.

At that moment, the Guard was busy piling up the remnant, readying them for transport out of the city where they could be burned.

"We did it!" Amelia cried, a triumphant smile on her beautiful face.

She was covered from head to toe in blood, but so were the rest of them. It would take quite a lot to clean up this mess and restore the city to order.

"We lost quite a few," Cathillian reported, "but we made it, mostly because of that plan of yours. It was dangerous to use her like that, but it turned out okay. If she hadn't been so weak by the time we called the lightning, she'd have killed us all, with or without that shield."

Amelia nodded, her eyes wide. "No shit. That's not a mistake I'll make again." She chewed on her lip. "We really need to work more with her. Damn, that girl has a lot of potential."

"Just a couple o' Chatty Cathies over here," Samuel remarked as he wandered up. "Ye act like we didn't just slaughter an army o' remnant. That's pretty normal fer the rearick, but yer people always seem weird after battle."

"Good point," Amelia shot back. "But we're happy! We survived! And we *didn't* lose a ton of men."

Samuel chuckled. "That's because of our girl. Speakin' of which, where is she? Last I saw her, she was headin' inta ground combat with Amelia."

Cathillian and Amelia looked around, seeing no sign of her anywhere.

"Arryn!" Cathillian shouted.

"Do you have enough strength to find her with magic?" Amelia asked, clearly worried.

Cathillian thought for a moment before nodding. He knelt and placed his hands on the ground, doing his best to sort everything out. Echo's call from overhead caught his attention.

He stood then, running toward her and jumping over bodies in the street to reach the area Echo was circling from overhead.

Striding into an alley, he saw that it looked largely untouched. It didn't seem to be affected as much as the rest of the city was, but he saw the bodies of several remnant lying on the ground just on the threshold of the street.

Farther in, he saw two puddles of blood.

Stepping over them, he knelt and placing his hands on the ground. He could tell it was Arryn's blood.

"She was here," he told them. "All this blood here is hers. There's no splashing or spattering, so there wasn't a fight. I'm going to guess she was unconscious when this happened, and they bled her out to weaken her."

He turned to see Amelia shaking her head, a look of terror on her face. "How can you be so calm? She could be *dead*! I'm getting the Hunters."

"No!" Cathillian warned. "You can't trust them, remember?

And believe me, this isn't enough blood to kill her. Not by a long shot."

"I don't care! I have to do something. I'm going to find a Hunter we can trust, then I'm going to go through the minds of anyone who fought in this area."

"Look around, lass," Samuel snapped. "Do ye see the Dean or the mystic anywhere? I don't know what the mystic looks like, but Talia is unmistakable. I ain't seen either. They took 'er."

"What do we do now?" Cathillian asked. "I can usually think of an answer for things, but this... I can't lose her."

Amelia took a deep breath, squaring her shoulders as she steeled herself. "I need to meditate like Julianne taught me. If they haven't gotten too far, I might be able to connect to her. It's possible I could see something through her eyes, make sure she's okay. Fair warning, though... I'm not that great. I'm a novice."

"If we can get even a hint of the direction they're traveling in, we can send Echo to scout after them," Cathillian offered.

"Sounds like this is the best plan we've got," Samuel confirmed.

"We'll find her," Amelia declared. "And when we do, we're not wasting any more time. We're ripping Talia's fucking head off."

ARRYN'S EYES fluttered open several times, and each time she caught a glimpse of some new surrounding before someone knocked her out again. She had no idea where she was or who she was with, though she was sure she'd seen Talia at least once.

What had happened? Had they won the war? The situation had looked promising last she remembered, when she came off the wall with Amelia just after having called the storm.

As Arryn slowly began to awaken again, she was painfully aware of the drastic temperature change. Her face felt as though it was burning from the cold.

She became aware of someone carrying her, someone warm she curled into as she fought the pain in her head. Even the throbbing behind her eyes and in her temples was nothing compared to what she'd felt when Scarlett had taken over her mind.

And there it was.

Her eyes snapped open as she remembered everything that had happened. Looking up, she saw that it was Jackson who had been carrying her.

"Well, good morning, sleepyhead." Talia's smooth, sing-song voice was both horribly loud and quiet at the same time.

Unsure how that was possible, Arryn pushed against Jackson, frantically looking around as she did. He set her down, and she toppled over into more than a foot of snow. Her eyes took in everything around her.

Talia's voice had seemed so loud because it was quiet there in the mountains of the Frozen North, and she'd seemed quiet because the sound had been absorbed by the thick snow and vast openness.

"Oh, hell," she muttered, fear in her voice. Not much scared Arryn, but at that moment she felt afraid.

She lifted her arms and threw them out in front of her, conjuring only enough power to shove Jackson back a few inches. As she stared at him, slack-jawed, she noticed the red-stained cloths that were wrapped tightly around her wrists.

"Oh, you don't want to move too quickly or forcefully, dear," Talia offered. "You'll tear open your stitches."

Arryn looked at her in confusion. "My stitches?"

"Well, we didn't want you waking up before you got to your new home, and we had to keep bleeding you along the way because, as it turns out, you have the ability to heal relatively fast even without actively calling your magic. I assume that's a druid thing?"

Arryn shook her head, unsure how to respond. "I... I don't understand."

Talia smiled as she leaned forward, her thick, black cloak fanning out over the untouched snow. "That's probably a side-effect of the blood loss. You're gonna be a little loopy for a while. I'll make things easy for you and explain."

There was a pause as Talia stood and walked over to Arryn, blocking the intense morning sun as she looked down at her.

"I need you out of my way if I'm going to accomplish what I want to. Killing you seemed like just letting you go. It would be too easy, so we decided it would be fun to bring you all the way up here." Talia motioned around her. "This is the Frozen North. Temperatures here are so cold that nothing can live. In other words, even if you waste your energy healing yourself—and it'll be at least a couple days before you can do that because your body will be fighting the cold—you'll end up starving to death.

"If you heal yourself enough to travel, you'll waste your energy. If you use enough magic to create food, you'll be forced to stay here because you'll be weak. If you create fire to keep warm, you'll be stuck here. Do you see a pattern? You're doomed, no matter what you do. You're going to die here. It's going to take a while, though, because you are one of those people who *refuse* to give up. You're going to use your hatred for me as fuel. But in the end... you'll die up here, cursing the day you shook my hand."

Arryn couldn't believe it. Talia hadn't only kidnapped her, she'd *really* gotten the best of her.

Talia and Jackson weren't the only ones present. There were several others from her group. She would have needed them to teleport as far as she had. They'd collectively used their powers to move Arryn north.

Memories of the other times she'd awakened started to come back. The random places. The random faces.

"How long have we been traveling?" Arryn asked.

"Three days," Talia replied. "We made it in six jumps. Every night we had to stop for food and rest and to make sure my *dearest* sister received proper care after the attack in Arcadia. Everyone was *so* concerned for you."

Arryn shook her head, her anger bringing with it a bit of comfort. She didn't feel quite so weak now that she was coming around to her situation.

"You bitch," Arryn spat.

Talia laughed, but it immediately cut off when she suddenly became excited about something. "Oh! I nearly forgot."

Reaching into her cloak, Talia pulled out the very box Arryn had risked her life to steal. Like the knife from Amelia's office, Talia had managed to find it and steal it back.

"Look familiar?" Talia asked.

Arryn nodded, enjoying feeling a bit more like herself. "Well, would ya look at that? It sure as shit does. You found my lockbox. Thanks! I've been searching all over for it. I can take it off your hands." Arryn completed her sarcastic remark by extending one of her weak arms as if she actually expected Talia to give it to her.

Talia shook her head and laughed. "You know, if you weren't completely against everything I stand for, I think I'd like you. You're quite funny."

Arryn snorted. "You should see me after having some of the Chieftain's wine. He makes it himself, the *drunkard*." She leaned forward, putting a hand next to her mouth as she quieted her voice for a moment. "He drinks too much with the young people because he says we think he's cool. Actually, if I'm honest, he *is* pretty cool."

Arryn laughed for a moment, leaning back and putting her weight on one hand in the snow like it was the most natural thing to do.

Never losing her smile, she said, "Hey, I have an idea! I'll bring you back some of his wine after I stop into the Dark Forest to grab an army of pissed-off, blood-thirsty druids on my way back to Arcadia. You'll *love* it. Really. It's *delicious*." Arryn placed her fingertips against her lips, kissing them before pulling them away and wiggling them in the air.

"One would assume you were drunk on it now," Talia told her, her voice reflecting slightly less amusement.

"Damn, I wish! You know, it's only been a few weeks since I arrived in the city, and I hadn't really expected to move again so soon. But you know? I think I like my new apartment. It's cozy, and it's a *lot* comfier here in the snow than in that lumpy-ass bed in my jail cell. Talk about bedhead! I looked *awful*! But from the looks of it, you know *exactly* what I'm talking about. Am I right?" Arryn smiled and pointed at Talia before motioning around her head at her hair.

Several of the group behind Talia had to stifle their laughter at Arryn's comments.

"That's enough," Talia snapped. "Even though I shouldn't because you're having *such* a good time here already, I'm going to show you something."

"Oh!" Arryn exclaimed excitedly. "I can't wait."

It was taking every ounce of energy she had to be a smartass, but once she saw how much it was getting to Talia, she couldn't hold back. It wasn't like she could attack her—

Or could she?

Arryn closed her eyes as she tilted her face up into the sky, acting as though she were enjoying the early rays of sunshine. It was colder than she'd ever felt before, but she shoved her hands down to the frozen dirt beneath the snow.

Cathillian had once told her that he could kind of recycle energy, using the naturally occurring energy in nature to pull into himself. Sure, it took power to pull it, but what was used was far less than pushing power out to heal.

He'd said that he could sense her ability to do it, but she'd never tried—until now.

It was slow at first, but after the first couple seconds, Arryn could feel a small amount of her energy returning.

"Did you pass out?" Arryn heard Talia's hard voice ask.

Arryn quickly pulled back, allowing her eyes to revert to their normal dark brown before opening them.

"No, but I wish I had. So, what did you want to show me?" Arryn asked.

Talia closed the box, a white envelope in her hand. "This is what you were after, I assume?"

She eyed the envelope. "Is that the letter Doyle delivered to you right around the time of the Battle for Arcadia?" Arryn asked.

Talia nodded.

"Then it is *indeed* what I was looking for. Again, I can take it off your hands. Really, it's no trouble."

Talia shook her head. "You're an idiot. What would you even do with it? You're stuck here, you...idiot."

"*Oooh*! Someone has a big vocabularyyy!" Arryn stretched out the last word, her voice soft and high-pitched as if she were talking to a baby.

Talia lifted her arm, rage on her face.

"Ah, ah, ah!" Arryn cautioned, wagging a finger in the air. "If you throw so much as a single fireball, you'll be stuck here with me. You need all your strength for jumping. I might not have the skill to do it, but I know how it works. You used a *lot* to get me here. Would you like me to tell you how we'll be spending our time if you stay?"

Talia growled. "No."

"Oh, but it's *super*-quick. Not gonna lie... It *also* sounds pretty fun. You see... You'll be spending your *grand* adventure here *dead*, and I'll be spending *my* time using your frozen corpse to sled down the side of the mountain." She put her hands in front of her, lifting and dropping them as if she had reins in her hand for emphasis.

"Have fun dying here in the wasteland," Talia said flatly,

turning as she placed the lockbox in one pocket and the letter in the other.

"Oh!" Arryn exclaimed. "I almost forgot! One more thing…"

"*What?*" Talia sighed as she turned, her eyes widening as she found Arryn standing behind her.

"This." Arryn threw her arm out and quickly yanked it back, causing Talia to hurl toward her by virtue of Arryn's telekinetic power.

Arryn spun out of the way just in time, punching Talia in the face and taking her down. They wrestled for a few moments before Talia grabbed Arryn's wrists. The wounds had closed, but hadn't yet fully healed, and Talia was easily able to jab her thumb through the stitches so that blood poured down her forearms.

Lashing out, Arryn quickly headbutted Talia in the face, who loosened her grip enough that Arryn could punch her one more time before rolling away. She needed to reserve her energy for what was to come.

She'd gotten what she was after.

"You crazy bitch!" Talia exclaimed as she stood, stumbling back to her group.

"*I'm* a crazy bitch? Fuck…" A confused expression crossed Arryn's face as she looked at the snow-covered ground before looking back at Talia. "What's that make you then?"

Talia stomped forward, but was quickly pulled back by the others. "You're going to die here. Alone. Freezing. Starving. I want you to think all about the people you left in Arcadia, because they're next. I'll kill them with my bare hands, and I'm going to watch their last breaths slowly escape them. Then… I'll go for the Dark Forest. I'll burn that motherfucker to the ground."

Arryn smiled—and judging by Talia's expression, it was not the response she'd expected.

"Good luck with *that*," Arryn said, amused. Talia shook her head, stepping back into line with her terrible friends. "I'll be seeing you *very* soon. When I do, I won't be alone. Promise." Arryn winked, and the group vanished in an explosion of magic.

It would take a few minutes before she could draw enough energy to stand, but she was confident that she could.

Reaching into her cloak, Arryn removed the letter Talia had shown her. "What an idiot," Arryn remarked out loud to herself as she opened the letter to find it addressed to *T* and signed by *A*.

It wasn't exactly proof, but it would go a long way toward doing what she needed it to. She just hoped her friends had been smart enough to continue their work on the city and would keep everyone else safe. She could take care of herself.

After about ten minutes, Arryn put her hands back in the snow and healed herself a bit more. Though it used less energy than a normal healing, it still used far more than she could risk, but it closed the wounds on her wrists and would allow her to stand. That was all she needed.

Tucking the letter away in her cloak pocket, Arryn stood and looked around, finding the south side of the mountain using the sun. Once she did, she took her first unsteady steps.

I don't *give up that easily, Talia. And I'm coming for you.* She took a few more steps, her eyes flashing.

I'm coming for ALL of you.

FINIS

AUTHOR NOTES - CANDY CRUM
WRITTEN AUGUST 8TH, 2017

Wow! Book two is now in the hands of JIT, and I can't believe it. Tomorrow is both release day for The Undying Illusionist as well as my boys' first day of school.

Brandon will be in sixth grade. And that will be in the 6th Grade Center—which is in this weird "in between", year-long purgatory between elementary and middle school. It's super weird and something I've never experienced, but from the sound of it, I think it will do him some good to have a transition!

Matt will be in fourth grade. I'm shaking my head right now thinking about these things! Unbelievable.

So, to celebrate all these new beginnings, we had quite a day. We spent the day with family—and my grandmother is hilarious, so it was great—and then we went to go see Spider-Man: Homecoming.

At the risk of gaining/keeping/losing some of you... I loved it! It was amazing. No pun intended (actually, yes... pun intended). I highly recommend it if you haven't seen it.

The last few weeks have been pretty crazy. A lot of driving. A lot of family time due to some unfortunate circumstances (which are A-OK now!). A lot of playing catchup on this fun book. It's been a long ride for a couple weeks, and I'm so happy to have all of you here with me.

I thank you guys all the time, but I'm going to do it again. Since this is book two, I can officially talk about what the KGU has done for me.

Blown my damn mind.

I saw review after review come in, and each one gave me that weird feeling you get when you can't decide if you want to jump for joy, or throw up because it's so awesome you can't handle it.

Actually... Now that I said it... I am pretty sure those are the same thing. Ha!

But seriously—It's been unreal, and I LOVE seeing those reviews coming in. I love seeing those comments coming in on posts on the Age of Magic fan page. I read them all, and I actually took some of them into consideration (the ones that offered suggestions) and put them into this book!

So, if you left a suggestion and you find it weird that the change miraculously appeared in this book...

Now you know why!

Also... I wanted to share a bit of a family story. One that I actually used as inspiration for a scene in this very book—one of my favorites actually.

In the first part of the book, Samuel and Ren are in a bar, and Ren is having a bit too much fun drinking. Almost all of that scene is fiction, but I was writing that day and I couldn't get, "summa muh bitch" out of my head.

For some reason, it just wouldn't go away. Then I remembered a funny story that my mom told me years ago.

My grandmother Candy McKinley (yep, same first name, and yep, the same one I mentioned above) was a foster parent. She had several kids over the years, but this story spawns from a sweet little boy and his hilarious big brother.

My grandmother went to the kitchen to fix breakfast for them and sat the youngest in the high chair which—at that moment—sat next to the fridge. When she opened the door, it opened toward the high chair, so the little boy was completely hidden right then.

She grabbed what she'd needed and closed the fridge—and found quite the surprise.

The little boy had been so curious to see inside, he grabbed hold of the fridge door and held on tight, trying to pull himself out.

My grandmother accidentally helped him.

When it closed, he'd been pulled out of his high chair and was hanging from the door, laughing. He'd ridden it all the way until it was fully closed.

His slightly older brother (around five years old) walked in the room, placed his hands on his hips, shook his head, and in all his tiny glory said, "Well, summa muh bitch."

My mom still laughs when she remembers that story, and I do, too because I think of the funny stories of my own kids.

So, that was what spawned that scene!

Funny kid things are my favorite, FYI. So, feel free to leave your own favorites as a "Hello" to me in the reviews! I'd LOVE to hear them. I'll even make a list of my top five and share them on my site. It'll be fun!

My personal favorite was my youngest, Matt, calling a peanut butter sandwich—and there is NO way you're ready for this one…

A "keekobody quits-switch." I literally had to pick up an angry toddler and hold him directly out in front of me while taking him from cabinet to cabinet so he could point it out. He's never living that one down, by the way.

But rounding back to the series and the awesomeness that is the KGU… You are all wonderful, and I truly feel blessed to be here. A BIG thank you for welcoming me, leaving amazing reviews, and just overall showing a huge amount of support.

All of you are badass.

Glancing back over this, I don't know if Michael will have to curb my excessive exclamation point addiction (he made it sound like a joke, but it REALLY is a problem!), but I have awesome news for you guys.

The title of book three will be (drum roll) The Frozen Wasteland!!!! I say we leave those. That's exciting news!

So, I will leave this here, and see you guys again in a couple weeks with the next one! <3

AUTHOR NOTES - MICHAEL ANDERLE
AUGUST 9TH, 2017

First, THANK YOU for not only reading this book, but sticking around and reading these Author Notes, as well.

Personally, I found it hilarious how much feedback we received about my editing Candy's excessive exclamation point problem (e2p2). This time, I didn't take one ep out. So, any of you ready to jump my case about it, you can chill...

This time.

I'm not making any promises NEXT book when Candy's... um, e2p2 problem... rears its ugly head again.

Just saying.

I'm blessed and I freely admit it. However, the blessing I'm speaking about is the chance to be the go-between the readers, and an author who is not only seeing sales, but fan *engagement* perhaps for the first significant time.

And changing a life as they receive the blessings.

You know, from people reaching out in reviews (talking directly to us in the reviews, not just talking about the book which is completely awesome as well) or on our Facebook pages, or shit, *wherever*. I've had a significant amount of fans say they appreciate our communication and the reality (for me anyway) is that I am *reactionary*.

Not majorly proactive.

Meaning (in a completely wrong sense of usage, but stay with me here) that I do put a few things up on Facebook and make comments. But if you, the fans, didn't write back, engage with us etcetera, then we would stop putting our content out there and talking.

Because, it would feel like I was talking in a deserted old cold, dank warehouse, which was crumbling down and I'd feel like I want to be anywhere else than where I was.

However, your replies, your comments, hell, your *SUPPORT* when I admit I'm having challenges writing every day to get the next book out *HELPS* significantly.

At some point, I can imagine someone is going to figure out that the story of The Kurtherian Gambit Universe is something that can be shared beyond the confines of our group. When that happens, I'm sure there will be a question that has to do with the 'secret' of the success.

Like hard-assed work is a secret? *Sorry, I digress.*

However, what they are truly asking is why what we did differently than others and part of the answer is we found a niche, a group of fans that are appreciative of our efforts. Fans helping us to keep going when the tough times hit so we can feel that dopamine slam when you read our books, give us those comments on Facebook or in reviews and ask us...

"WHEN THE HELL IS THE NEXT BOOK?"

Yeah, it occasionally sucks to hear that after putting out twenty books in twenty months, but you know what?

It's like a drill sergeant who is in your face, *pushing* you to be the best recruit / soldier / whatever you can be.

You might hate what they are yelling, but you *KNOW* their heart is in the right place.

So yeah, I'm ready for the truth, and my book is coming out

August 23rd you red-faced, yelling at me (but completely *awesome*) sonsabitches!

You are the reason Kurtherian is kicking ass and taking names.

And I love you all.

Michael

BOOKS BY CANDY CRUM

TALES OF THE FEISTY DRUID
with Michael Anderle

The Arcadian Druid (01) - The Undying Illusionist (02) - The Frozen Wasteland (03) - The Deceiver (04) - The Lost (05) - The Damned (06) Into The Maelstrom (07)

THE THERIAN CHRONICLES
with Amanda Browning

The Dark Professor (1) The Therian Prince (2)

CONNECT WITH THE AUTHORS

To see ALL of Candy's different books check out her website below

Website:
http://www.candycrumbooks.com

Facebook
https://www.facebook.com/groups/thecandyshopgroup/

Michael Anderle Social

Website:
http://www.lmbpn.com

Email List:
http://lmbpn.com/email/